———————————— ★ ————————————

"YOU SAID HER SISTER WAS MURDERED?"

"Strangled." He shook his head. "A horrible thing. A genuine tragedy. I always liked Cathryn. A really sweet girl, one of the world's true innocents."

"Who killed her?"

"Some kind of burglar. A maniac, according to the police. They haven't found him yet."

"They have a suspect?"

He shook his head. "I don't think so."

"You've seen this postcard they found?"

"Yes. A picture of Taos Pueblo."

"What was the date of the postmark?"

"The twenty-third of September."

"Was there a message on the card?"

"Just one line. 'The flower in the desert lives.' And then her signature. Melissa's."

———————————— ★ ————————————

"Mr. Satterthwait is a . . . persuasive writer . . ."

—*New York Times*

"Croft is an engaging character . . ."
—*Minneapolis Star-Tribune*

Also available from Worldwide Mystery by
WALTER SATTERTHWAIT

AT EASE WITH THE DEAD
WALL OF GLASS

Forthcoming from Worldwide Mystery by
WALTER SATTERTHWAIT

THE HANGED MAN

A FLOWER
IN THE
DESERT

Walter Satterthwait

W🌐RLDWIDE.

TORONTO • NEW YORK • LONDON
AMSTERDAM • PARIS • SYDNEY • HAMBURG
STOCKHOLM • ATHENS • TOKYO • MILAN
MADRID • WARSAW • BUDAPEST • AUCKLAND

This book is dedicated to my daughter, Jennifer

A FLOWER IN THE DESERT

A Worldwide Mystery/December 1993

First published by St. Martin's Press, Incorporated.

ISBN 0-373-26134-9

Acknowledgments

Thanks to the staff at the Santa Fe Public Library for their help. Thanks to J. W. Satterthwait and to my agent, Dominick Abel. Thanks to Anita Battat for her help with the computer and for her sage advice. Many thanks, and another birthday card, to Reagan Arthur at St. Martin's, for her endless patience while answering questions and tolerating bad jokes. For information on electronic surveillance, thanks to Michael Peros and his Privacy Electronics in Pinellas Park, Florida. Thanks to Carol Mothrer for the loan of her paintings. Thanks to Ada Dryce for her company and the use of her washing machine. Thanks to Josiah Thompson, whose excellent book *Gumshoe* provided many valuable insights. Thanks to Miriam Davidson, whose book *Convictions of the Heart,* also excellent, did the same. And thanks once again, and a Hatlo Hat-tip, to Jonathan Richards and Claudia Jessup, who've been good friends through the occasional patch of thick and the protracted periods of thin.

There is a faith that is primarily belief. This kind of faith calls for definitive doctrines from which guiding objectives and priorities can be derived. And there is a faith that is primarily trust. This kind of faith expects to be guided by a unifying presence that enlivens each moment, breaks all borders, gathers us into communion with one another, and addresses us in all we meet. For faith as belief, it makes sense to ask how all we presently encounter can be used to achieve our (or God's) objectives; the present must be sacrificed to the future. For faith as trust, the future we hope for must emerge out of a fulfilled present; to treat any being or situation we meet only as a means to be used or as an obstacle to be eliminated attacks the historically unique liberating power with which every person and every community is endowed.

—Jim Corbett

PART ONE

PART ONE

ONE

THAT OCTOBER, the weather couldn't decide what to do with itself. Some days it arrived gray and bleak and pensive. Ponderous leaden clouds leaned overhead, their bellies slumped against the peaks of the Sangre de Cristo Mountains; polar blasts of wind sent stiff black leaves blindly scrambling down the streets. People were bundled up in parkas and mufflers, and when they met, on the Plaza, along the sidewalks, they kept their shoulders hunched and their hands in their pockets, and through clenched teeth and fixed smiles they blew hurried little puffs of vapor at each other.

Other days, the weather arrived sleek and sassy. The air was warm and it had a glitter to it, and a fizz. Only one or two clouds trailed across the taut blue sky, each fluttering brilliant white from the shoulders of the mountains like an aviator's scarf. Sunbesotted, people stood around wearing summer slacks and summer skirts and grins that were grateful and a little bit guilty, the grins of children who had pulled a fast one on their parents. They licked ice cream cones and they sipped sodas and they were very vocal about the wonderfulness of the climate, and in their voices you could sometimes hear a hint of self-congratulation at the wisdom they had shown in choosing to live here. In its own way, perched as it was in the high desert, Santa Fe was an island; and in our own way we all shared an islander's narrow pride of place.

There had been, a few weeks ago, some snow. Not much here in town, only a few uncertain flakes, quickly gone. But from my office window, sitting with my boot heels propped atop the sill, I could see it lying up there along the sunny ski basin, a fine bright dusting of confectioner's sugar configuring the ridges. I was sipping a soda myself, a Dr Pepper, and I was wondering, as I often did, how Rita was doing.

When someone knocked at the door, I felt a tiny flicker of annoyance: reveries weren't supposed to be interrupted. But reveries don't pay the rent, and I swung my feet off the windowsill, swiveled around, parked the can of soda on the floor beside the chair, and called out, "Come in."

He made his entrance by opening the door, stepping in, and then pushing it shut behind him with an easy effortless grace, as though he'd been shutting that particular door behind him, effortlessly, all his life. In his midforties, he was tall, maybe an inch taller than I was, which put him at six feet three in his black cowboy boots. He was wearing neatly pressed gray cavalry twill trousers, a snug black snap-button silk shirt, and a gray suede jacket that looked soft enough to spread on bread. He had narrow hips and broad shoulders and the physical self-assurance of a bank manager with a black belt in karate. His thick black hair was wavy, his big brown eyes glittered, and his smile was bright and white and probably insured. He looked like your basic Hollywood heartthrob. Which is exactly the way he was supposed to look, since that was exactly what he was.

"Mr. Croft?" he said, and his voice was the same rich baritone that had once or twice rumbled from the speaker of my television.

"Yes."

"Roy Alonzo." The introduction was unnecessary, and he knew it, and that may have been why he smiled a man-to-man smile as he strode gracefully across the room, his arm outstretched. He hit his mark on the far side of the desk and I stood up and we shook hands across the desktop. I caught the faint scent of something that someone on Madison Avenue had probably described as bracing, or manly. "I know I don't have an appointment," he said, "but I wondered if you could spare a few minutes of your time."

"Of course," I told him. "Have a seat."

He stepped back, lowered himself gracefully into one of the two clients' chairs, gracefully tugged up the knees of his trousers, and sat back, gracefully crossing his legs, right ankle over left knee. The cuffs of the trousers rose far enough along the sides of his boots to display the elaborate custom stitching in the supple leather.

I sat down. I have what might be a curious reaction to these movie and television stars. We get a fair amount of them floating through Santa Fe; some of them, preferring our oxygen to the assorted carcinogens of Los Angeles, have built homes here. Whenever I meet them, I feel for a moment as though they were somehow more real, more substantial than I. Sitting opposite Roy Alonzo, it seemed to me that it was he, up till now a tiny figure strutting across a cathode ray tube, who was three-dimensional and alive, while I had abruptly become merely an image, black and white and two-dimensional, flickering on a flat silver screen. I suppose that I found this fairly irritating.

Alonzo, his arms resting gracefully along the arms of the chair, looked around the room and then turned to me with another smile, this one wry and self-amused. "You know," he said, "I probably shouldn't admit it, but this is the first time I've seen a real private detective's office."

I smiled back. "Not like the office on 'Valdez!'?" "Valdez!" was the name of the private-eye series he'd starred in. Once a week, as Rick Valdez, he had plowed a bare-knuckled path through clutters of thugs and clusters of commercials, stopping along the way to pick up Significant Clues and distressed damsels with attractive overbites.

His smile became a grin. "No. It's a lot cleaner."

"This is only Monday."

He laughed a rich baritone laugh that was perhaps a bit louder, and lasted perhaps a bit longer, than the remark deserved. Possibly he was nervous. Or possibly he was trying to convey the notion that he was nervous. Actors can do that.

He looked around the office again, the big brown eyes thoughtfully narrowed.

I said, "How can I help you, Mr. Alonzo?"

He turned to me and smiled again. The smile this time was sociable and engaging. He had a wide variety of smiles, apparently. Maybe by the time he left I'd get to see all of them. "A friend gave me your name," he said.

"Which friend might that be?"

He shook his head. "Doesn't matter. Someone whose judgment I trust. He said you were honest and dependable."

I nodded. Who was I to argue with such an assessment?

"He also said you were discreet."

"Did he mention brave, clean, and reverent?"

He laughed again, and again the laugh sounded slightly forced. The laughter faded, and he rubbed his fingertips reflectively at the corner of his square chin, and then he looked at me with his eyes narrowed and his brow sincerely furrowed. The preliminaries were over, it seemed, and now we were Getting Down to Business. "Mr. Croft, you know about my wife? My ex-wife?"

"No," I said. "What should I know about her?"

He appeared puzzled. "You don't know about the divorce? The court case?"

I shook my head.

"It was all over the papers," he said. "*People* did a cover story."

I shrugged. "My subscription ran out."

He stared at me for a moment, blankly, and then he surprised me by laughing once more. The laughter this time sounded more genuine. "Typical, isn't it?" he said, and held out his hands, showing me his palms. "Celeb sees himself, once again, as center of universe." He gave the word *celeb* a small, scornful spin. For just a moment he seemed like a real person, unaffected and unrehearsed, and I almost liked him. And then, reaching behind his head, he scratched at the back of his neck and he gave me an abashed smile, just the way Jimmy Stewart used to do it. "All I can say is that when you're stuck in the shit, back in L.A., it seems like everybody in the world knows about it."

I shrugged. "Out here in the boondocks, we sometimes miss a thing or two."

"You're lucky."

"Suppose you tell me about it," I said.

He nodded. He took a deep breath, let it out. "Right," he said. He nodded again. "Right. My wife and I, Melissa, we divorced two years ago. It wasn't an amicable divorce. Melissa wanted everything. The house, the car, all the stocks and bonds. Everything. And she wanted our daughter, Winona."

I nodded neutrally. Something that over the years I've gotten fairly good at.

"Well, her lawyers talked to my lawyers, and hers were a little more bloodthirsty than mine, and the upshot was, Melissa got pretty much what she wanted. Including Winona."

"You say you went to court?"

He shook his head. "Not then," he said. "We settled. Easier that way, all around. I got weekend visitation rights. I used to pick up Winona on Fridays, after school, and I brought her back to the house—Melissa's house now—on Sunday morning."

I nodded.

"Last year I started seeing someone else. Shana Eberle. Not in the business—she designs clothes. A terrific woman. Smart and funny, and caring—really a remarkable person, and she absolutely loved Winona. And Winona adored her. They got along beautifully." He smiled with a kind of mock ruefulness. "Sometimes it almost made me jealous."

I smiled back, my standard-issue smile, and I nodded some more.

He took another deep breath. "Well," he said, "it certainly made Melissa jealous. She called me up one Sunday night and told me to get rid of Shana—'that filthy bitch,' she called her—or I'd never see Winona again."

I nodded.

"Well," he said, "that pissed me off. What right has she got to dictate how I live my life? We're divorced. We're both free agents now. Each of us has a right to see whoever we want to." His baritone had risen to a tenor.

"You explained all that to Melissa," I said.

"Yeah." He smiled bitterly. "I explained all that to Melissa. She refused to listen to reason. She was screaming at me over the phone. Shouting, cursing. She was totally hysterical."

"Why would she react so strongly to this woman?"

"It wasn't this woman, it wasn't Shana in particular. It could've been any woman. Melissa doesn't want me involved with anyone."

"Why not?"

He raised his eyebrows and showed me his palms again. "The way she is. If she can't have me, then nobody else can have me either."

"It's you and Eberle she's jealous of, not Winona and Eberle."

He nodded. "Exactly."

"Was she a jealous woman before the divorce?"

He nodded. "It was one of the problems in our marriage. One of the major problems."

"Did you give her reason to be jealous?"

"She didn't need reasons. It's just the way she was."

Which didn't, of course, answer my question. "Who filed for the divorce?"

"She did. But that doesn't make any difference. Not to Melissa. She's not satisfied. She's not happy with stripping me of the house, most of the investments, everything else. She wants me miserable. And she wants me miserable and alone."

I nodded. "So. You refused to stop seeing Eberle. What happened?"

"Phone calls. All week. Every single day. Hysterical phone calls. Vicious phone calls. Either I got rid of the bitch or I'd be sorry. And then, the next Friday, when I came to pick up my daughter, Melissa told me that Winona was sick. She wouldn't let her leave the house. I told her that I could take care of Winona at least as well as she could, but she refused to let her go. Wouldn't even let me see her."

"So you did what?"

"I notified my lawyer. He told me not to worry, he'd take care of it. And then on Monday, Melissa and her lawyer went to the police and accused me of abusing my daughter."

"Abusing," I said.

His mouth was grim. "Sexually abusing. Molesting. My own daughter."

I nodded again. Neutrally.

He leaned toward me. "Do you have any idea what it feels like for someone—for your ex-goddamn-wife—to accuse you of something like that?"

"No," I said.

"It feels like shit. Like absolute goddamn shit. Here's a woman I lived with, a woman I loved, a woman I supported, a woman I was still supporting, and she could turn around and do that. It was goddamn sick."

He sounded entirely sincere to me. But sincerity was what, as an actor, he was paid to deliver. "How old is Winona?" I asked him.

He winced. "She turned six in July. She was five when Melissa started all this."

I nodded again. "I did read something about it. I didn't follow it very carefully." I didn't follow it at all. I seldom read about celebrities, and I never read about child abuse.

"Five years old, Mr. Croft. Can you imagine what an accusation like that could do to a five-year-old girl!"

"No," I said. I didn't really want to.

"It was a mess," he said. "Melissa sued to deny me visitation, I countersued for defamation of character. It went on for months. Lawyers, doctors, social workers, judges. A circus. A nightmare. And poor Winona was in the middle of it. Finally, though, the appellate judge ruled that there was no evidence of abuse. Naturally—there had never been any abuse. Anyway, afterward, Melissa went off to South America for a few days, to lick her wounds. I had to go off to Europe myself that month. When she came back, she picked up Winona and the two of them disappeared."

"Disappeared?"

"Vanished. No one's seen either one of them since then."

"This was when?"

"Middle of August. August the seventeenth. As soon as we knew what Melissa was up to, my lawyer and I hired a private investigator to track her down. He had no luck."

"Why come to me? And why now?"

"Melissa had a sister in L.A. Cathryn Bigelow. Last week, Cathryn was killed. Murdered. I was in New York when I learned about it, and I had to fly out there. While they were investigating her apartment, the police found a postcard from Melissa, a postcard that was postmarked in Albuquerque. All the Santa Fe mail is postmarked in Albuquerque—you know that, right?"

I nodded. "So is all the Albuquerque mail."

"Sure, but we have a house here in Santa Fe. Had a house. It's mine now, part of the settlement, a little place out in La Tierra. But Melissa has contacts here in town. Friends, people she trusts. She doesn't know all that many people in Albuquerque. She was here, in Santa Fe. I'm sure of it. And it's possible that she's still here."

"Has she come to Santa Fe since the divorce?"

"Yes. A couple of times. She stayed at The Cloisters." An expensive guest ranch north of town. "But I've already checked there, and no one's seen her."

"Let's go back a bit. You said her sister was murdered?"

"Strangled." He shook his head. "A horrible thing. A genuine tragedy. I always liked Cathryn. A really sweet girl, one of the world's true innocents."

"Who killed her?"

"Some kind of burglar. A maniac, according to the police. They haven't found him yet."

"They have a suspect?"

He shook his head. "I don't think so."

"You've seen this postcard they found?"

"Yes. A picture of Taos Pueblo."

"What was the date of the postmark?"

"The twenty-third of September."

"Was there a message on the card?"

"Just one line. *'The flower in the desert lives.'* And then her signature. Melissa's."

"*'The flower in the desert lives'?* Does that have any special significance?"

"Not that I know of." He shrugged. "Probably some private thing between Cathryn and Melissa."

I nodded. "So what is it you'd like me to do, Mr. Alonzo?"

He frowned. "Well, that's pretty obvious, isn't it? I want you to find Melissa and Winona, and I want you to bring my daughter back to me."

I shook my head. "I'm sorry," I said. "I can't do that."

TWO

"YOU'RE A SNOB, JOSHUA."

"The guy was a major asshole, Rita."

"I rest my case," she said.

The two of us were in sitting on the sofa in Rita's living room. From there, as we sipped our tea, we could look out through the French doors and across the patio to the west, where the sun was turning into a plump ripe peach as it glided down the sky toward the distant slopes of the Jemez Mountains.

I said, "From the time he came into the office until the time he left, he was busy auditioning. He was playing a part. He was playing three or four parts."

"Maybe he sensed what a tough critic he was dealing with. Maybe he wanted to dazzle you with his virtuosity."

Above a long, flowing, navy blue skirt she wore a pale blue satin blouse that contrasted nicely with her smooth dark skin and the thick tumble of her hair, as black as a raven's wing. Gone now was the wheelchair in which she'd spent the days of the past three years. In its place, at the end of the sofa, stood a stainless steel walker. Using the walker must have been difficult for Rita, and painful: she never used it while I was around. Whenever I arrived at the house she was already sitting on the sofa, and when I left she was still sitting there.

"First of all," I said, "he made it sound like his ex-wife had cleaned him out when they got the divorce. California is a community property state, just like New Mexico. Either he kept half of what they had, or he gave it away in the settlement. If he gave it away, she must've had something on him."

"He did tell you that he had a house here in Santa Fe."

"And he made that sound like a little old shack by the railroad tracks. It's in La Tierra, Rita. There aren't any railroad tracks in La Tierra. They're against the zoning laws."

She smiled at me over her teacup. Her smile wasn't something that happened only to her lips. It happened to her large black eyes, too, and it put a glow behind the smooth skin of her face; and it put a kind of taut emptiness in my chest. "Joshua, there's no zoning law against his trying to get your sympathy."

"No law against my withholding it, either."

She smiled again, sipped at her tea. "Would you have been so hostile if Alonzo hadn't played a private detective on that television program?"

"I wasn't hostile. I was a prince. Polite. Respectful. Completely professional."

"Why is it, then, that he wanted to punch you in the nose?"

I shrugged. "Macho posturing, I suppose."

"His or yours?"

I took a sip of my tea. Lapsang souchong. "Do you want to hear the rest of this or not?"

"Desperately," she said.

Roy Alonzo had frowned when I told him I couldn't help him. "What do you mean?" he said.

"I mean that I won't involve the agency in a sexual abuse case. They're messy, and they only get messier, and there's never any final way to determine the truth. The medical evidence, if there is any, is ambiguous—the first doctor says yes, the second doctor says no. The testimony of the child is suspect. And so, obviously, is the testimony of the parents. Both parents."

"What's all that got to do with anything? I just want you to find my daughter."

I shook my head. "I'm sorry, Mr. Alonzo. I won't take the case."

"You won't take the case," he repeated, his voice flat.

"No. If you'd like, I can give you the name of a good private investigator here in town, someone who'd be happy to take it."

"Someone who doesn't have your scruples, you mean."

"Scruples don't enter into it."

He leaned slightly forward in his chair. "Listen to me," he said. "A little over a year ago, I was on top of the world. I had a top-twenty series on a major network—the only Hispanic in the history of television who's ever carried a prime-time hour by himself. That may not mean a damn thing to you, but it was something I took a lot of pride in. And I had a big-budget feature in the chute. It was a go. I had a lock on it, points in the gross, the video, the cable, everything. We're talking, conservative projections, something like two or three million dollars. Today, I don't have diddly.

Even though I proved in court that I never laid a finger on Winona, not that way, even though everyone knew that the whole thing was a crazy lie of Melissa's, my career was shot. Suddenly I was a leper. The series was canceled, the money people flushed the feature. I've spent nearly every dime I had on lawyers, fighting this. My entire life is in fucking turn-around. All I have left is my daughter, and now she's gone."

"I understand that, Mr. Alonzo."

"You have children?"

"No."

"Then you don't understand a fucking thing." He frowned again, shook his head, sat back in the chair. "All right. Look. Forget I said that." He took a deep breath. When he spoke, his voice was level and his face was open. "I want my daughter back. I don't want to hurt my ex-wife, I don't want revenge. All I want is to get my daughter back."

"Like I said, I'll be happy to give you the name of a competent private investigator here in town."

He nodded, his eyes narrowing slightly. "Explain to me why you won't take a child custody case."

"I already did."

"Try it one more time."

"Because I like to be on the side of the angels, and there's no way, in a situation like this, for me to determine where that is."

"Listen to me, Mr. Croft," he said calmly, earnestly. "I give you my word that I never abused my daughter. I swear to God that I never once touched her."

Once again, he sounded entirely convincing. But, once again that was exactly the way he was supposed to sound. As George Burns said, sincerity is the most important thing—if you can fake that, you've got it made.

"I'm sorry," I told him.

He was leaning forward in his chair. He nodded. "So," he said, "what you're doing, basically, is calling me a liar."

"What I'm doing, basically," I said, "is telling you I won't take the case."

His face had closed up the way it did on television whenever Rick Valdez discovered that during the next few minutes of airtime, he would be wading through a puddle of thugs. He stood, moved away from the chair, planted his feet. "All right," he said. He held out his hands, palms up, and flicked his fingers at me. "Come on."

I sat back and smiled up at him. Partly, I was genuinely amused; but partly, too, I suppose, I was trying to needle him. It's not only the make-believe P.I.s who're capable of asshole-ism. "Mr. Alonzo, seems to me you've already had enough lawyers and court appearances. You sure you want to waste your time with an assault and battery charge?"

He showed me still another of his smiles, this one curled at the corner with scorn. "That the way you handle things, Croft? You hide behind your lawyers?"

"Whenever I can."

He put his hands on his hips, cocked his head slightly back, the better to look down at me. "I heard you were a *man*."

I nodded. "Got a certificate to prove it."

"You look like a goddamn pussy to me."

"Then both of us could be in serious trouble."

His smile vanished and his eyes narrowed. He leaned forward and put his hands, fingers splayed, along the edge of the desktop. "I'm not through with you, Croft." His voice, low and menacing, was the voice that had sent spasms of fear rippling through the pimps and dealers and grifters who inhabited "Valdez!" "I know people in this town. I know a lot of people. Big people. Important people. I can make your life very unpleasant."

"You already have," I told him. Some folks, without even trying, bring out the best in me.

He reached across the desk for the front of my shirt. I slapped his hand away and he nearly went sprawling across the blotter. No big deal; leaning forward like that, he was off balance.

As he pushed himself back, righted himself, I said, "Let's not forget those lawyers."

He adjusted the lapels of his jacket, straightened his shoulders. He took a deep breath. "I'll see you again, Croft."

I nodded. "I look forward to it."

He turned, stomped across the room, tore open the door, strode through it, and slammed it shut behind him, just like Kirk Douglas in *Gunfight at the O.K. Corral.* Or maybe it was like Gregory Peck in *Duel in the Sun.* Hard to keep track sometimes. Anyway, it was a swell exit.

SMILING SADLY, Rita shook her head. "Joshua," she said, "do you think you'll ever grow up?"

I smiled. "I doubt it, Rita. I'm having too much fun being an adolescent."

"An occasionally obnoxious adolescent."

"Jeepers," I said. "*He* started it."

She shook her head. "Sometimes I think there's something worrisome about this need to be a wiseass."

I nodded. "Maybe so. Things probably would've gone better if I'd just duked it out with the guy. Knocked out a couple of million dollars worth of dental caps. Had *his* lawyers screaming assault and battery."

"I'd like to think that there was some other option. Something besides beating him up."

"I should've shot him, you think?"

"Perhaps you could've been a shade more diplomatic."

"Diplomacy would've been wasted on this guy, Rita."

She sipped her tea. "Possibly not only on him."

I smiled. "Ah, Rita. You play pelota with my heart."

We talked for a while longer, but since what we were talking about was the business, and since there hadn't been much of that lately, it wasn't for a very long while. Before I left, I asked her, as I always did, how it was going.

She knew what I meant and, as she always did when I asked, she smiled. "Fine," she said.

"So when do we get to go down to the Plaza?" Rita hadn't been off her property since she'd returned from the hospital, where the doctors had plucked a .38-caliber bullet from her spine. For three years now she'd been telling me that she wouldn't go into town until she could walk there.

"Soon," she said. As she always did.

With my usual maturity and sophistication, I resented this. Partly, because getting answers to questions was what I did for a living, and I wasn't getting them from her. And partly, I suspect, because by refusing to answer me she failed to allay the anxieties I felt about her recovery. Crippled, she had depended on me. When her legs were working once again, would she use them to walk out of my life?

These were secret, selfish, chicken-shit anxieties, and I wasn't especially pleased to find them floating around my soul. But self-knowledge rarely leads to self-esteem.

"You let me know," I told her.

"I will, Joshua."

It was around seven thirty when I left. I drove over to Furr's Cafeteria in De Vargas Mall, pigged out on chicken-fried steak and home-fried potatoes and tossed salad, then picked up a six-pack of cold Pacifico at Albertson's and drove home.

At a little after nine o'clock, while I was reading yesterday's *New York Times* and sipping the good Mexican beer, someone knocked at the front door.

I set the newspaper on the end table, stood, crossed the room, flicked on the exterior light. There was a time, years ago, when I used to open the door without looking through the peephole. But opening the door onto one or two unpleasant surprises had changed that. Now, a glance through the hole showed two men standing out there, both of them distorted by the fish-eye lens, their bodies elongated, their faces bulbous. One of them I recognized, the other I didn't. The one I didn't recognize was a small, slight, white-haired man in his sixties. The one I recognized was Roy Alonzo.

For a moment, I wondered whether I should trot back to the bedroom and snare the Smith & Wesson from the shoebox at the back of the closet. Alonzo and I had not parted as compadres. Maybe he and his friend had turned up here to cause me grief.

But Alonzo hadn't impressed me as much of a threat this afternoon, and the little white-haired man didn't impress me as much of a threat right now. Probably, with a bellyful of beer and chicken-fried steak, I wasn't much of a threat to these two, either; but I figured that if worse came to worst I could always sit on them.

I opened the door.

As soon as I saw the older man clearly, I did recognize him—and I realized that he was very much of a threat indeed. His name was Norman Montoya. I had met him once, a year or two ago. According to the state police, and the federals, he was responsible for most of the illegal things that went on in northern New Mexico, from petty vandalism on up to drugs and murder.

When I'd last seen him, he'd been sitting back against the curve of his hot tub, streamers of steam rising off his naked shoulders. Now he was wearing a natty cashmere topcoat, opened, and, beneath it, a gray three-piece suit with pinstripes so subtle they might have been imaginary. His shoes were black brogues, polished to a mirror shine. I liked the brogues. On formal occasions, most of the males in New Mexico wore cowboy boots. Norman Montoya, whose family had been here since the conquistadors, wore brogues.

He nodded to me. "Good evening, Mr. Croft. A pleasure to see you once again." He turned to Roy Alonzo. "Tell him, please."

Alonzo frowned. He put his hands up, a gesture that seemed at once supplicatory and defensive. "All right. Look. I was out of line this afternoon. I apologize."

"Very good," said Norman Montoya, as though to a reasonably competent but not particularly bright child. "Now, please, wait in the car."

Alonzo took the dismissal well, certainly better than I would've taken it. He only blinked, nodded, shoved his hands into the pockets of his gray twill trousers, then turned and stalked down the steps.

Norman Montoya said to me, "May I come in?"

THREE

As Norman Montoya entered my living room, I offered to take his topcoat.

"Thank you, Mr. Croft," he said, "but I shall keep it." He smiled. "Old bones are never warm."

I nodded. "Have a seat."

He sat down in the armchair. I sat down opposite him, on the sofa.

"He is my nephew," said Norman Montoya. His voice was as smoky as I remembered it, and as well modulated. "My oldest sister's son."

"Roy Alonzo is your nephew?"

He smiled once again. "Even television actors must have relatives, Mr. Croft."

Maybe, but usually they don't have an uncle who's the Hispanic Godfather of New Mexico.

"And you appreciate," said Norman Montoya, "that with family, sometimes it is necessary for one to impose oneself."

"And how," I asked him, "are you planning to do that?"

"I have already done so. It was I who suggested to Roy that he contact you."

"Why me?"

"Because when we met, you and I, some time ago, I found you to be a serious person."

"Serious."

"Yes." He smiled. "Despite a perhaps unfortunate fondness for childish humor."

I nodded. "Mrs. Mondragón would probably agree with you about that."

Another smile. "Mrs. Mondragón is a woman of no small discernment."

I nodded. "That she is. But tell me, Mr. Montoya. What is it, exactly, that I can do for you?"

He shrugged lightly. "I should think it obvious. I should like you to reconsider your refusal to help locate my nephew's daughter."

"Did your nephew tell you why I refused?"

"Yes. And your reasons are excellent." A small quick wince of distaste flickered across his face. Except for a slightly aquiline nose, his features were even, fine-boned, aristocratic. He would have made a good Roman emperor. Or at least a good-looking one. "A situation like this, it is extremely unpleasant. For everyone. But always, Mr. Croft, the one who suffers most, no matter what the truth might be, is the child. In this case, the child is my sister's granddaughter. And it is the child whom I wish to protect."

"I can appreciate that, Mr. Montoya, but—"

He held up his right hand. Like the rest of him, it was small but well shaped. "Please, Mr. Croft. Hear me out. What I propose to you is this. I propose that you accept me, rather than my nephew, as your client. I propose that you investigate the disappearance of his wife and child, and also that you attempt to determine the truth of the other matter. If you in fact discover that my nephew has actually"—once again he winced slightly—"interfered with his daughter, then I should be grateful if you told me. You have my word that such an interference will never occur again."

"The California courts said he didn't."

He nodded. "And I hope they were correct." He smiled his small slight smile. "But permit me not to rely too heavily upon a decision made in the courts. Particularly in California." I've never met a New Mexican who had a great deal of respect for the state of California.

I said, "You believe that he's capable of abusing his daughter?"

He looked at me thoughtfully for a moment. At last he said, "I told you once that I was a Buddhist, did I not, Mr. Croft?"

"You did, yeah." In his enormous hilltop mansion up north, while the two of us sat in his huge hot tub before a wall of double-glazed glass that looked down a steep river valley draped with mist. He owned the valley.

"As a Buddhist," he said, "I believe that no one of us is evil. We are each of us, finally, an aspect of the same thing—call it what you will—God, Self, Buddha-nature. And yet there are evil actions in the world. Evil patterns. And through our ignorance, or our anger, or our greed, these are patterns into which some of us, into which perhaps any one of us, may fall."

I nodded. "Is that a yes?"

He smiled. "Yes, Mr. Croft. I believe that he might be capable. But is he in fact guilty? I should be inclined to think that he was not."

"All right," I said. "Let me see if I understand this. You want me to locate Roy Alonzo's wife and daughter, or try to. You also want me to find out, if I can, whether Alonzo actually abused the girl. If he did, then you want me to tell you, so you can prevent him from doing it again. How exactly do you plan to do that?"

Another smile. "I detect, in your voice, a note of wariness. Do you believe that I would do so by an exercise of violence?"

"Mr. Montoya," I said, "I know you well enough to know that you're a man of strong convictions. I don't know you well enough to know exactly what those convictions are." I thought, *There you go, Rita, how's that for diplomatic?*

Norman Montoya produced a light easy laugh, something a bit more complicated than a chuckle but a bit less exuberant than a guffaw. "Fortunately," he said, "I am a man who has had virtually no convictions whatever in the state of New Mexico."

This was apparently an example of Hispanic Godfather humor. It was my first. I wasn't altogether overwhelmed by it, but the thought did occur to me that smiling might not be a bad idea.

Norman Montoya smiled back, and nodded. "Ah, you indulge an old man, Mr. Croft. I thank you for your kindness." He smiled again, his eyes twinkling now. I've read about eyes twinkling often enough, but I've never actually seen them do it before. "But, yes," he said, "to answer your question. Assuming past abuse, how would I prevent it in future? First, by providing for both the mother and the daughter. They would want for nothing. And second, by suggesting to my nephew that he never see either one of them again unless he undergoes some sort of psychotherapy."

"'Suggesting'?" I said.

"Strongly suggesting," he said. "There will be no need for violence. My suggestion, I like to believe, carries a certain amount of weight with Roy."

I nodded. "When you say 'providing for' the mother and the daughter, what do you mean, exactly?"

"Providing for them financially."

"On whose terms?"

He smiled. "I set no terms, Mr. Croft. I am concerned only with the welfare of my great-niece."

"So your support would be open-ended, independent of wherever or however Mrs. Alonzo chooses to live?"

"Precisely."

"*If* I discover that Roy Alonzo abused the girl. Even if he did, it's probably impossible to prove it. The courts couldn't."

He nodded. "I understand this. I would accept your recommendation, whatever it might be."

"That puts an awful lot of responsibility on my shoulders."

He nodded again. "And upon mine."

"Yours are probably used to it."

"All of us must accept some responsibilities, Mr. Croft."

"I generally like to pick the responsibilities I'm going to accept."

"As you will here. You are perfectly free to reject this offer and the responsibilities it entails."

I smiled. "And no hard feelings."

Once again he returned the smile. "And no hard feelings. You would be of little help to me if you were operating under duress. If you prefer not to involve yourself, I will, regretfully, find someone else."

I nodded. "Suppose I involve myself and it looks to me that your nephew didn't abuse the girl?"

"Of course, as I told you, I believe that this would be the case. If it is, and if you can locate Mrs. Alonzo and the child, I should like you to act as go-between and attempt to construct an arrangement that both Roy and his former wife would find workable."

"Something else the courts couldn't do."

"But often, in the courtroom, people find themselves taking a stance from which they cannot, publicly, withdraw. I know that Roy will be more flexible now than he was then. Perhaps the same will be true of his former wife."

"Maybe. Maybe not."

"We shall never know, shall we, Mr. Croft, unless we locate the woman. And, as we sit here so casually discussing it, perhaps she and her daughter are in jeopardy."

"Do you have any reason to believe that they're in jeopardy?"

He shrugged lightly. "A single woman and a young child? In hiding? Trying desperately to avoid the legal authorities? What would be more likely than their being in jeopardy?"

I nodded. "I'll reconsider taking on the case. On two conditions. The first is that Mrs. Mondragón agrees. The second is that when I locate Mrs. Alonzo, *if* I locate Mrs. Alonzo, I don't disclose her whereabouts. Not to you, not to anyone. I'll contact her, I'll explain your offer. I'll act, as you put it, as a go-between. If she decides she wants to buy into the game, fine. But if she decides to pass, then it's over. I leave it alone. And you leave it alone."

He pursed his lips thoughtfully, but I noticed, once again, the twinkle in his eyes. "If you succeed in locating her, what is to prevent me from hiring someone else to locate the two of you?"

I smiled. "The Code of the West?"

Norman Montoya chuckled once more. His eyes still twinkling, a slim, slight, Hispanic Santa Claus, he smiled at me. "Will you take my word, Mr. Croft, if I give it?"

"Is your word any good?" When you say that to someone like Norman Montoya, even when he's in Santa Claus mode, you say it with a smile.

Still twinkling, still smiling, he said, "If I tell you *yes,* how will you know I'm not lying?"

"I suppose I won't. Maybe I should reconsider my reconsideration."

"Do you mean to tell me, Mr. Croft"—he smiled—"that even if I gave my word, and even if you accepted it, you would not take precautions against my having lied to you?"

I smiled. We were doing a lot of smiling tonight, the two of us. A couple of old buckaroos sitting around beaming at each other. "No," I said. "I don't mean to tell you that."

"Very good." He nodded approvingly. "And I do give you my word. My word, you will discover if you inquire, is good. And I do accept your conditions. If she refuses to negotiate with Roy, I will make no further attempt to contact her. So long as you make clear to her that whether she negotiates with Roy or not, I should like to offer my assistance to her and her daughter."

I nodded.

"Would it be appropriate now to discuss your fee?"

"After I talk to Mrs. Mondragón."

"And when will this be?"

"Is Alonzo still outside?"

"Yes. In his car. We arrived separately."

"He'll accept the conditions that we've discussed?"

"Yes."

I nodded. "Then I'll call her now."

He stood. "Very well, Mr. Croft. I thank you, and I shall await your answer outside."

"JOSHUA," Rita told me over the phone, "you said you never wanted to take a case like this."

"I think we might be helpful here. And I think that in terms of protecting the girl, everything is pretty much covered."

"Can you trust Norman Montoya?"

"I honestly don't know," I said. "But if I can find the girl and her mother, I think I can find them without leaving a trail that anyone else could follow."

"Because your heart is pure?"

"Because my heart is tricky."

"Well, just in case, I'll have Paul draw up a contract specifically for Mr. Montoya." Paul Gallegos was our lawyer.

"Thanks for the vote of confidence," I said. "Paul can't put together a contract that forbids Montoya from hiring another investigator."

"No, but if it's important to Montoya that he's perceived as a man of his word, and his word is given on paper, then perhaps he'd be less likely to violate it."

"Worth a try, I guess."

"Thanks for the vote of confidence."

FOUR

THOUSANDS OF FEET below us, the parched tan plains of western New Mexico slowly rolled away. Here and there a conical hill, looking like the sand-blasted nub of some ancient volcano, rose from the wasteland and cast a crouched, hunchbacked shadow in the slanting light of early morning. Down the hillsides gullies wound and twisted, fanning out across the empty flats into pale brown lacework deltas, dry as bone now, but reminders of the sudden spring showers, swiftly gone. Ahead of us, small as a sparrow, a phantom black airplane skimmed along the bleak khaki surface, exactly matching our speed.

Only fifteen minutes out of Albuquerque, sitting back in the thickly padded first-class seat, sipping my freshly squeezed orange juice, I was already beginning to regret accepting this case.

For one thing, I've never been very fond of Los Angeles. It's always seemed to me about as appealing, and about as substantial, as a cheap wedding cake.

For another, I couldn't stomach the idea of child abuse, sexual or otherwise. Back when I started working with Rita, it had been my idea, not hers, that we refuse any cases in which it might be involved. This was partly because of their ambiguity—as I'd told Alonzo, to me it seemed unlikely that anyone outside a family would ever be able to determine what truly went on within it.

But there was another reason. You can't live at the close of the twentieth century and not be aware that human beings are capable of a savagery that would make a hyena gag. No animal on earth is capable of the frenzy that we bring, blindly, merrily, to one another: the rapists, the racists, the serial killers, the ideologues, the genocidal lunatics. But nothing, no other kind of cruelty, bothers me as much as the cruelty visited, all too often, by parents upon their children. It's the ultimate violation, a betrayal of love by power, and I don't like to think about it. Out of basic gutlessness, I prefer to pretend that it doesn't exist. And I hoped, probably as much for my sake as for his, that Roy Alonzo was innocent.

Certainly, sitting with his uncle in my living room last night, he had once again seemed innocent. After I'd asked them both if I could get them anything, a drink, a coffee, and both had refused, Alonzo had said to me, "Listen, Croft, I mean it. I acted like an asshole this afternoon."

I nodded agreeably because I entirely agreed with him. "Yeah, well," I said, "there's a lot of it going around. I've had a touch of it myself from time to time."

"And I want to tell you how much I appreciate your changing your mind about looking for Mel."

I noticed two things. That his wife was Mel now, not Melissa. And that he hadn't interrupted his earnestness to react to, or maybe even register, my response. He was still playing a part, still reading lines. Well, it didn't necessarily mean that he was lying. Maybe he simply didn't know any other way to tell the truth.

I said, "You do understand, Mr. Alonzo, that it's Mr. Montoya who's hiring me?"

"Sure, sure. Absolutely."

"He's the one I'll be reporting to. If you've got any questions about the progress I'm making, you'll have to ask him. Are we clear on that?"

"A hundred percent. I just wanted you to know how glad I am that you'll be helping us out."

"Thanks." I lifted my notebook and my Pilot Razor Point from the end table. "What I'll need first of all," I told Alonzo, "is the basic list of friends and relations."

"People here or people in L.A.?"

"Let's start with Los Angeles."

AND SO ON TUESDAY afternoon, after a change of planes in Phoenix and another hour of flying time, there I was, starting with Los Angeles. The regret that I'd been feeling in the air didn't let up when I reached the ground. LAX, Los Angeles International Airport, is as big as a fair-sized city, and the bustle of its passengers had me immediately nostalgic for the austere silences of New Mexico. Los Angeles is the sort of place that produces instant nostalgia for somewhere else. For almost anywhere else.

At the Hertz counter I traded my signature and a peek at my credit card for a '91 Geo and a bored smile from the redheaded woman behind the counter, who could have been, who probably had been, a Miss Citrus or a Miss Diesel Fuel back in Clearwater or Omaha. They flock here from all over the country, these astonishingly beautiful young women, and sometimes for years they beat their wings against the screen door, hoping desperately that it will open and let them flutter into that bright white beckoning light. Not many of them make it.

The Hertz bus trundled me to the parking lot where my car awaited. Above a grim flat commercial wasteland of discount furniture stores and auto repair shops, the sky was dullish chrome yellow. At its edges it had darkened to a sooty brown, like an old newspaper about to burst into flame. The air was warm and tasted like it had passed through too many lungs and too many machines.

It's become a cliché that the city of Los Angeles is a prefigurement of the end of the world, but clichés are clichés for a reason. Once upon a future time, after all the trees had burned and all the animals had died, we humanoids would be standing in line beneath a smoky yellow sky, and we would learn that today we wouldn't be receiving our ration of coal tar derivatives, because the coal tar had run out.

Thinking such sanguine thoughts, I took the San Diego Freeway north in sixty-mile-an-hour bumper car traffic until I got off at Sunset. I drove past UCLA and through Beverly Hills, cool complacent estates hidden up there behind the trees, gardens slung with bougainvillea, jasmine, rose. Then I was in Hollywood, amid the drugstores and the burger stands and the sleaze shops, each building looking as though it had been designed by a different mad architect. I passed Moorish castles and Venetian palaces and Mediterranean villas, an eerie landscape spangled with limp palm trees and bright gaudy billboards. Only the billboards seemed real.

Ed Norman had moved his offices since I had last been in Los Angeles. His new operation was on Gower, and it occupied the entire top floor of a twelve-story building. I rode the elevator up to twelve and stepped out into the lobby. Was greeted by silver linen wallpaper, silver shag rugs. Behind a black lacquered desk, a beautiful blond receptionist with a spectacular tan—a former Miss Blue Grass, from her Kentucky accent—took my name. After silently noting that it belonged to nobody in The Industry, she spoke it into a telephone, then told me with a bored smile to take the hallway down to the door at the end. I thanked her. She gave me another bored smile and went back to working on her screenplay.

I walked down the hallway. Maybe, behind the doors I passed, investigators were busy interrogating witnesses and poring over clues, but if they were, they were doing it silently. The only sound was a very faint background drone, barely audible, like the hum sometimes made by neon lights.

At the end of the hallway there was a door with a brass plaque set about three quarters up. EDWARD W. NORMAN, it said. PRESIDENT, it said. I knocked on the door and it buzzed and I pushed it open. I stepped into a small anteroom, more silver linen walls, more silver shag carpeting, to the left a gray sofa and a black lacquered coffee table that held copies of *Newsweek* and *U.S. News & World Report*. To the right, behind another black lacquered desk, sat a brunette in a gray skirt and a white blouse. She was a tanned and extremely well-endowed young woman who, from my vantage point, seemed to consist entirely of profiles. The smile she presented was a definite improvement on the smiles I'd received so far today. It was bright and open and it contained no boredom at all. Much more exposure to that smile and I'd be forced to tell her, reluctantly, that my heart was promised to another. In a soft, pleasant voice, she informed me that Mr. Norman was expecting me and that I should go right in. I noticed, as I passed by her, that her eyes were green. I opened the office door.

Inside, white linen on the walls, white shag on the floor. The desk, lacquered in white, wasn't quite as big as a cabin cruiser. Neither was Ed Norman, who stood up behind it and then walked around it, smiling at me and holding out his hand. Beyond the desk, framed in the big picture window, stood the Capitol Records Building, one of L.A.'s monuments to American good taste.

Six feet four inches tall, Ed Norman was a black man with an uncanny resemblance to the young Harry Belafonte. The current Harry Belafonte also possesses an uncanny resemblance to the young Harry Belafonte, but Ed's resemblance was uncannier—maybe because Ed was about two feet wider at the shoulders. Today those shoulders were neatly encased in a conservative gray suit of tropical-weight wool whose tailoring was so sleek it could have been genetically engineered.

He squeezed my hand. "How's it going, Joshua?"

"Fine," I said. "I can see that things are a little rough for you right now." I looked around the office. "If I can help out, a shoulder to cry on, a ten-spot till next Thursday, you let me know."

He smiled. "It's all front. Tinsel and glitter, like everything else in town. So how's Rita?"

"She's fine. Fine. She's out of the chair, you knew that?"

He grinned. "Yeah." He shook his head. "Jesus, that's great. I can't tell you how pleased I was when I heard."

I nodded. "Me too."

"Would you like something to drink? Coffee? Tea? Something stronger?"

"Tea, sure. Thanks."

He leaned back against the desk, tapped a button on his phone, and said, "Bonnie, could you bring us a pot of tea, please?" He tapped the button again, lifted a manila folder off the desktop, turned back to me. "Take a seat." He nodded to the long white sofa.

We sat down on it and he stretched back, propped his Florsheims atop the coffee table, and reached into his shirt pocket and plucked out a pack of Marlboros. He turned to me. "You're still not smoking?"

"Seven years now."

"You're not going to get all prissy on me if I light up?"

I shrugged. "Your office. Your lungs."

He smiled and stuck a cigarette between his lips, tossed the pack to the coffee table. "At least you're not a Born-Again Breather. Quite a few of those here in town." He slipped his hand into his suit coat pocket, slipped it out holding a gold Dunhill lighter, flicked the lighter, lit his cigarette, returned the lighter to his pocket. He took a long deep drag that probably left nicotine stains along the soles of his socks. I felt the ex-smoker's mixed feelings of contempt and envy.

"Okay," he said, exhaling. He opened the folder against his lap. "This is what I've been able to put together since this morning, when you called. It's not a lot, but it should get you started." From the folder he lifted a sheath of computer-form paper, the sheets still connected to one another, the sprocket strips still attached. He looked at me. "Tell me something. I didn't ask this morning because I don't function too well before that first cup of coffee. But why is it that Rita didn't do the search herself?" He sucked on his cigarette.

"The search?"

"The database search." Exhaling a cumulus of smoke, he lifted the computer paper. "For all this."

"I never asked her. I thought that you being out here, you'd be able to find the stuff more easily."

He smiled a tolerant smile. I knew it was a tolerant smile because I got a lot of those from Rita. He leaned forward, flicked his cigarette ash into a round onyx ashtray. "Joshua, most of this has been retrieved from databases that're accessible from anywhere in the world. And Rita is one of the best on-line investigators in the business. I send business to her by modem all the time. I know three or four other P.I.'s who'd be lost without her. She does it all—prejudgment and postjudgment asset searches, corporation and limited partnership information, state and federal court records. I could use one of my own people, but Rita's faster and better. She goes whizzing through those gateways like she was wearing roller skates." He inhaled on the cigarette.

"Gateways?" I said, beginning to feel like a fool.

"Information gateways. DIALOG. BSR. CompuServe. They provide access to five or six hundred different databases." He frowned. "You don't talk to Rita about all this?"

"Rita handles the computers," I said. "I'm the one who hustles the bad guys into the alley and pounds the shit out of them."

He was looking at me. I had no real idea what was going on beneath the surface of his handsome black face, but I had a sense that it was something like puzzlement, and perhaps even something like pity.

By then my transformation into fool was feeling fairly complete. I had known for years that Rita played around with a computer. *Played around* being my perception of what she did. I'd even known that from time to time she helped out other agencies, searching for information in what I had assumed was a single database. But I'd had no notion at all that she did this so extensively and so frequently.

My first reaction was to wonder why she hadn't told me. My second reaction was a variation on this, a variation distorted by a sudden, full-blown attack of the weasely unease I'd been feeling lately: why was she keeping secrets from me?

I nodded to the sheaf of computer paper in Ed Norman's hand. "So what do we have?"

Ed had the grace to pretend that nothing had happened. "Okay," he said briskly. He looked down. "Roy Alonzo. Born in Carlsbad, New Mexico, in 1946. Did elementary and high school there. Grades okay, nothing spectacular. Interest in drama. Played football, first string. No apparent trouble, no arrests. Went to Reed College, out in Oregon, in 'sixty-five. Head Start Program. Drama major. Graduated in 'sixty-nine. Once again, grades okay but not spectacular. No trouble, no arrests. Toured for a while with some improvisational group—'' He looked up. ''More of this, or shall I cut to the good stuff?''

''What's the good stuff?'' Was she planning to abandon the agency and go full time into this computer investigating?

''In 'seventy-eight,'' said Ed, ''there was a story going around that he was nearly busted for statutory rape. The girl was fifteen. Her parents got paid off and backed away. Or so the story goes.''

''How reliable is the story?'' Why else would she hide from me what she was doing?

Forget it for now, I told myself.

Ed shrugged his heavy shoulders. ''No arrest was made, no charges were ever brought. Alonzo was here in L.A. by then, and his career was coming along pretty well. He was also a certified stud, if you believe the fan magazines.''

''You bet I do.'' How could she let Ed Norman—and at least three or four other P.I.'s—know things about her that I didn't?

He smiled. ''From the source I talked to, I get the impression that there *was* a young girl, but that she didn't look anything like fifteen. One of those precocious little numbers with a twenty-three-year-old body and a forty-five-year-old soul. In fact, assuming it did happen, the whole deal could've been something she set up. Or her parents did. According to the story, they were perfectly happy to take the money and run.''

''It's a wise father who knows his child.'' Forget about it. Deal with the case.

He nodded. ''I believe I read that somewhere.'' Ed had once taught English at a small New England college.

I smiled. The smile felt a bit wan. ''What else do you have?''

Someone, just then, knocked at the door. Ed called out, ''Come in,'' and the door opened. A tea caddy entered the room, followed by the young woman from the anteroom. I stood up as she pushed the table toward the sofa. She was taller than I'd thought and she looked more voluptuous in a businesslike skirt and a demure white blouse than anyone has a right to look. I wondered if she kept secrets from people.

''Joshua,'' said Ed, smiling up at us from the sofa, ''this is my associate, Bonnie Nostromo. Bonnie, Joshua Croft.''

She smiled that remarkable smile again. Her eyes, in the natural light from the window, now seemed blue. ''Pleased to meet you.''

''And pleased to meet you.''

She smiled the smile once more and then turned and walked back to the door and out through it, closing it behind her. *Walking, through,* is really too prosaic a term to describe accurately the pneumatics and mechanics of her movement.

Ed, grinning, had been watching me watch her.

"Attractive woman," I said, feeling suddenly like a lickerish old man on a park bench.

He nodded. "A friend of mine—an unredeemed sexist, of course—described her as having the kind of body that made you proud to be a mammal."

"Proud to be a biped, too. And listen, just exactly where do you go to redeem your sexists?"

He smiled. "She's got a rated IQ of 160. She's wasted as a secretary—she's only filling in this week as a favor to me. She's one of the best surveillance people I've got. In another year she'll have her P.I. license. A year or two after that, and she'll probably open an agency of her own."

"Does she have an older sister? One with an IQ closer to mine? Something in the double digits?"

Ed raised his left eyebrow. I've always found this, probably because I've never been able to do it myself, an irritating habit. "Are you really in the market, Joshua?" He had known Rita and me for a long time now.

"No," I admitted. "Not really." I took a deep breath and nodded to the computer printout. "Okay. What else do we have on Roy?"

"No more dirt. You already know most of the rest. The divorce from Melissa Bigelow Alonzo in 'eighty-seven. The court battle in 'eighty-nine, her accusing him of sexual abuse, him denying it."

"He was found not guilty."

"The jury liked his doctor."

"Better than hers, you mean."

"Right."

"You figure him for guilty?"

He shrugged. "No way to know."

I nodded to the manila envelope. "You have transcripts in there?"

He shook his head. "Press coverage. *L.A. Times.* We can get the transcripts if you want them."

"Let's wait on that. Why don't you tell me about Melissa Alonzo."

FIVE

"MELISSA ALONZO," said Sergeant Bradley, sitting back in his swivel chair, his fingers laced comfortably together beneath the round, comfortable swell of his belly. He shook his head. "I got nothing to do with her. Like I told your buddy Norman, you should check with missing persons. Or the FBI."

"Why the FBI?" I asked him. "Why are they involved? There's no kidnapping here. She was the daughter's legal guardian."

"Hey," said Bradley, and showed me the palms of his meaty hands. "I look to you like a PR guy? Ask someone at the Bureau." He put a nice ironic twist on the word *Bureau.*

Like a lot of homicide cops, Bradley was a big man who had gotten bigger over the years. The extra weight comes from cheeseburgers and tacos and pizzas eaten on the run, and occasionally from the booze some of them use to wash away the memory of what it was they were running to, and running from.

Unlike most homicide cops, except for Meyer Meyer and Kojak, Bradley was completely bald. The shiny scalp of his big round head was dented here and there, as though bullets had bounced off it. Like the rest of him, it was untanned. So far, he was the first person I'd met in Los Angeles who didn't look like he spent the afternoons basting himself at the beach.

Ed Norman had told me that Bradley was a tough cop, but a fair one.

"That sounds," I had told him, "like the whore with a heart of gold."

Ed had smiled, and blown some cigarette smoke out across the room. "People in this town start playing out their lives the way they see them up on the silver screen."

"Terrific," I'd said. "He'll be crusty and colorful, and we'll start out hating each other's guts, but by the end of the second reel we'll establish a grudging respect for each other."

"I doubt it," he'd said. "You'll probably still hate each other's guts."

So far, I'd seen no reason to doubt Norman's prediction. For ten minutes I'd been sitting across a desk from Bradley in his cubicle at LAPD, and I'd learned nothing.

I asked Bradley, "Is there anything you can tell me about her sister's murder?"

"They got copies of the *Times* in the library. And look. You tell me you're looking for Melissa Alonzo. How come you want to know about her sister?"

"One sister disappears, and then a few months later the other sister is murdered. It seems to me possible that there's a connection."

He chuckled and his round belly, encased in a tight-fitting yellow polyester shirt, bounced up and down. "What're you? Mannix?"

I smiled amiably. I could feel the corners of my mouth working at it. "Sergeant, I'm not asking you to reveal anything about your investigation. All I'm trying to do is locate Mrs. Alonzo and her daughter. Maybe there isn't any connection. But if there is, and I locate her, then maybe she'll be able to provide information that could help you."

Grinning, Bradley shook his head. "Jesus. You're worse than Norman. You used to teach college too?"

"Home Economics."

He chuckled. He looked down at his desk, shrugged, looked back up at me. "What the hell. I can waste a half hour. But let's get the ground rules straight."

I nodded. "Go ahead."

"Your New Mexico license isn't worth jackshit here. Far as we're concerned, you're just another citizen. We get a complaint you're harassing anyone, you're history."

I nodded. "I can live with that."

"You do any surveillance, you report it to us. First. Before you start. Otherwise, you get noticed, we're gonna pick you up. And the odds are, friend, you're gonna get noticed."

I nodded.

"And you find anything, any single solitary thing, that points at somebody for the Bigelow killing, you bring it to me before you take another breath."

I nodded. "If I learn anything, I'll let you know."

"Because, my friend, if you don't, you are going to be extremely sorry."

A bit of overkill in the threat department, I thought, but didn't bother pointing out. He was establishing territory, laying down spoor in the corners of his realm. I said, "I understand, Sergeant."

"I hope so." He sat back in his swivel chair, hooked his hands behind his neck. Hector Ramirez, a friend and a Santa Fe cop, frequently did the same thing. Maybe the two of them had read the same manual. "Okay," he said. "What you wanna know?"

I got out my notebook, my pen. "Cathryn Bigelow. When was she killed?"

"Last week. October the second. Wednesday."

"Time of day?"

"Coroner figures between eight and nine in the morning."

"When was the body found?"

"Around twelve. She didn't show up for work, didn't answer the phone. A friend came by from the library to check on her. That's where Bigelow worked, the library. Friend saw the body through the kitchen window, called us."

"She was strangled."

Bradley nodded.

"And she was tortured." I'd gotten that from Ed Norman.

Bradley nodded.

"How, exactly?"

"*Exactly?*" Bradley mimicked. "You get a kick out of that shit?"

"Was it sexual torture, the kind that might be done by a psychopath? Or was it the kind of torture designed to make her talk?"

Bradley smiled sourly. "And reveal the present whereabouts of her sister, Melissa Alonzo?"

"For example."

"Alonzo disappeared two months ago. Why would the guy, whoever he was, wait all this long?"

"Was it sexual torture, Sergeant?"

He shook his head. "No." Then he grinned at me, evilly. "You want details?"

"No. But maybe, if you're willing, I'd better get some."

"He beat her. Then he tied her up. To a kitchen chair. Hands, feet, body. Gagged her with a kitchen towel. Then he started on her fingernails with a pair of pliers." He said all this flatly, watching me for a reaction.

I said, "Did she talk?"

He shrugged. "She still had some fingernails left."

"He strangled her with what?"

"A belt, probably."

"It wasn't on the scene?"

He shook his head.

So, after using it to choke away her life, the killer had calmly slipped it back around his waist. Nice.

"There was a postcard found," I said. "From her sister, postmarked in Albuquerque on September the twenty-third."

He nodded.

"You have it?" I asked him.

"It's in the evidence locker."

"*The flower in the desert lives.'* Does that mean anything to you?"

He shook his head.

"And that was all that was written on the card?"

He nodded. "That and her signature. Melissa."

"Any other kind of evidence? Prints? Fibers?"

Bradford grinned. "Jeez, you're a regular Sherlock Holmes."

"Was there any?"

"That's privileged information."

"All right. Is Melissa Alonzo a suspect?"

"Everyone's a suspect until they prove they aren't." This is what most cops believe to be an unwritten amendment to the United States Constitution.

"So you're actively looking for her?"

"Not me."

"Who then?"

"Talk to the FBI. Guy named Stamworth."

"I still don't understand why the FBI is involved."

He shrugged. "Talk to Stamworth."

"You don't really think that Melissa Alonzo tied up her sister and ripped off her fingernails?"

He shrugged. "Could of happened."

"You believe that it did?"

He shook his head.

"So what do you think happened?"

"A crazy."

"Why the fingernails? Why would a crazy want her to talk?"

Another shrug. "Who can figure crazies. We had a guy here last month, took a hammer to his landlady because she was sending death beams at him. From her microwave."

"What about Bigelow's associates? Boyfriends? Family?"

"No associates, no boyfriends. Worked as a librarian out in Brentwood. Never went out. Never did anything. Little Miss Muffet."

"How old was she?"

"Thirty-four."

"And the family?"

He smiled. "You figure Mom and Dad aced her because she didn't call 'em on the weekends? And look. Like I said before, how's this gonna help you find Alonzo?"

"I don't know. Do you know anything about a woman named Edie Carpenter?"

He grinned. "Know the story about her husband. You heard it?"

I had, from Ed Norman, but Sergeant Bradley was enjoying himself. Time for a bit of bonding here. I shook my head.

"Scriptwriter," he said, lowering his arms and putting them along the arms of his chair. "Successful. Big bucks. Edie's an actress, a second stringer, gets chewed up by the giant bug fifteen minutes in. Anyway, Carpenter marries her. Two days later he decides to kill himself." He shrugged, grinned. "Maybe Edie's too much for him. What he does, he's got one of those fax machines can send the same fax automatically to a bunch of people, one after the other. So he writes his bye-bye note, So long, sayonara, I'm splitting, and he sticks it in the machine, tells the machine to send it to everyone he knows. This is maybe thirty people. Close friends, right? Then he goes into the library and eats his Colt Commander." He grinned, shook his head.

I smiled. Once again, I could feel the muscles of my face holding the smile in place. "Where was Edie?"

He grinned again. "Getting lessons from her tennis pro. Horizontally."

"A marriage made in heaven."

"Yeah."

"What about the people he sent the faxes to? Any of them try to reach him?"

Another grin. "At three in the afternoon? In L.A.? They were all doing lunch."

I made myself smile again. "No connection between Edie and Cathryn Bigelow?"

He shook his head. "You gonna be talking to Edie?"

"She was a friend of Melissa Alonzo's."

Grinning, he ran his right hand over his shiny dented scalp. "Ask her something for me."

"What's that?"

"Ask her if she kept the fax machine."

DRIVING UP the winding turns of Laurel Canyon Boulevard, past the elms and the eucalyptus, I went over what Ed Norman had told me about Melissa Alonzo. It was better than going over what he'd told me about Rita. And what Rita hadn't told me about herself.

Melissa came, Ed had said, from Old Money. Old Money in Los Angeles is about two hundred years younger than Old Money in the East, but then things happen faster here. Her grandfather, John Bigelow, had originally put the pile together, mostly in real estate, and her father, Calvin, had added to the heap. With holdings in L.A. and the San Fernando Valley, Calvin was still involved in real estate, but he'd broadened his base to include a construction company and a bank or two.

His daughter Melissa graduated from Beverly Hills High School in 1972; afterward, she put in two years at UCLA. In 1975, at the age of twenty, she married a William Lester, some twenty-five years her senior and a business partner of her father's. While not as short-lived as Edie Carpenter's, this had been another marriage that wasn't made in heaven—Bigelow and Lester divorced a year later. Amicably, said Ed Norman.

Living in a Malibu condo paid for by her father, drifting from one nondescript secretarial job to another, taking an occasional course in political science or sociology, Melissa was, according to Ed, the kind of "rich young liberal who doesn't really come alive until she finds herself a cause." The cause Melissa found was called Sanctuary, a nondenominational group that aided refugees from Central and South America. From 1979 until she disappeared, she worked for them as a volunteer, and it was at a benefit dinner for the group that she met her future husband, Roy Alonzo.

"Sanctuary was Alonzo's pet charity," Ed had explained. "You have to understand, Joshua, that the heavy-duty actors and actresses here in town, the big stars, they're not the shallow, superficial beings you may think they are. Oh, they may blow thousands of dollars on real estate and Ferraris and nose candy, but deep down, you see, they're deeply committed human beings. Every one of them—above a certain tax bracket, anyway—has a charity of his own. Usually he's the spokesperson, and usually it's a disease of one kind or another."

He inhaled on his cigarette. "Well, by the time Alonzo was making enough cash to afford a charity of his own, all the really good diseases were taken. About the only thing left was postnasal drip. Alonzo decided to go with Sanctuary instead. It firmed up his standing in the Hispanic community, and it put him in solid with the Hollywood young guard."

I had asked him, "Sanctuary is a bit leftish?"

Smiling, Ed exhaled cigarette smoke through his nose. "In a very civilized, socially conscious way. Somewhere slightly to the right of Greenpeace, maybe."

"Being involved didn't hurt Alonzo's career?"

He smiled again. "So long as the receipts keep coming in, it's perfectly okay for you to dabble in lefty politics. Or in witchcraft, for that matter. The bottom line in this town, Joshua, is the bottom line."

I smiled back at him. "I hope I never get quite that cynical."

"Then maybe," he had told me, smiling, "you'd better head back to Santa Fe as soon as you can."

Over the next few years, Ed said, Melissa had gone, usually with other members of the group, on fact-finding missions south of the border: Nicaragua, El Salvador, Guatemala. She had continued her work with them after her divorce. It was, in fact, just before her most recently scheduled trip, back to El Salvador, that the appellate court had decided in favor of her ex-husband and his visitation rights. Melissa had gone anyway, two days later, the second of August, leaving her daughter, Winona, with her sister in Brentwood. She returned to Los Angeles on August 17, picked up Wynona, and disappeared the next day.

I had asked Ed, "Bank accounts, credit cards?"

"She closed out her accounts on the eighteenth, checking and savings, for a total of about five grand. Converted some stocks into cash, another four grand. She left all her plastic behind. No action on any of her cards since she left. Left her driver's license, too, and her passport."

"Her car?"

"She left it at the airport. Took a cab home, took another cab to her sister's house."

"She's being careful," I said.

Ed nodded.

"She was able to raise only nine thousand in cash?"

"Her lawyers, the trials, ate up most of what she had."

"She couldn't borrow a ruble or two from Mom and Dad?"

"Dad stopped paying her an allowance after she married Alonzo. He disowned her after she went to the police with the story about Alonzo's sexual abuse."

"Why?"

Ed shrugged. "Bad publicity?"

"Alonzo told me that the P.I. he hired had been able to put her with a woman named Elizabeth Drewer, a lawyer."

Ed nodded, inhaled on his Marlboro, exhaled. "You know anything about Drewer?"

"According to Alonzo, she's a connection to something called the Underground Railroad. People across the country who help women and children who're running from the kind of thing Melissa Alonzo was running from."

Another nod from Ed. "Drewer doesn't deny it. Doesn't admit it, either. But she's an industrial-strength feminist, and she's very vocal about the way the courts have handled child abuse."

"You think Alonzo could've disappeared down their pipeline?"

"It's possible. They'd be able to provide her with papers, a new name, safe houses."

"Seems a rough way for a poor little rich girl to travel."

Another shrug. "Maybe she thought the alternative was rougher."

THE HOUSE I WANTED was on a side road at the top of the mountain. Hidden from the street by a small forest of maples and elms, lying at the apex of a semicircular asphalt driveway, it was a long, low, Spanish-style structure that, if it hadn't looked as though the peons had finished erecting it just yesterday, might have been built back in the seventeenth century. I parked the rented Chevy and followed the flagstones to the front door, which was about eight feet tall and four feet wide, built of solid oak and braced with strips of antiqued black wrought iron. There was no doorbell. In the center of the door, at chest level, was a wrought iron clapper. I raised it and banged it down once. I half expected the door to be opened by Zorro.

It was opened by a maid. A real maid, in a real maid's cute little frilly black outfit that displayed quite a lot of very good leg. She was young and attractive, her features even, her hair in tight black curls, and she was, like maids were supposed to be, extremely pert. But probably, with the kind of salary she made, she could afford to be pert. She cocked her head, smiled, and she said, "Yes? May I help you?" She spoke without a French accent. This was, for me, a major disappointment.

"I'm Joshua Croft," I told her. "I have an appointment with Mrs. Carpenter."

"Yes," she said. No accent at all. The neutral, nonregional inflection of a television anchor. She smiled pertly. "Please come in."

SIX

I FOLLOWED HER down the hallway, across a living room with a floor big enough and a ceiling high enough for a soccer match, past plush cream-colored furniture and across plush cream-colored carpeting. I didn't look around for a fax machine, and I was conscious that I wasn't looking around for a fax machine.

She stopped before an open pair of French doors and turned to me. "Mrs. Carpenter is waiting for you by the pool." She gave me another smile and then flounced pertly away. Anxious, no doubt, to get back to her screenplay. Or put in a margin call.

I stepped through the doors and out onto a redwood deck. Up here, two glass tables, both surrounded by redwood chairs, sat beneath bright yellow parasols. To the left, across a swath of lawn so green it looked as though it had been spray painted this morning, the view of the city was spectacular. Or it would've been, if the city—and the sea, which was presumably out there, too, somewhere below the four o'clock sun—hadn't been buried beneath a blanket of smog. The stuff stretched out to the blur of horizon, sooty and yellow and somehow threatening, like a vast alien creature slumbering while it waited for feeding time.

Straight ahead, however, the view actually was spectacular. Lying on a white towel atop a redwood chaise, in front of a brilliant aquamarine swimming pool, was a slender woman. Her hair was thick and red. She wore a bikini bottom that was almost as large as a slingshot, and she wore a dark, even tan, and she wore nothing else. Her left hand was draped across her eyes, her hand hanging free, fingers limp. I admired the curve of her wrist very much. I admired all her curves, and she had quite a lot of them.

I crossed the deck, went down two steps to the lawn, and crossed that. "Mrs. Carpenter?" I said.

She moved her arm, turned her head, and slowly looked me up and down as though she were trying to guess my weight, or assess my stamina. Feline cheekbones, dark green feline eyes, a wide red mouth. "Croft?" she said.

I admitted that I was.

She nodded toward a redwood chair. "Grab a seat."

I sat.

She was somewhere in her thirties, maybe even in her forties, but she was fighting it, and she was winning. She was in remarkable shape, so far as I could see, and just then I could see fairly far. The muscles of her thighs were long and sleek beneath the oiled brown skin, the muscles of her stomach were slightly ridged. It was a body that had seen a certain amount of exercise. All those tennis lessons, possibly.

When she sat up and swiveled slightly to her left to raise the back of the chaise, her breasts swiveled with her, too firm to be constructed entirely of human flesh. She sat back, put her arms along the arms of the chaise. Her breasts stared at me. I tried not to stare back.

She smiled. "What can I do for you?"

I smiled. Engagingly. I was developing, like everyone else in this town, a nice repertoire of smiles. "Well," I said, "you could try putting on a shirt."

She glanced down at her breasts, glanced back up at me. Smiled again. "Never seen tits before?"

"Once," I said. "I haven't been the same since."

She looked me up and down again. Maybe she was admiring my Wrangler shirt, my Levi's, my Luchese boots. She said, "You're not gay, are you?"

"Not even giddy."

She smiled again, and then she shrugged. As her shoulders moved, her too perfect breasts slipped mechanically up and down. "What, then?"

"Mrs. Carpenter," I said, "you're an extremely attractive woman. Obviously, you take your body seriously. I take it seriously, too. The problem is, it's a bit distracting right now. I've got this job to do. I'm supposed to ask you questions about Melissa Alonzo, and, in order to do that, I have to talk. I find it very hard to talk when my mouth is filled with drool."

She laughed. Much as I had admired her body, I hadn't really liked the woman herself until she laughed. It was a good laugh.

She said, "Nicely done," as though I'd passed a test of some kind. Perhaps I had. With her left hand she reached down and lifted from beside the chaise a thin white muslin blouse. As she stretched her torso to ease it over her head, more muscles slid and tightened beneath her taut brown skin.

At least an hour every day, more likely two hours, working with free weights and Nautilus both. That was the only way anyone could put together, and keep together, a body like hers.

She shook loose her thick red hair, sat back, put her arms again along the arms of the chaise. "Better?" she smiled.

Not by much. Pointed brown nipples still peered at me from beneath the loose, gauzy material. I nodded anyway. "Thanks."

She smiled again. "You're so welcome." Clearly, she thought I was entertaining. But that was good. That was part of my master plan.

"So," she said. "What's this about Melissa?"

"Do you have any idea where she might be?"

She shrugged lightly. "None. Just like I told everyone else. You're working for Roy?"

"No," I told her.

"Who?"

"Someone who's concerned about Melissa and her daughter."

She smiled, and this time the smile was slightly sour. "Ever heard of Mary Chatsworth?"

"No."

"A television actress. A very pretty girl. I knew her. Some psycho, a fan, hired a private detective to find out where she lived. When he got the address, he drove over to her house and shot her. He killed her."

I said, "No one wants to shoot Melissa Alonzo."

"How do I know that?"

"My guileless face?"

She smiled, shook her head.

I told her.

"Roy's uncle?" she said when I finished. "And he wants to know if Roy was fiddling with Winona?"

"Yes."

"Melissa said he was. I believe her. Roy's a slime bucket."

"But you never witnessed any molestation?"

"I would've said so in court if I had." She smiled another sour smile. "But then again, it's not something you do in front of witnesses, is it?"

"You had contact with Melissa during the time of the trials?"

She shrugged. "A phone call now and then."

"When was the last time you saw or heard from her?"

"Day before she left for South America."

"In August?"

She nodded.

I asked, "You saw her or you talked to her?"

"Talked to her."

"What was her mood like?"

"Angry. Furious. Who could blame her? The court'd just told her she had to let Roy see Winona. Unsupervised visitation. Which was the last bloody thing in the world she wanted."

"She went off to El Salvador anyway."

"The trip'd been arranged for months. Melissa took all that charity business very seriously. Central America. Starving refugees. Trying to save the world." She shrugged. "She should've spent more time trying to save herself."

"Did she suggest to you then that she might disappear when she came back?"

"No," she said. Slowly, casually, she crossed her long legs. "just like I told everyone else."

I thought she was lying. I could've been wrong—I often am—but behind the overly causal movement of her legs I sensed a sudden concealed tenseness, a closing off.

"Who else asked?" I said.

"Who didn't? Roy. The police. That silly little detective Roy sent over. The group she was involved with, Sanctuary. Even the FBI. Twice."

"An agent named Stamworth?"

She nodded. "The second time. A week or two ago. He was a long cool drink of water." She smiled. "Or at least he thought he was. I wasn't thirsty at the time." Her glance slid up and down my frame again, as though she were suggesting that her thirst might have increased since then.

"Stamworth talked to you recently? When, exactly?"

She shrugged. "The end of September sometime. I don't remember the exact day."

Why had Stamworth been asking about Melissa in September? "What did he want?"

She frowned slightly. "Something to do with illegal aliens. I didn't pay much attention. I didn't care much for Stamworth. He was a jerk."

"Is Sanctuary involved with the movement of illegal aliens?"

"They're a bit too chic for that." She shrugged. "But I really wouldn't know. I don't pay much attention to do-gooders, either." She smiled. "It's not my style, doing good."

I showed her my own smile in return, the neutral one. "Did Melissa contact you when she came back to Los Angeles?"

"No." Once again, I thought she was lying.

"How did you learn she'd disappeared?"

"Roy called me and asked me if I'd seen her. The police talked to me later. Then the rest of them. It's been a damn procession."

"Did she contact you at any time afterward?"

"No."

"No calls, no letters? No postcards?"

"I got a card she sent me from El Salvador. A few days after she came back. It'd been delayed in the mail, obviously. From some town called Santa Isabel. Just your basic postcard. Hello, how are you, see you soon."

"Nothing since?"

"No."

"Does the phrase *'The flower in the desert lives'* mean anything to you?"

From her reaction, I could understand why her acting career had never gotten much past the giant bugs. She concentrated, frowning, for a beat too long before she shook her head and told me, "No."

And a good director would've told her not to pause, as she did, before she asked me, "What's *that* supposed to mean?"

"I was hoping you'd know."

She shook her head. "No. Doesn't mean anything to me."

"Roy Alonzo claims that Melissa instigated the sexual abuse charge because she was jealous of the woman Roy was seeing."

Another sour smile. "Roy's full of shit. Melissa couldn't care less about that bimbo."

"Which bimbo might that be?"

"Shana Eberle. Christ. Talk about a star-fucker."

"You know her?"

"Everyone in town knows her. *Has* known her, in the biblical sense. She's humped everyone but Lassie." Another smile. "And we're not really sure about Lassie. She's keeping mum."

"You're saying Melissa isn't a jealous woman."

"Jealous of Shana Eberle?" Amusement and scorn showed in the wide red mouth, the dark green eyes. "She thought it was a joke."

"Is she normally a jealous woman?"

"No more than most."

"How jealous is that?"

Her face tightened slightly in annoyance. "What's jealousy got to do with anything? She was divorced from the scumbag, the marriage was over, she was getting on with her life. And then she found out what her asshole ex-husband was doing to Winona. It tore her up. It would've torn anybody up. What Roy did to Winona was *vile*. But I can tell you one thing, she wasn't jealous of Shana Eberle."

"All right," I said. "She isn't a jealous woman." But I assumed, from all the smoke Edie Carpenter was putting out, that she was. Perhaps she hadn't actually been jealous of Shana Eberle; but if she had been, I wouldn't learn about it from Edie. "What kind of woman was she?"

She frowned. "How do you mean?"

"What's she like? I don't know her, Mrs. Carpenter. I need to get some kind of a handle on her. I need to know who she is. Maybe then I can figure out where she's gone. The two of you were friends."

"Friends, but not all that close."

"What's she like?"

"She's a do-gooder. Your typical kindhearted cheerleader. Very sincere, very sweet, and just a teensy-weensy bit boring."

Friends, but not all that close.

I asked, "How did you meet her?"

She smiled. A small, self-amused smile that told me she was keeping secrets, and didn't mind letting me know that she was. "At a party."

"What kind of party?"

She shrugged. "Who can remember L.A. parties?" But the smile, although diminished now, was still there. I was supposed to guess why, apparently.

I said, "She was married to Roy at the time?"

She nodded.

"Did you ever meet her sister, Cathryn?"

She shrugged lightly, dismissively. "Once. She joined us for lunch. Mousy little thing. A librarian."

She said this as though the single word somehow encapsulated the woman's entire life. As though it were an epitaph.

I started disliking her again. "You do know," I said, "that she was murdered last week."

Nodding, she said, "I read about it. This town is getting worse than Chicago in the thirties."

"Were Cathryn and Melissa close?"

"They were sisters. They kept in touch. But close? It looked to me like Cathryn wasn't close to anyone." Abruptly she narrowed her green eyes. "You don't think that Cathryn's getting killed has anything to do with Melissa?"

I said to her the same thing I'd said to Bradley, the homicide cop. "One sister disappears, the other's killed a few months later. It's possible there's a connection."

She looked off for a moment, thoughtfully. For the first time I believed that what she was doing was genuine and not a performance. Then she shook her head, looked back at me. "People are getting killed in Los Angeles all the time."

"But they're not related to Melissa Alonzo."

"How could what happened to Cathryn have anything to do with Melissa?"

"I don't know yet. Maybe it doesn't."

"It doesn't," she said. "It couldn't." I got the impression that I wasn't the only one she was trying to convince.

"If it does," I said, "Melissa Alonzo may be in danger. Her sister wasn't just killed. She was tortured. Probably for some time."

Her face was closed, shuttered. She didn't want to believe me, didn't want to listen. Perhaps she felt that if Melissa actually were in danger, then she herself might be partially responsible. Melissa, therefore, could not be in danger.

I said, "I'm trying to help Melissa, Mrs. Carpenter. If you know anything at all about where she might be, where she might've gone, you'd only be doing her a favor by telling me."

She shook her head. "I told you. I haven't got any idea."

I asked her, "What do you know about Elizabeth Drewer?" Dazzle them with a sudden change in the questions. Interrogation 101.

We were back to performances once again. To demonstrate concentration, she paused longer than she should have. "A lawyer, isn't she? One of the firebrand feminists."

"She's supposed to be connected to the Underground Railroad."

She demonstrated puzzlement.

"They help women in Melissa's position," I said. "Women who're trying to keep their children away from abusing fathers."

She nodded. "I read about them, I think. *People* magazine."

Maybe I should renew my subscription. "Did Melissa ever mention them to you?"

She uncrossed her legs, drew up her right knee. Another lie approaching? "No," she said.

"Never mentioned Elizabeth Drewer?"

"No."

"And you have no idea where she might've gone."

"Like I said."

"All right," I said. "Thank you, Mrs. Carpenter."

"Edie," she said. She smiled. "Are you off duty now?"

"Nope." I stood. "Back to the salt mines." I reached into my shirt pocket, plucked out my card and my Erasermate. On the back of the card I wrote down the name of my hotel. I handed her the card. "I'll be there tonight. If you think of anything that might help me locate Melissa, could you give me a call?"

Smiling, she tapped the card with a long red fingernail. "Are you sure I can't offer you a drink? Something else?"

I ignored the intentional broadness of that *something else*. I smiled back. My guileless smile, deliberately obtuse. "Thanks, I appreciate it, but I've got an appointment. Maybe some other time. And if Melissa does contact you, anytime in the future, could you give her my Santa Fe number?"

"You know," she said, smiling, "you could do pretty well in this town."

"How's that?"

"You don't have any appointment. You haven't looked at your watch since you sat down. You're a damn good liar, Croft."

I grinned down at her. "You're not bad yourself, Edie."

She stared at me for a moment, and then she laughed. It was still a good laugh. She looked me up and down again. Then she showed me that she was the second person I'd seen today who was able to raise a single eyebrow. "Well," she said, "that remains to be seen."

SEVEN

I *DID* HAVE an appointment, but it wasn't until six thirty. I thought I might have time to pick up some California fast food—an abalone tortilla, maybe, or an escargot-and-pineapple pizza. But the traffic was terrible, bumper-to-bumper cars breathing frustrated hydrocarbon sighs at each other, and I spent over an hour getting to the beach. At the entrance to Malibu Colony, the guard found my name on his clipboard, told me that Mr. Arthur was waiting at the Alonzo house, and explained how to get there.

As I drove down the street, I could smell, through the open window of the Chevy, the astringent tang of brine and kelp, and even here, out at the farthest reaches of Civilization As We Know It, the quintessential Southern California scent of automobile exhaust.

For the most part, the houses along the shore side of the road were alike—narrow, two-story buildings of weathered gray shingle, some of them looking like they'd been imported from Cape Cod or Fire Island, all of them so close together you could spit from your window into your neighbor's margarita. All sat with their backsides facing the street and their fronts facing west, so their owners could enjoy an expensive view of sea blurred by smog. Beyond the houses, where the sun should have been, the sky was a dull apocalyptic red, as though out there on the gray Pacific, beneath a pall of dense yellow smoke, a city were afire.

The Alonzo house was newer than most of the others, a long, modernistic structure that looked like irregularly shaped boxes of cedar and glass, jumbled together by a very large hyperkinetic child. A spotless black Mercedes 250-SL, its top down, was parked in the shade of the carport. I pulled the Geo in beside it, got out, walked over to the unprepossessing wooden door, and pushed the doorbell.

After several long moments, the door was opened by a man wearing black leather loafers, lightweight gray wool slacks, an open vest of the same material, a dark blue silk shirt with the sleeves rolled back, and a silk tie of gold and red with its Windsor knot loosened and tugged down, all of which made him look like a straightforward, no-nonsense kind of guy. Maybe he was. He was in his early thirties, tall, and in very good shape. His shirt—and presumably the vest and the missing suit coat—had been cut to display the nicely defined curve of his pectorals. His wavy hair was brown and so was his Tom Selleck mustache. He was tanned.

"Croft?" he said.

I admitted I was.

"Chuck Arthur." Unsmiling, he held out his tanned hand. I shook it. He didn't move from the doorway and he didn't invite me in. He said, "I'm not sure why I agreed to this."

"Maybe because you're concerned about Melissa Alonzo and her daughter," I said.

"I *am* concerned. Damned concerned. I hate to think of the two of them out there, on the run. But I'm still not sure that talking to you is a good idea."

"I'm not the enemy, Mr. Arthur. I told you over the phone, my primary interest is in delivering Mr. Montoya's message to Mrs. Alonzo."

He looked at me for a moment, expressionless. "Well," he said finally. "Come on in."

We went down the passageway, passing several closed doors—storage space, perhaps, or slaves' quarters.

The air smelled of wood polish and cleanser, like an obscure museum, often cleaned, seldom visited. Our footsteps, echoing faintly back from ahead, clipped the silence into hollow fragments.

The passageway opened up into a sunken living room with white sectional furniture surrounding a large rectangular stone fireplace, also white. Abstract paintings, their colors muted in the dim light, hung on the white walls. Above the fireplace, an enormous inverted funnel of stainless steel chimney climbed to the faraway beamed ceiling. We walked down some polished tile steps, crossed the brick floor of the living room, walked up some more tile steps to the terrazzo floor of the dining room, past a round white-enameled wooden table circled by white-enameled wooden chairs, and through an opened sliding glass door to a glass-enclosed porch. Beyond them, another sliding door, partially opened, led out onto a redwood deck that held, along the side abutting the house, a pair of ficuses in large terra-cotta pots. The floor in here was oak, bleached and waxed, but the furniture once again was white, a metal table and three metal chairs padded with white corduroy cushions. Draped from the arched back of one of the chairs was a gray suit coat.

Chuck Arthur stood for a moment, hands in his pockets, looking out of the wall of glass at the smudged red and yellow bands in the darkening sky. If you didn't know what caused them, they might have been pretty—a soft, distant, impressionistic blur of color. The tide was out, and a few people, mostly couples in shorts or rolled-up trousers, walked along the smooth brown sand. Out on the water, some motorboats loafed across the gray. In the sky, some seagulls soared.

"You picked a fine time to visit Los Angeles," he said without looking at me. "This is the worst smog I've ever seen. It never used to get all the way out here, to the beaches. You could stand here, anywhere along the coast, and you could see practically all the way to Hawaii." He frowned. "It gets worse every year." He was killing time, I thought, postponing a possible confrontation.

He turned, stepped over to the entryway, pushed a button. Above us, a neon light flickered for an instant, then glowed, filling the room with that artificial brightness that seems, while there's still some light in the sky, thin and paltry and sad. "Have a seat," he told me.

I sat down on the far side of the table and he sat opposite me, in the chair that held his suit coat. "All right," he said. "You're looking for Melissa Alonzo."

"That's right."

"And, according to you, you're not working for her ex-husband."

"Right."

"This story about Alonzo's uncle. I hope you don't mind if I tell you that I still find it a little difficult to believe."

"I don't mind," I said. "Sometimes I have problems with it myself. But like I said over the phone, you can call Martin Durham in Santa Fe. He'll verify everything."

"I did call him, and he did." He smiled a small, wry smile. "But I'm a lawyer myself, remember. I don't necessarily have to believe everything another lawyer tells me."

I smiled. "Even when he used to be a governor?"

He smiled back. "Especially then." His face became expressionless again. "You said you intended to act only as a go-between, without telling Mr. Montoya where Melissa is. If you do find her, what will prevent him from hiring someone else to follow your trail?"

"For one thing, I'll keep looking for her."

He thought a moment, then nodded. "After you find her, you mean."

I nodded. "I won't contact him until I've moved on a reasonable distance from wherever she is."

A faint smile. "Is that ethical?"

I shrugged. "I told Mr. Montoya that I'd do whatever I could to guarantee Melissa and Winona's safety."

"You'll be charging him for work that you won't actually be doing."

"I can live with that. So can he."

Another faint smile. "Are you always so relaxed about overcharging your clients?"

"Not always," I said. I smiled; I was careful to smile. "But then I'm not a lawyer."

He laughed. There was some surprise and some reluctance in the laughter. "Is that your standard technique for lowering a witness's defenses? Insulting his profession?"

"When I think it'll work."

He looked at me, smiling thoughtfully. Then he nodded. "All right. What can I do for you?"

"You represented Melissa in her divorce, as well as the custody thing."

"Yes."

"I imagine you got to know her fairly well."

He shrugged lightly. "Inevitable, given the nature of the case."

"What did you think of her?"

He seemed surprised. "Why?"

"I don't know the woman. And knowing something about her, about the kind of person she was, might be helpful."

Another small, wry smile. "The psychological approach?"

"Yeah. They said in the correspondence course that it was a good way to go when there was nobody around to beat up."

He smiled. Again he looked at me thoughtfully for a moment, and again he made up his mind. "Melissa Alonzo," he said, "is one of the bravest women I've ever known."

He said it with a casual matter-of-factness that was more impressive, and more believable, than an intense conviction. That told me a few things. It told me that possibly he cared for Melissa beyond the boundaries of the lawyer-client relationship. And it told me that, because he might, I'd have to be careful with the questions I asked him. It told me, too, that I'd have to be careful with the answers he gave. He might not consciously lie to me, but if he were involved with Melissa, or if he'd wanted to be, his attachment to her might color his perceptions. I glanced at his left hand. No wedding ring.

It could be. Even lawyers, I had heard, can make fools of themselves for love.

And so, I had heard, can private detectives.

"Brave how?" I asked him.

"She has this...she has a really remarkable inner strength. She's—you've seen pictures of her? You know what she looks like?"

I nodded.

His eyes were brighter now and his face was animated. "Well," he said, "here's this slight, slim woman—she's in her thirties but she looks like a teenage girl—and you think, Jesus, a strong breeze would blow her over. She's very open, very unguarded, very... innocent. Almost an Alice in Wonderland figure. And she gives you the feeling that she could be hurt extremely easily. And she *could* be. She *is*. She's certainly sensitive, and she's certainly had more than her share of pain and disappointment. But beneath all the other qualities there's an amazing strength of character. All through the trial, with reporters badgering her, her family ignoring her, her husband lying through his teeth up on the stand, she never broke. She had some rough moments. She had some extremely rough moments. A couple of times there I thought she was gone. I thought she'd crumble. But she always picked herself up and got on with the business at hand. She's an extraordinary woman."

I nodded. I no longer wondered whether the man had been attached to Melissa. Any lawyer learns early on to hide his feelings. And a divorce lawyer can see people at their worst, at their most wounded, their most malicious. A lot of divorce lawyers become hardened. He hadn't. Or, if he had, something about Melissa Alonzo had caused him to open his shell to her. And now to me.

"And she was a wonderful mother," he said. "Caring. Supportive. Protective of Winona without trying to smother her."

"After the trial," I said, "or during it, did Melissa ever talk about running off with Winona?"

He considered his answer. Finally, expressionless once again, he said, "I'm sorry. That would have been privileged communication. I can't answer that question." He was trying, I thought, to walk a line that wound precariously between his legal ethics, his residual wariness of me, and his desire to help find Melissa. But he must have known that by refusing to answer the question, he was permitting me to assume that Melissa had in fact mentioned the idea of running off.

I said, "Can you tell me if she ever discussed the Underground Railroad with you? A network that helps hide women and their children?"

He shook his head. "I'm sorry. I can't answer that either." Which again, if I was reading him correctly, probably meant that Melissa *had* discussed the Railroad.

"Were you surprised when Melissa vanished?"

"Yes," he said—more at ease, apparently, now that he could answer without playing games. "Completely surprised. We had an appointment at my office on the twenty-third. The twenty-third of August. She was due back the twenty-first. When she didn't show up, I tried to reach her. When I couldn't, I . . . I made a few inquiries. That's when I learned that she'd gone."

"You didn't know that she'd come back early from El Salvador?"

"No." He frowned slightly. That still rankled. Or still hurt.

"Did you try to locate her?" I said.

"I know a private detective. He's worked with me from time to time. I asked him to see what he could find." He made it sound casual, an offhand request to an old friend. Both of us knew that locating someone who doesn't want to be located is not an offhand kind of job.

"And what did he find?"

"Nothing."

"Have you heard from her since she left?"

He took a deep breath, the kind you take when you try to fill an emptiness in your chest that has nothing to do with oxygen, and already I knew what his answer would be, and I knew that I believed it. "No," he said. "Nothing."

He looked out the window. The blur of red and yellow was gone now. Except for a faint luminescence in the west, the sky and the sea were a dull seamless sheet of lead.

I asked him, "Does the phrase *'The flower in the desert lives'* mean anything to you?"

"No," he said to the window. He turned to me. "Should it?"

"Maybe not. It's just a phrase that's come up. Did Melissa ever talk with you about her involvement in Sanctuary?"

"Nothing specific. We talked about it in general terms. She was very serious about helping those people." He shrugged, and his shoulders seemed to have gotten heavier. "As I said, she's an extraordinary woman."

He looked off to the window again.

"In your mind," I said, "there's no doubt that Roy Alonzo was guilty of sexually abusing Winona?"

He turned, and his face was flushed. For a moment I thought he was going to hurl aside the table and jump me. I braced myself. Then he sat back. "You haven't read the trial transcripts," he said flatly.

"Not yet."

"Read them. There's no doubt whatever that Roy was guilty."

I nodded. "You understand that I had to ask."

He stared at me, and finally his face softened and he nodded. He looked out again at the leaden sea.

I said, "Would you mind if I looked around the house now?"

He turned to me. He managed a weak, ironic smile. "Do you think the police haven't looked around? The FBI?"

"An agent named Stamworth?"

He nodded. "Some nonsense about Melissa being involved with illegal aliens. He went all over the house. So did the police."

And so did you, probably, I thought. I said, "Maybe they weren't looking for the right things."

He nodded lifelessly. His voice without tone, he said, "The psychological approach."

"Yeah. That."

"Go ahead. The bedrooms are upstairs. I'll wait here."

THERE WERE THREE BEDROOMS on the second floor. The first might have been Roy Alonzo's bedroom at one time, if he and Melissa had slept separately. Now it was obviously a guest room, as characterless and as impersonal as a room at the Marriott. A white-enameled dresser, a white-enameled nightstand supporting a brass three-way lamp, a double bed with a chenille bedspread, a fairly good Navajo rug on the hardwood floor, an empty closet. Two framed paintings, both Southwest landscapes, hung on the wall. They were signed *Sedgewick,* a name that meant nothing to me. A door led into a bathroom smelling of the floral-scented soap, sculpted into hearts and eggs, that filled a small wicker basket on the windowsill.

I got the feeling that whoever had put the bedroom and the bathroom together—and I assumed it was Melissa—had done so without much enthusiasm. They were moderately comfortable, but they were perfunctory and prosaic, as though she hadn't really expected guests, or particularly wanted them.

I broke the bedroom into quadrants and searched each of them. Found nothing useful. Did the same in the bathroom, and found the same.

The master bedroom smelled very faintly of Jean Naté. It had a beamed ceiling and, like the porch downstairs, a glass wall that faced the sea. Pale yellow satin drapes, pulled shut now. A king-size bed lounging in a sleek brass frame and covered with a white satin bedspread. Two white Flokati rugs on the floor. A long oak dresser. Atop that, facing the bed, a twenty-one-inch color television, a VCR, a large jewelry box, a single photograph in a silver frame. Obviously taken by a professional photographer, this showed a young baby, presumably Winona, gurgling merrily at the camera. There were no photographs of anyone else. No Roy Alonzo, no grinning friends, no beaming grandparents.

On the wall above the bed was another Southwest landscape, also signed *Sedgewick,* this one a Cinemascope view of Monument Valley. A bit gaudy, I thought, but technically well done. John Wayne would've liked it. There were two other paintings in the room, to the left of the television. These were much smaller, both about six inches by twelve, and each was a view from a doorway into the interior of a room, one of them a parlor, the other a kitchen. The light in each had a Vermeerish quality, glinting off polished surfaces of tile and wood, and the paintings themselves, precisely detailed, had a quiet elegance and a slightly haunting quality, as though the rooms were inhabited by smiling ghosts, just out of sight. They were signed *D. Polk.*

The paintings and the yellow drapes were the only touch of color in the room. Everything else was white or off-white, monotoned, making the place seem stark, almost sterile. As though Melissa had been reluctant to reveal herself by committing to blues or reds or browns, plaids or checks or stripes.

I searched the room, and then the dressing room and then the bathroom, which held a sunken hot tub large enough to bathe a Buick. At the bottom of one of the dresser drawers, I found a pair of handcuffs. A nice toy. I wondered what the earlier searchers had made of those. I wondered what I made of those.

There was none of the other grim paraphernalia of bondage: no riding crops, no choke collars, no clamps or clips or shiny leather straps. Maybe there had been, and the cops had removed it. But wouldn't they have taken the cuffs as well?

In the jewelry box, which held mostly costume stuff, rolled gold and paste, I discovered that a few of the slots in the velvet, slots which still bore the impression of jewelry, were empty now: some earrings and some rings were missing. Melissa might have taken them, possibly pawned them; or possibly they'd been lifted by someone else. The cops. Stamworth. Chuck Arthur, for all I knew.

All I knew was approximately nothing.

I found nothing to indicate that a man, any man, had ever once set foot in the room. I found no note from Melissa Alonzo that described her current location.

The final bedroom was a surprising contrast to the rest of the house, a giddy explosion of color. The walls were pink, banded toward the ceiling with lavender, covered all over with appliqués of laughing cartoon characters, teddy bears and rabbits and Smurfs and the entire Disney contingent. The curtains were red, patterned with large black dots, like the wings of a ladybug. Braided, multicolored throw rugs were scattered around the floor. And stuffed animals were everywhere: along the walls, along the bright yellow bedspread, sitting and lying and slouching in the blue plastic bookshelves.

I looked around and, once again, I found nothing. I sat down on the bed, picked up a brown rabbit. It seemed old, older than the toy of a six-year-old, its plush worn down to the thread in spots, its long ears limp. Perhaps it had once been Melissa's.

I glanced around the room. It was cheery, festive—happy. I wondered whether Melissa, whose decorating had been so restrained throughout the rest of the house, who seemed to have denied a fondness for color and patterns, as though perhaps she were hiding herself, had felt suddenly liberated when she designed this room for her daughter.

I looked down into the shiny brown glass eyes of the rabbit. He didn't know the answer. Or if he did, he wasn't telling.

EIGHT

WHEN I GOT back downstairs, Arthur still sat staring out at the sea, which was invisible now in the blackness. His face, reflected in the glass wall, was empty.

He glanced at me, silently watched me circle the bar, turn on the light, and enter the kitchen. It had all the cooking toys, and then some—a restaurant-quality gas oven and stove, a microwave-convection oven, a Cuisinart, a blender, rows of Sheffield knives, ceramic pots holding an assortment of metal spatulas and wooden spoons, a deep freeze filled on one side with uncooked roasts and steaks and chops and hams and fish, and half filled on the other with leftovers carefully wrapped in aluminum foil and carefully labeled: pot roast, coq au vin, pork in ginger sauce. The cabinets were packed with expensive crockery and an impressive array of herbs and spices. Someone had removed all the perishables from the refrigerator, but it still contained a forest of commercial sauces and condiments: green chili jam, blueberry preserves, mayonnaise, three imported mustards, curry paste, mango pickle, lime chutney.

From all of this I deduced that Melissa had been something of a cook. Or that Winona had been. Or that the two of them had hired someone who was.

At the end of the bar, an answering machine sat beside a cordless telephone and its base. The indicator said that there were no messages, which meant that someone, at some time, had retrieved whatever messages might have been on the tape. But most of these machines don't erase the most recent messages, even after they've been retrieved, until they record over them to receive a new one. I pushed the button. There was a silence, someone not speaking after hearing the outgoing message, then a beep. Another silence, then a series of three beeps, to let me know there were no more messages available.

I fiddled with the machine until I found the button that played the outgoing message. I pushed it. A woman's voice, flat, nonregional, announced the phone number and asked the caller to leave a message.

Melissa's voice, presumably. Melissa herself was off somewhere, but here in Malibu her disembodied voice was still mechanically greeting callers.

The voice told me nothing about its owner. I hadn't expected it to; people are usually a bit constrained when they're recording a message into their machine.

After the tape rewound, I opened the machine, fumbled the tiny cassette out of its berth, carried it around the bar and out to the porch.

Chuck Arthur said, "Jesus, that gave me a start. Hearing Melissa's voice on the machine like that."

"When the police were here," I said, "did they take anything from the house?"

He shook his head. "No. Nothing."

"Did Stamworth?"

"No."

"Has anyone, that you're aware of? Have you?"

"No, of course I haven't. No one has."

I nodded. "You wouldn't happen to have a mini tape recorder, would you?"

He frowned. "In the car."

I would've bet on it. Would've bet that he had a cellular phone, too. And a laptop computer. Maybe he and Rita had modemed together.

"Could you get it?" I asked him.

"Why?"

I held up the cassette. "After you retrieve your messages, the answering machine rewinds the tape to the beginning. Any new messages are recorded over the messages already on the tape. But if there're more old messages than new ones, some of the old ones, the ones that haven't been recorded over, will still be there. The machine won't play them, because it only plays the messages that've come in since you last retrieved. But they're still there."

He looked at the cassette. "And you think that'll help, listening to the messages?"

"Let's find out."

ONCE I'D LOADED the cassette into Chuck Arthur's minirecorder and turned it on, the first thing that Arthur and I heard was Melissa's outgoing message. I glanced across the table at Arthur. He was staring down at the machine, his lower lip caught between his teeth, his head slightly cocked. Suddenly, as the message ended, he reached out, lifted the machine from the table, and hit the Stop button.

I looked at him. "Why?"

"This is a patent invasion of privacy." He held the recorder tightly in his hand—his tanned knuckles were white. Beneath his mustache, his mouth was set.

"You're her attorney," I said.

"Yes, but you're not."

"Come on, Arthur. We both want the same thing. We both want Melissa and Winona safe and sound. The cops can't find her, the FBI can't find her. Your private detective couldn't find her. Did he think to check the tape?"

He frowned.

"No," I said, "he didn't. So already we're ahead of the game, the two of us." Bonding.

"The police must've checked it."

"Maybe they did. And maybe they didn't—I don't think they put a real high priority on finding Melissa. You were here when Stamworth searched the house?"

He nodded. "He listened to the machine. I watched him. But he didn't take out the tape."

Penalty against Stamworth. Five yards. Stupidity.

"When was this?" I asked him.

"Two weeks ago. He said he was investigating a connection between Melissa and illegal aliens."

"Melissa's sister was killed last week. Did you know that?"

"Yes."

"Did you ever meet her?"

He frowned, probably wondering where I was going with this. "Once. At court. Afterward. Just for a moment. I got the impression that she felt she wasn't supposed to be there. She was nervous. Worried that someone might see her talking to Melissa."

"Who?"

He shrugged. "The press. And then it would get back to their parents. Melissa was the black sheep in her family. Her father's a stubborn old goat. He was furious about the court case, and he'd disinherited Melissa. Cathryn wasn't supposed to contact her."

"Did Cathryn ever contact you, let you know that she'd heard from Melissa?"

"No." He looked at me, his eyes narrowing. "You're suggesting that Cathryn's death *is* connected to Melissa somehow."

"No one else seems to think so. And maybe they're right. But what if they're wrong? Wouldn't that suggest to you that Melissa and Winona might be in danger themselves?"

He said nothing. He looked down at the recorder in his hand.

"Look," I said. "I'm good at what I do. I don't have the resources that the cops and the feds have, but I don't have their bureaucracies either. And I'm a stubborn bastard. I'm going to find Melissa and I'm going to make sure that she and her daughter are okay, whether you help me or not. But if you do help me, I just might be able to find her a little faster."

It was a good speech, and I believed most of it.

So did Arthur, apparently. He took another deep breath, frowned again, and then, without a word, he leaned forward, set the machine on the metal table, and pushed the Play button.

The two of us listened to what I'd heard before—the two blank spots on the tape in which someone, or two someones, had hung up after Melissa's outgoing message. They were followed by a faint metallic click, and then three more hang-ups separated by beeps. The faint click came again, then a man's voice, one I thought I recognized:

"... *check in with you later. Bye.*"

I reached out, hit the Stop button. "That's you?" I asked Arthur. "That's your message?"

"Yes."

"Any way of telling when you left it?"

He shook his head. "I generally left the same message whenever I got her machine. Is it important?"

I shrugged. "Maybe. When was the last time you left a message?"

"On the twenty-third," he said. "The day she was supposed to come to my office."

I hit the Play button. The machine beeped and then a woman's voice said, *"Mel? Hi, this is Deirdre. Give me a call when you get a chance."*

I turned off the machine. I asked Arthur, "You know a Deirdre?"

He shook his head.

I hit the Start button. Another beep, then a different woman's voice, in Spanish, urgent, and trembling with something like fear. *"This is Juanita. I have just heard, Melissa. Call me right away."*

I stopped the machine, looked at Arthur. "What about Juanita?"

Frowning, he shook his head. "That was Spanish?"

"Yeah." I translated it for him.

He was still frowning. "Did she sound frightened to you?"

"Maybe. Hard to tell. Did anyone take Melissa's messages while she was in El Salvador?"

"I don't know. She had a woman come in, but I don't know what kind of arrangement they had."

"Do you know the woman's name?"

"Not offhand. It's a Spanish name. Not Juanita. I can find it. My secretary makes out her checks."

"You're paying Melissa's bills?"

"It's only temporary," he said, a bit defensive. "I'm billing her account."

"At her request?"

"Someone had to take care of it. She can settle when she comes back."

I nodded. The electricity was still on, so presumably he was paying that, too. And probably some kind of maintenance fee to keep Melissa in good standing with the Colony. He had to know that he had no legal obligation to pay anything, and that Melissa had no legal obligation to pay anything back, when she returned. If she returned.

"The woman's still cleaning the house?" I asked him.

"Once a week."

"Could you get in touch with her? Find out if she's checking the messages now, and if she checked them while Melissa was in El Salvador?"

He nodded. "I'll call her tonight."

"Thanks." I hit the Start button. We heard a beep, and then a deep, rumbling actor's baritone, angry. *"Where the hell are you, Melissa?"*

I turned off the tape player. "That's Roy Alonzo."

Arthur nodded.

"The beeps," I said, "mean a separation between a set of messages. That little click means that we're moving from one set of messages to another. An earlier set."

"So this set may be from the twenty-third. Alonzo and I were still trying to reach her here."

"Yeah." I hit the button. Another beep, and then:

"Melissa, are you back yet? This is your mother, dear. Call me, would you?"

A beep, a pause, another beep, then the metallic click. Then:

"Call me, dear." Melissa's mother again.

A beep. Then: *"Hi, Mel. This is Deirdre. I just got your message. I'm back home, and I'll be here all night, so give me a call if you can."*

A beep. Then: *"Melissa, this is Chuck Arthur. Would you call me sometime tomorrow morning? I'd like to talk to you before we go to court. Bye."*

I shut off the machine. "Can you remember when you left that?"

"Well, obviously," he said, "it had to be during one of the trials. The divorce or the child abuse case."

"Usually, when you left a message, did you call yourself Chuck or Chuck Arthur?"

"Chuck Arthur." He frowned. "I may've given you the wrong impression. What we had, Melissa and I, was only a professional relationship."

However much he might have wanted it otherwise. I nodded. I hit the Play button. A beep sounded. Then Roy Alonzo's voice came racketing out of the tiny speaker, higher in register now, and shredded with anguish:

"How can you do this, Mel? How can you do it to me, how can you do it to Winona? How can you tell all these lies you're telling!"

NINE

"AND WHAT DID Arthur say to that?" Rita asked me over the phone.

"He wasn't very concerned," I told her. "He pointed out that Alonzo was an actor. And also that there was no way of determining exactly when the message was left. Roy might've left it back in the beginning of all this, when he still thought he could persuade Melissa she was wrong."

"And what do you say?"

"About Roy abusing Winona? I can't say anything yet, Rita. So far, everyone I've talked to is in Melissa's camp, more or less."

"Arthur's planning to get back to you about the cleaning woman? The one who might've written down Melissa's messages?"

"He already has. He called me tonight. She checked the machine twice, she says. Once on the fifth, once on the fifteenth. No messages. Everyone must've known that Melissa was out of the country. The woman, a Carlotta Garcia, still goes to clean once a week, and there haven't been any messages since August."

"Did Melissa return to her house before she disappeared from Los Angeles?"

"Apparently. Arthur got a locksmith to open up the place. The police came along with them. She'd left a bunch of clothes on the closet floor. The cleaning woman says they weren't there on the fifteenth. Presumably Melissa grabbed some new clothes and took off."

"Were there any messages on the machine when Arthur and the police went in?"

"No. According to Arthur."

"So. Melissa probably checked her machine when she returned from El Salvador on the seventeenth. Arthur's right. The calls from him and Deirdre and Juanita probably came in on the twenty-third of August."

"What it looks like."

"And Melissa was gone by then."

"Right."

"You'll have to find Deirdre and Juanita."

"No shit, Rita."

"You'll find them. Have you checked her phone records for August?"

"Arthur has the bills. He'll fax them to the service tomorrow."

"We need our own fax machine, Joshua."

"Right. We'll talk about it later." And perhaps we'd talk about a few other things, too.

"You always say that, Joshua."

"A creature of habit."

"A creature of bad habit."

"But nonetheless charming."

"What are you doing tonight?"

"I thought I'd just lie here on the bed and pine for you."

"That sounds very productive."

"It's a very nice bed, Rita. Maybe you could fly out here and examine it. It might contain clues. It might contain me."

"I'm sure it's a wonderful bed. It's too bad you'll have to get out of it to meet with Ed Norman in half an hour."

"Ah. So you talked to Ed." Learning that she'd talked to him only underscored what I felt, had been feeling all day, about Rita and her secrets.

"Briefly," she said. "He called to say hello."

"If you already knew I was meeting him, then why ask what I'm doing tonight?"

I could hear the smile in her voice. "Just checking to see if your level of invention was up to par. When are you talking to Elizabeth Drewer?" Trust Rita to get back to business.

"Tomorrow morning."

"Good. Who else are you seeing?"

"Guy named Hatfield. He's the chairman for the group Melissa was involved with. Sanctuary. And Melissa's parents, if I can get in touch with them. They haven't returned my calls."

"You're still planning to fly back tomorrow night?"

"Unless something turns up."

"But right now your feeling is that Melissa disappeared somewhere along the Underground Railroad."

"Yeah. That's the impression I get, talking to Carpenter and Arthur. She didn't want Alonzo anywhere near her daughter, and that may've looked like the only way out."

"There *is* another possibility."

With Rita, there usually was. "And what's that?"

"We're assuming that she's running from Roy Alonzo. But she was down in El Salvador just before she disappeared. It's still a politically volatile country. Perhaps something happened to her down there. And perhaps that's what she's running from. You said that Arthur was surprised when she disappeared without contacting him. If you're right, and Melissa had already discussed the Railroad with him, why wouldn't she talk to him before she used it?"

"I don't know."

"And why did she return early from El Salvador?"

"Beats me."

"Didn't you say that Carpenter had received a card from some Salvadoran town?"

"Santa Isabel."

"Santa Isabel. I'll look into it."

"On the database?"

"Yes."

"Well," I said. "Good luck." I didn't put much conviction into the words. I didn't think Rita would learn anything important, no matter how well she maneuvered through her databases. Or perhaps I didn't want her to.

"Thank you," she said. She didn't put much conviction in her words, either. "I'll see you on Thursday. Give my regards to Ed."

I wanted to ask her why she hadn't told me about her being an internationally famous computer wizard. I wanted to ask her if she was planning to leave the agency and set up a business of her own.

I didn't. I said, "I will," and I said, "Goodbye," and I hung up.

I NEVER GOT A CHANCE to give Rita's regards to Ed Norman. He never showed. I waited twenty minutes in the bar downstairs, trying not to listen to people at nearby tables as they talked expansively about packages and product and Julia and Warren. I sipped at my Jack Daniel's and wondered how many of these deals were real and how many were sheer fantasy. In a town built upon fantasy, it was probably impossible to say. I doubted whether any of these tanned stalwarts in Armani jackets actually knew for certain themselves.

Also, I spent some time pouting. Was Rita going to leave the agency? After all the time we'd spent together? After all that we'd meant to each other? Or after all, at any rate, that she'd meant to me?

I knew, a part of me knew, that Rita's leaving was unlikely. Probably unlikely. Not terribly likely. But the possibility did exist, and self-pity will burn whatever fuel is available. I was working myself into a pretty good brood when someone, a woman, said, "Mr. Croft?"

I looked up, and then I stood up. For a moment I didn't recognize her. Dark-haired, blue-eyed, stunning, she wore a short red dress as tight and shiny as the peel of an apple.

"Bonnie Nostromo," she said, smiling. "We met today at Ed's office."

"Of course. Good to see you. Have a seat."

Holding a small red purse in her left hand, she lowered herself into the chair opposite me with an efficient, liquid grace—no small feat, considering the dress she wore.

As though reading my mind, she smiled her memorable smile when I sat, and she said, "This isn't what I'd usually wear to a place like this. I was working on something when Ed got in touch with me. He had to run up to La Jolla, an emergency, and he couldn't get through to you."

I'd been on the phone most of the evening, trying to reach Melissa Alonzo's parents, and then talking to Rita.

I said, "So Ed sent you instead?" Your professional detective is trained to make these startling intuitive leaps.

She nodded. "I've got some of the information you asked for. Edie Carpenter, the Underground Railroad, Elizabeth Drewer."

A cocktail waitress materialized to my right. "Can I get the lady something?"

I was a tad disappointed to see that Bonnie Nostromo smiled as genuinely at the waitress as she'd smiled to me. She ordered a club soda and lime. Not a designer water, I noted, and I was vaguely, irrationally pleased. I ordered another Jack Daniel's.

As the waitress left, Bonnie opened her purse, took out some folded sheets of paper, opened them. "Can you read shorthand?" she asked me.

I shook my head. "I sometimes have trouble with basic English."

She smiled. I noted that she wore no ring on the fourth finger of her left hand. "I'll translate," she said. "Which first? Carpenter?"

"Why not?" Her breasts, firm and round beneath the taut red fabric, had almost certainly never been touched by a surgeon. Except perhaps by an off-duty surgeon, and then, no doubt, with enthusiasm and a sense of enormous good fortune.

"Do you want it all?" she said. "History? Career?"

"Not unless it connects to Melissa Alonzo."

"You want the dirt, you mean."

"I collect it. I've got a big ball of it at home."

She smiled. "I know the feeling. You never know what you're going to find under the rocks, do you?"

"Except that it's almost never gold."

Another smile. I noticed that she had an attractive overbite, just like the women on "Valdez!" I wondered if she had a boyfriend. Did women still have boyfriends these days, or only Significant Others? Did they keep secrets from their Significant Others? "No gold here," she said. "The story is that Carpenter's a swinger, kinky, into S and M, very big time."

"We're talking what?"

"Leather. Whips. Private parties. Mistresses, masters, slaves. The usual sad nonsense."

I remembered Edie Carpenter's smile when she told me she'd met Melissa at a party. I remembered the handcuffs I'd found in Melissa Alonzo's dresser.

I said, "The usual?"

"It's not that uncommon here. L.A. La-la Land. Everything and anything is possible. These people, Carpenter's playmates, they're all rich. Upper-upper-middle class, lower-middle age. They've got all the toys they've ever wanted, and they still feel hollow. Some of them try to fill up the hollowness by acting out their sexual hang-ups. They have get-togethers. Parties. They play whatever role turns them on."

The waitress brought our drinks and I asked her to put them on my tab. She was agreeable.

As she left, I asked Bonnie, "Carpenter organizes these?"

"Sometimes, so the story goes. Sometimes she's only a participant."

"And what role turns Carpenter on?"

She sipped at her soda. "Mistress. Dominatrix."

I nodded. "She'd look good in leather." She certainly looked good out of it. And so, it occurred to me, would Bonnie Nostromo. "Is there anything to tie Melissa Alonzo to these soirées?"

"Nothing definite. This is all gossip, Mr. Croft. Gossip is one of the major currencies in this town. But a lot of it is counterfeit."

"Joshua. Please. You're making me feel upper-upper-middle aged."

She smiled that smile again. "Joshua."

Maybe I should invite her up to my room. We could discuss all this in private. I could explain some of the finer points of investigative work.

"What's the *nothing definite?*" I asked.

"Old stories. Secondhand, thirdhand. Stories that Roy and Melissa Alonzo would show up once in a while."

"As participants?"

"From what I gather, one is more or less compelled to participate. If you're a participant, you're not likely to go telling stories about everyone else."

"Everyone else could tell the same stories about you."

She nodded. "But as I said, this is all second- and thirdhand information."

"Do we know what sort of roles Roy and Melissa favored?"

"Roy, according to the stories, was the dominant, Melissa the submissive."

"Those are the technical terms?"

"Those are the terms these people use. Sadist and masochist are passé."

I nodded. "Okay. Tell me about the Underground Railroad."

What she told me was that the people responsible for its organization were careful and smart. A woman and a child in need of help—occasionally a man and a child—first contacted them through an intermediary. Who, in Melissa Alonzo's case, might well have been Elizabeth Drewer. They, whoever they were, would request convincing proof that sexual abuse had been committed. If they determined to their satisfaction that it had, and that the woman had attempted every legal means to protect the child, and had failed, they would provide her with instructions. How to vanish, leaving behind no trail. Where to go. How to get there: often by bus, sometimes in a private car with a driver, a "conductor," who was part of the network.

From what Bonnie had been able to learn, there were four loosely structured but interlocking networks, one in the Northwest, one in the Northeast, and two in the South.

As she talked, I regarded Bonnie Nostromo's face, her blue eyes, her mobile, intelligent features. I wondered if she'd ever considered vanishing from Los Angeles. Ever considered, for example, relocating to a small, quaint Southwestern town...

"Sometimes," she said, "they can zigzag, the mother and child, up and down the country, moving from one safe house to another. Go to Boise, Idaho, and then Las Vegas, and then Rockford, Illinois, and then New Orleans, or wherever, before they finally settle down."

"Why zigzag?"

"There are some states where the network hasn't organized any safe house."

"These people, the Railroad, they provide papers? ID?"

"Usually. Birth certificates, some of them forged. Some obtained from public records."

"They visit cemeteries, find names whose birth dates match."

She nodded. "And with the birth certificates, they can get drivers' licenses, Social Security cards."

It was the classic method for obtaining false papers. "So who are they? The organizers?"

She sipped at her soda. "No one seems to know," she said. "There are supposed to be four or five of them. Elizabeth Drewer might be one."

"Who runs the safe houses?"

She shrugged. "They call themselves 'keymasters.' Some of them, apparently, are old sixties radicals. Some of them are children's rights advocates. Some are just sympathetic families—sometimes the wife, sometimes the father, has a history of having been sexually abused."

"Where are we getting all this information?"

"Off the databases. Magazine articles."

"People?"

She smiled. "Among others."

I'd put the check in the mail tomorrow.

"Okay," I said. "Elizabeth Drewer?"

"She's one of the most vocal supporters of the Railroad here in California. Or at least here in Los Angeles. And, as I said, she may be one of the organizers. Rumor says she is. But so far the FBI hasn't been able to prove it. She's extremely bright. Ed says you're talking to her tomorrow."

I nodded.

She said, "I'd suggest you don't try to bullshit her. She's also extremely tough."

"I'm the soul of guilelessness," I said. And then I asked her, guilelessly, "Would you like another soda?" Maybe the bubbles would go to her head and I could sling her over my shoulder and cart her off to my lair.

She shook her head. "No thanks. Got to run. I was supposed to meet a friend of mine over an hour ago."

Ah.

I said, "One more thing. In all this checking you've done, did you run across anyone named Deirdre? Or a woman named Juanita?"

She shook her head. "No. Are they important?"

"I don't know yet."

"No. Sorry." She folded the sheets of paper, which she hadn't once looked at while she spoke, slipped them back into her purse, and smiled. "It was a pleasure talking to you. I wonder if I could ask you a really big favor?"

"What's that?"

"Could you tell Rita, Mrs. Mondragón, how much I admire her work? We've talked, over the phone and over the modem, but I've never really had a chance to tell her that I think she's just amazing."

Wonderful. I nodded. "I'll do that," I said.

TEN

I LAY ON THE BED staring at the photograph Roy Alonzo had given me back in Santa Fe.

It showed a woman in jeans and a sweatshirt and running shoes leaning back against a low adobe wall, brown hills studded with piñon and juniper rolling off into the background. The sky was blue, as it usually is in New Mexico. The woman squinted against the sun, and her arms were folded together beneath her breasts, and her legs were crossed, and she stood with her hip canted a bit stiffly, as though she felt awkward being photographed. Her pale, fine blond hair fell straight to her shoulders, making her look, as Chuck Arthur had said, like an Alice in Wonderland figure. Her smile, like her pose, was a bit stiff. She had been thirty-three when the picture was taken, but looked much younger. Perhaps because the stiffness, the awkwardness, made her appear tentative, vulnerable, even somewhat lost.

Melissa Alonzo.

And now in fact she was lost.

Where are you, Melissa? On a bus somewhere right now, you and Winona huddled together on a hard flat seat, hurtling through the darkness down a long empty highway? Do you miss your hot tub? Your Cuisinart? Your handcuffs? Your peace of mind?

Did Winona miss her rabbit?

And *who* are you? A poor little rich girl? A political activist? A wife fighting to save her daughter from a monster of a father? A woman driven by jealousy and spite? A bored Hollywood homemaker with a fondness for an occasional bout of S and M?

Taken together, all the snippets of information I'd collected—none of them supported by any hard facts, except a nice house and a pair of handcuffs—didn't jell into the young woman who stood there poised so awkwardly against that adobe wall, beneath that bright New Mexican sun.

I was still staring at the photograph when someone knocked at the door to my hotel room.

I looked at my watch. Five after twelve. Five after one back in Santa Fe.

Bonnie Nostromo? Swept away by my charm, she'd decided to forgo her boyfriend?

I rolled off the bed, crossed the room. There was no peephole set into the door, but, so far as I knew, I hadn't antagonized anyone in Los Angeles.

I opened the door without asking who might be out there.

The man standing outside the door was tall and broad shouldered, and he wore a pale yellow shirt, a Countess Mara tie, and a dark gray three-piece suit that had probably made several thousand silkworms extremely proud, or extremely frazzled. The coat was so exquisitely tailored that, unless you were looking for it, you might never notice the very faint bulge under the left shoulder. I could afford a suit like that if Rita and I had gone through an exceptionally good month, and my landlord had let the rent slide.

His ruggedly handsome face was square, with a firm, determined jaw neatly bisected by a manly cleft. His eyes were brown and steady. His hair was dark brown and curly. He had a splendid tan. I was beginning to believe that everyone who worked in L.A. had been hired from Central Casting, and that none of them had ever heard of skin cancer.

He smiled politely and said, "Mr. Croft?"

"Yes."

"Jim Stamworth. FBI. May I come in?"

I looked at my watch, to see what his reaction might be.

He smiled politely again. "Just a few questions. They won't take long."

I nodded. "Come in."

He came in and I gestured toward the two overstuffed chairs by the window. He walked across the room and sat down in one, gave a gentle tug to the knees of his slacks, and crossed his legs, left ankle over right knee. Shiny silk socks that matched his suit, sleek black leather slip-on shoes. Italian, probably.

I sat down in the other chair, stretched out my legs and crossed them ankle over ankle. I'd kicked off the boots when I arrived in the room and I was wearing white cotton socks. Taiwanese, probably.

I said, "What can I do for you?"

He smiled politely again. "We understand that you're attempting to determine the whereabouts of Mrs. Melissa Alonzo."

"We?" I said.

"The Bureau."

"Do you have any identification, Mr. Stamworth?"

Another polite smile. "Of course." He reached into the inside pocket of his suit coat, slipped out a black eelskin billfold, opened it, handed it to me. His hands were nicely manicured.

The photo on the ID looked like him, although not quite so ruggedly handsome. Nothing in the world could look quite so ruggedly handsome. I handed the billfold back and he returned it to his pocket. I asked him, "What's the FBI's interest in Mrs. Alonzo?"

Still another polite smile. "It's two pronged, actually. One team is attempting to locate her because by removing her daughter from Los Angeles without permission, Mrs. Alonzo put herself in violation of a court order. By crossing state lines, she put herself within the jurisdiction of the Bureau. My own concern, however, is somewhat different."

"How so?"

"We have reason to believe," he said, "that Mrs. Alonzo might be able to assist us with an ongoing investigation into the movement of illegal aliens into the United States."

"Assist you how?"

"We have evidence which suggests that Mrs. Alonzo, through her involvement in a certain political group, may possess valuable information about such activities." He still hadn't run out of polite smiles. Nor polite evasions. "Now, Mr. Croft, may I ask the questions for a while?"

"Sure," I said. "Which certain political group?"

He shook his head slightly, still smiling. "My turn, I believe."

I shrugged. "Go ahead."

"Who was it that employed you to locate Mrs. Alonzo?"

"I'm sorry," I said. "But I'm not at liberty to discuss that." I don't know why I didn't tell him; I'd told everybody else, and if he really wanted to know, he could find out without too much trouble. I was probably just being a jerk.

He managed another polite smile, but I had a feeling he was nearing the end of his supply. "Mr. Croft," he said, "under both state and federal law, a private investigator has no claim to the privilege of confidentiality."

"Unless he's working under retainer for an attorney."

"And are you?"

"Martin Durham in Santa Fe." Before Norman Montoya had left my house last night, he'd called the lawyer and told him that I was now, technically, working for Durham. Told him. Martin Durham, a former state senator, a former governor, and one of the most expensive and powerful lawyers in New Mexico, had immediately agreed. I said, "I'm afraid you'll have to talk to Mr. Durham."

Stamworth surprised me by finding, somewhere in his reserves, yet another polite smile. He slid a small eelskin notebook from his shirt pocket, and then a Montblanc ballpoint pen. He flipped open the notebook and wrote something in it. Durham's name, possibly. Possibly a reminder to get his shoes buffed.

He looked at me and his handsome face went ruggedly serious. "Mr. Croft," he said. "Shall we be frank?"

"Let's."

"I have no interest in Mrs. Alonzo's flight from California, per se. My only concern is our illegal-alien investigation. As a matter of fact, if Mrs. Alonzo should be disposed to cooperate with us in this matter, I think I can safely say that the Bureau would be inclined to... ignore, shall we say, the matter of her flight from California. And even, perhaps, assist her in a relocation of some sort."

"You'd work a deal with her."

He smiled broadly, apparently gratified by my quick understanding. His teeth were very white. "Exactly," he said. "But in order to arrange this, of course, we need to contact Mrs. Alonzo."

"And so far you haven't."

"Precisely. Now, we've checked you out, Mr. Croft, you and Mrs. Mondragón. From the records we have available, the two of you appear to run an exemplary private agency. You, personally, seem to be an intelligent and determined investigator. I'm hoping that you'll be disposed to cooperate with us."

"Work a deal with you."

He smiled, gratified once more. I was coming along nicely. "It's always a good thing," he said, "to have a friend or two at the federal level."

That was the carrot. I wondered how long it would take him to bring out the stick.

"And naturally," he said, smiling, "it would be a shame *not* to have a friend or two at the federal level."

Not long. It was a stick wrapped in velvet, but it was a stick.

"Let me ask you something," I said.

"What?"

"CPA or law?" The FBI recruited only CPAs and attorneys.

He smiled. "Law."

I wasn't surprised. CPAs don't usually have so large a reservoir of polite smiles.

I said, "Who are these illegal aliens you're interested in?"

Another smile. "To quote you, Mr. Croft, I'm not at liberty to reveal that."

"Fair enough," I said. I was tired. I stood up. "It's been a pleasure talking to you, Mr. Stamworth. Maybe we can do it again sometime."

"Sit down, Croft," he said. The reservoir was empty. His voice was hard.

I smiled. "Do you have a warrant? Search? Arrest? Anything?"

"I can get one."

"On what basis? What just cause?"

"I'll think of something."

"You do that. In the meantime, you're leaving and I'm going to bed. Good night."

Still sitting in the chair, he looked down at the floor, examined the carpeting for a while, then looked back up at me. "Let's not get off on the wrong foot," he said. "I'd appreciate a few more minutes of your time. Believe me, this is as much for your benefit as for mine."

I doubted that, but I sat down anyway.

He studied me for a bit, and then he said, "I assume you have some conception of Bureau agents as storm troopers, swooping out of the night to grab terrified families of poor starving migrant workers."

"I don't have any conception of Bureau agents at all." Except for a suspicion that this particular agent was about to start laying down a scam.

"That might've been true," he said, "back in the old days. But we've changed. We've cleaned up our act. We—most of us, anyway—believe in due process. We believe that the ends don't justify the means."

I smiled. "Didn't I hear you mention something about a warrant?"

His polite smile resurfaced. "I regret that. Sometimes unfortunate things are said in the heat of the moment."

He studied me some more, his handsome features thoughtful. Finally he said, "I'm going to take a chance with you, Mr. Croft."

"Golly," I said.

If he heard the sarcasm, he ignored it. "I'll need your word that what I'm about to tell you will never be repeated to anyone."

"I can't give it. Mrs. Mondragón will have to know everything I know."

"Excepting Mrs. Mondragón."

"Fine."

He nodded. "You've heard of Sendero Luminoso?"

"Shining Path," I said. "Terrorists. Or guerrillas. Or freedom fighters, depending on your point of view. Peru?"

"Peru. And no matter what they call themselves, they're terrorists pure and simple. We have reason to believe—and I'm talking solid evidence, not hearsay—that a cadre of Shining Path terrorists has infiltrated itself into the United States, disguised themselves as illegal aliens from Salvador and Guatemala and utilizing the various underground groups that assist such people."

"And why is a Shining Path cadre sneaking into the United States?"

He shook his head. "I'm sorry, Mr. Croft, truly sorry, but that comes under the heading of national security. Suffice it to say that, on the evidence we possess, the threat they represent is immediate and quite real."

"So you think Melissa Alonzo is involved with a group of terrorists."

"Not wittingly, we believe. We have no reason to think that Mrs. Alonzo sympathizes with these people. We suspect she knows nothing about their intentions and their true identities. But we do believe that she may possess information as to their location."

"And what is it you want me to do?"

"We'd be very grateful if you gave some serious consideration to apprising Mrs. Alonzo of the situation, assuming you do manage to contact her. If you can persuade her to get in touch with us, you'll be doing both Mrs. Alonzo and yourself a great favor."

I nodded. "Okay," I said. "I'll give it some serious consideration."

He smiled politely once more. He reached into his coat pocket, slipped out his eelskin billfold again, took from it a business card, handed me the card. "I can be reached at that number anytime, night or day. If you do locate Mrs. Alonzo, please ask her to call me."

I nodded noncommittally.

He stood up. "Thank you for your time, Mr. Croft."

He held out his hand and I shook it. I asked him, "What about Cathryn Bigelow?"

He frowned. "What about her?"

"Does her death have anything to do with Melissa's disappearance?"

Another frown. "Why should it? From what I understand, the police believe that a psychotic is responsible."

"Is that what you believe?"

"I haven't given it any thought. The two things have nothing to do with each other."

I nodded.

"Well," he said. "I hope we'll be hearing from you. Or from Mrs. Alonzo."

"We'll see."

He showed me his polite smile one more time, in case I'd forgotten what it looked like. "So we shall," he said.

After he left, I lay for a while on the bed staring at his card. It was an expensive card, heavy off-white paper, embossed black print. *James B. Stamworth, Special Agent, Federal Bureau of Investigation.* The phone number was a local call, prefixed by 213, L.A.'s main area code.

Like Stamworth himself, the card seemed a bit too expensive. The man wasn't picking up tailored silk suits and Montblanc pens on an FBI agent's salary. Maybe he was an independently wealthy young swell who'd decided, as a lark, to become a crimebuster. The FBI, for all I knew, was riddled with independently wealthy young swells in silk suits.

But I doubted it. And the shoulder rig bothered me. According to a Santa Fe friend, a gun buff who followed such things, the FBI these days was partial to hip holsters, and usually they filled them with the Smith & Wesson .38 or, on more merry occasions, with the Smith 9-millimeter automatic. The bulge under Stamworth's carefully tailored suit suggested something larger. A Glock, maybe. Or a Scud missile.

And I really couldn't see the FBI dividing its forces, setting up a two-pronged operation, to look for one woman. A woman who, after all, was hardly Ma Barker.

And Stamworth's story about the Shining Path cadre sounded like something that had been slapped together, on an off day, by the Brothers Grimm. The last I heard, the Shining Path people were too busy toppling the Peruvian economy to worry about exporting terrorism, or anything else, into North America.

But if Stamworth wasn't FBI, then who was he? And how had he managed to track me down so quickly?

Sergeant Bradford, the L.A. homicide cop, knew where I was staying. But Bradford, even if he actually bought Stamworth's FBI story, hadn't seemed particularly disposed to cooperate with the Bureau.

Edie Carpenter knew, but why would she notify Stamworth? Why would Chuck Arthur?

Stamworth had claimed that he—they—had checked out me and Rita. That might have been smoke. But if it wasn't, it argued some sort of organization behind him.

Or did it? Maybe he was a computer whiz, like Rita.

In any event, it seemed to me that Stamworth was probably not what he claimed he was.

But even if he wasn't FBI, he could very well be from some other obscure branch of the federal government, which meant that he could have already arranged a tap on the hotel phone.

ELEVEN

ELIZABETH DREWER looked exactly like what she, and possibly what *People* magazine, claimed she was. In her early forties, with close-cropped and curly salt-and-pepper hair, wearing a navy blue skirt and a matching coat, a pale blue blouse and a red and blue Hermès scarf, she was the perfect picture, almost the stereotype, of a tough, businesslike woman attorney. She didn't have a tan, but maybe, even in L.A., tough, businesslike women attorneys weren't supposed to

Her face was lean, her nose narrow and pointed, her mouth thin. It was a face that, when animated, would be attractive; but when guarded, as it was now, seemed pinched and disapproving. She was tall and angular, filled with a wary nervous energy, and she held and she moved her body as though it were a vaguely irritating but necessary apparatus into which she'd slipped that morning, like a suit of armor. Perhaps when she got back home, she clambered out of the thing, and her bright restless spirit, suddenly loosed from the burden of flesh, flittered and swooped from room to room.

Her eyes were brown and they had been unfriendly since I sat down opposite her on Wednesday morning, across a desk littered with computer printouts and legal texts and a sprawl of file folders. The rest of the office was impeccably neat, but this wasn't much of an accomplishment, because the rest of the office was all bookshelves, every one of them packed with law books. One small window looked out onto a small courtyard that held a single dispirited palm tree shading a patch of Culver City gravel. It was the office of someone who hasn't experienced a great deal of financial success, possibly because she didn't care much about it.

"Look," she said when I finished explaining my reason for invading her life, "let's cut the shit." Sitting back in her swivel chair, holding a yellow Bic pen between the first two fingers of her right hand, she tapped it against the edge of her desktop, rapidly, steadily, like a speed-freak drummer in a rock band. "First of all, even if I *had* been contacted by Melissa Alonzo, which I don't for a moment admit, the nature of the attorney-client relationship precludes my discussing it. You're familiar with the word *precludes?*"

I smiled pleasantly. "Maybe if you spelled it."

"Secondly," she said, "I don't like private detectives. I've had too many nasty experiences with them."

I smiled pleasantly again. It was only slightly more difficult this time. "Mrs. Drewer—"

"Ms.," she said, without losing her steady beat against the desktop.

"Ms. Drewer." Of course. "I only accepted this case because it seemed to me that Mrs. Alonzo"—she frowned, I smiled apologetically and silently cursed the person who had invented that ugly word—"*Ms.* Alonzo might be in danger. Her sister was killed last week. It's possible that there may be a connection between the sister's death and Ms. Alonzo's disappearance."

"What evidence do you have to support that contention?"

"None. But it's not a contention. If I'm contending anything, I'm contending that it's a possibility."

"It's an unlikelihood. Melissa Alonzo disappeared almost two months ago." Still tapping against the desktop, she said, "You're working for Roy Alonzo." It wasn't a question.

"No," I said.

Her thin lips moved slightly in something that was more a sneer than a smile. It suggested that she knew more about this particular situation than I did, and probably more about most other situations, as well. "Really?" she said. "For who, then?"

For whom, I nearly corrected her. I didn't. We might have sat there all day, taking turns correcting each other's speech. "For his uncle." I explained the arrangement I'd made with Norman Montoya.

"You expect me to believe that?" she said. The small superior sneer hadn't left her lips.

I was beginning to suspect that Elizabeth Drewer and I would never exchange girlish confidences. "What I expect and what I hope are two different things," I said. "I was hoping that you'd give me the benefit of the doubt."

"The benefit of the doubt," she repeated, and bitterness made the words curl up at the edges. "That's what the judge gave Roy Alonzo. Do you know what Roy Alonzo did to his five-year-old daughter?"

"I know what he was acquitted of doing."

"If you'd read the transcripts, you'd know that the evidence was absolutely conclusive." She swiveled the ballpoint, held it as though it were a pen and not a drumstick, and then knifed its point against her desk blotter, once, sharply. "Winona testified that her father forced her to commit fellatio." She knifed the penpoint against the blotter again. "Winona's hymen was ruptured." Another stab. "There was evidence of rectal scarring."

Involuntarily, I winced. "Why did the court decide that the abuse hadn't occured?"

She turned the pen into a drumstick again, began tapping it. "Because the judge couldn't believe that such a thing was possible. No father, no upright male citizen, could ever commit those terrible acts. And since it was impossible—despite the incontrovertible evidence—Roy Alonzo was given access to his daughter."

"There must've been conflicting medical testimony."

"Oh, naturally there was. Alonzo paraded his two paid physicians past the judge. Hired guns." She smiled a small bitter smile. "Like yourself."

"Ms. Drewer," I said. "I know you're convinced that Roy Alonzo sexually abused his daughter. For all I know, you're right. But suppose you're wrong. Suppose Melissa Alonzo invented all this, out of anger or spite."

"She didn't invent the medical evidence."

"The medical evidence is open to interpretation. And suppose that once Melissa made the accusation, the process she set in motion made it impossible for her to retract it. Suppose she got caught up in something she never intended. Suppose Roy Alonzo is innocent."

She had been waiting for me to finish, and not patiently. Still tapping her pen against the desktop, she said sharply, "I don't deal in suppositions."

"If Roy Alonzo is innocent," I said, "if he didn't abuse his daughter, a father has been separated from his child for no good reason. And his child is being dragged around the country, living like a fugitive, afraid to answer the door, afraid to answer the telephone. She's a six-year-old girl. If Roy Alonzo is innocent— even if he isn't—should any six-year-old girl have to live like that?"

Eyeing me, still tapping: "What makes you think that the girl is living like a fugitive?"

"I'm assuming that she and her mother are somewhere along the Underground Railroad."

"It sounds to me like you're awfully fond of assumptions and suppositions."

"From what I understand, the people in charge of the Railroad are sincere and dedicated. They honestly believe they're doing the right thing. And probably, in most cases, they are. But they're still only people. They can make mistakes."

"No matter what you may have heard," she said, "I can't speak for the Underground Railroad. But from what *I* understand, their screening process is extremely thorough. And if they've assisted Melissa Alonzo, they haven't made any mistake. That was as clear cut an example of sexual abuse as I've ever seen."

"You said yourself that at least two doctors disagreed."

"I also said they were hired hands."

"But what if the Railroad did make a—"

She stopped tapping her pen. She leaned forward and narrowed her eyes. "Listen to me. I was an abused child myself. I married a slimeball who abused my daughter when she was three years old. It's an insidious pattern—abused children become abusers themselves, or marry men who are. Not always, but often enough. Too often. In any case, I know *personally* the kind of psychological damage that sexual abuse can cause. And if it were up to me, if I *did* have any say into who was helped by the Railroad, and if there were even the remotest possibility that the child in question had been subjected to abuse, I'd say help her. Get her away from the father. *Immediately.* Anything, even living like a fugitive, is better than that. Better than even the *possibility* of that. And, frankly, if it were up to me, I'd see to it that every man convicted of sexual abuse was legally castrated."

I opened my mouth to say something, but she wasn't finished. She was summing up, and I was merely a member of the jury.

"And in the case of Winona Alonzo," she continued, "there's not the remotest possibility that she *wasn't* sexually abused." She sat back, folded her arms beneath her breasts. Thank you, ladies and gentlemen.

I nodded. Time to change direction. I said, "Once a mother and a child are being moved along the Railroad, is there any way for someone to contact them?"

She shrugged, her shoulders stiff, her armor locked tightly into place. "Why ask me?"

"Because I'm assuming that you have some connections with people in the Railroad."

"Another assumption," she said flatly.

"Look, Ms. Drewer, no matter what you think, I'm not the enemy." I'd been saying this a lot lately. "I'm trying to help Melissa and Winona Alonzo. Let's phrase it hypothetically. *If* a woman and a child were being hidden by the Railroad, would there be some way for someone to contact them?"

She shugged again. "Possibly."

I reached into my blazer pocket, took out the envelope carrying the letter I'd written this morning, at the desk in my hotel room. I sat forward, laid the envelope on her desk, sat back. "That's a letter to Melissa Alonzo. It outlines the arrangements that Norman Montoya is prepared to make on her behalf. The envelope is open, you're welcome to read it. It also includes my Santa Fe office number and address. And my home phone number. Melissa can call me at either place, anytime. If I'm out, she can leave a message."

"If I accept that," she said, "my acceptance might imply that I was in some way aiding and abetting a fugitive."

"Then don't take it," I said. "Leave it on the desk. Maybe Melissa Alonzo will wander in here and pick it up."

She glanced down at the envelope, her face empty, her body immobile.

I asked her, "Did Melissa ever mention a woman named Deirdre? Or a woman named Juanita?"

She smiled sourly. "I told you. Even if I had been contacted by Ms. Alonzo, the nature of that contact would be confidential."

I stood. "Thanks for your time, Ms. Drewer."

She looked up at me. "You won't find her," she said.

"I'll find her," I said. But I said it less out of genuine belief than out of a sudden childish desire to pierce that brittle armor she hid behind.

I didn't succeed. She only sat there and smiled up at me, smiled her small superior smile.

I left.

CALVIN BIGELOW, Melissa's father, hadn't returned any of the phone calls I'd been making since yesterday, so I decided to try the personal approach. Bigelow Realty was in Century City, across town. I took Santa Monica Boulevard, the rented Chevy scooting demurely alongside sleek Rolls-Royces and Jags and Mercedes-Benzes. Mostly Benzes, sedate sedans and sporty convertibles, although I noticed an occasional low-slung Ferrari slinking by. The

Ferraris would've been a novelty in Santa Fe. The kind of people who own Ferraris in L.A. buy Range Rovers when they move to Santa Fe, so they can demonstrate their pioneer spirit.

Today a breeze was straggling in from the sea and the smog had scattered. The air smelled stale, as though it had been pumped there from some vast underground storage tank, but the sky overhead was bright blue and the windows on the skyscrapers sparkled like diamonds. Or at least like rhinestones. Los Angeles, I decided, wouldn't be a bad place to live, if you liked living among a lot of tall buildings and a lot of tanned people.

Calvin Bigelow's office was in one of the tall buildings, on the top floor, and his secretary was one of the tanned people. In her mid-twenties, regulation beautiful, she wore a white ruffled blouse, a small black bow tie, frosted blond hair, and a pair of designer glasses with stems that dipped down to her angled cheekbones before sweeping up to the top of the lens frames. I suspected that the lenses were plain plastic, a prop to make her look more like a secretary and less like a cupcake.

Maybe Ed Norman was right. Maybe L.A. made everyone cynical. Or maybe I was just feeling somewhat sour after my encounter with Elizabeth Drewer.

I gave her my name and asked to see Mr. Bigelow. She was polite but dubious, despite the tie I'd put on downstairs in the marbled lobby. One of the three ties I owned, it was red silk, and I was mildly distressed to discover that it hadn't swept her off her feet.

She told me, her feet firmly planted somewhere beneath her large Danish Modern desk, that Mr. Bigelow was busy at the moment and didn't see anyone without an appointment. I suggested she let him know that I was here, and told her I'd wait. I sat down on a long gray tweed settee and picked up a copy of *National Geographic*. It was the classic September 1986 issue. I was just getting excited about the Pacific island of Nauru, where a mountain of bird guano provided the citizens with one of the highest per capita incomes in the world, making it something like Los Angeles, when the secretary told me that Mr. Bigelow would see me now.

Nauru and the bird guano would have to wait.

TWELVE

CALVIN BIGELOW'S OFFICE was twice the size of Ed Norman's. Two walls, paneled in dark wood, held framed paintings of ships running with the wind, sails taut, and framed photographs of prosperous people shaking hands and grinning at each other. Prosperous people evidently did this fairly often. The other two walls were lightly tinted glass, providing a lovely panoramic view of some tinted windows on another tall building. At the angle where the glass walls met, an enormous oval desk of mahogany or teak sat, and behind it, turned into a silhouette by the light beyond, sat Calvin Bigelow.

He didn't stand during the fifteen or twenty minutes it took me to cross the expanse of ivory-yellow carpet. He didn't stand when I reached the desk. He looked up at me, his arms atop the desk, his fingers laced, and he said, "I let you in so we could get this over with. You've got three minutes." He nodded to a chair to my right. "Sit," he said.

I sat down and admired the scale model perched atop his desk. It was a sailing yacht, a ketch, a beautiful boat, built to sit low in the water and slice through it like a saber.

"Mr. Bigelow," I began.

"Your phone message said you wanted to know about my daughter," he said. "I have no daughter. I lost the only daughter I had last week. A vicious, brutal, unnecessary death. I know nothing about Melissa Alonzo. I have no information about the woman, and no desire to obtain any. That should satisfy you. If it doesn't, you'll have to ask elsewhere."

Closer up, in better light, I saw that he was a beefy man in his sixties. His wavy white hair was combed back from a precise widow's peak. His face was dark, but a bright florid red rather than the usual California tan. It was the kind of ruddy complexion that came from standing at the tiller while the wind and the spray beat at you and the sun drummed down. Or from three-martini lunches. The pouches beneath his hazel eyes and the tracery of veins across the bridge of his nose suggested the latter. Still, he had clearly been a handsome man at one time, and even now he was a man of presence.

"Mr. Bigelow," I said. "I can understand your grief at the death of your daughter. I honestly regret having to intrude at a time like this. But I believe it's possible that the death of your daughter Cathryn and the disappearance of Melissa may be connected in some way."

He unlaced his fingers and put his hands along the edge of the desk. His face had gotten redder. "That is absolute, utter horseshit. Cathryn was killed by a maniac. A psychotic. How dare you imply that she had anything to do with Melissa?"

"She was apparently in contact with Melissa."

"*Melissa* was in contact with Cathryn. One goddamn postcard. Cathryn would never have contacted Melissa. Never. She knew what Melissa is, knew what kind of life she leads."

"What kind of life is that?"

"Depraved. Abandoned." He started to say something, then looked at his gold mariner's Rolex. "Your time is up," he announced.

"Mr. Bigelow, maybe you've got good reason to feel the way you do about your daughter. But aren't you concerned about your granddaughter?"

He stabbed his thumb at a button on his desk. He turned to me, his florid face set. "I told you. I know nothing, and I care nothing, about Melissa Alonzo. And I know and care nothing about any member of her family."

"We're talking about a six-year-old girl, Mr. Bigelow. A six-year-old girl isn't responsible for the kind of life her mother leads. You can't just let her—"

He slammed his hand down against the top of his desk. "Don't you goddamn tell *me* what I *can* and *can't* do! I don't have to take that, not from some goddamn slimy private eye in goddamn *cowboy* boots! You get the fuck—" He turned toward the door and then gestured toward me, abruptly, with his thumb. *"Get him out of here,"* he growled.

I turned.

I hadn't heard them come in. Both of them wore sleekly styled khaki rent-a-cop uniforms. Italian, probably. One of them was big and slope-shouldered, his belly sagging like a beanbag over his belt. The other was small and wiry and he moved very nicely on the balls of his feet. He was the one carrying the police baton, slapping it lightly into the palm of his left hand. He was smiling and his eyes were eager.

"Well now, Ace," he said, smiling as he floated lightly across the carpet, "guess it's time for you to say your goodbyes and come along like a nice little boy."

I stood up and reached into my blazer. The short rent-a-cop stopped moving forward and stopped smiling. He blinked nervously—neither he nor his friend was wearing a gun. I took out a business card, set it on Calvin Bigelow's desk. "If you change your mind," I told Bigelow.

Without looking at me or the card, Bigelow said to the guards, "Throw him out."

The short rent-a-cop made a mistake then. Maybe he resented my causing, and seeing, his brief flicker of fear. Maybe, like Bigelow, he didn't like my cowboy boots. Whatever the reason, he grabbed at my left arm with his left hand and raised the baton in his right.

It had been a bad day for me, first Elizabeth Drewer and now Bigelow and his Keystone Kops, and I was not in the best of moods. I went with the force of his pull, throwing him off balance, then slammed the heel of my hand up into his jaw. His teeth clicked and his eyes went loose. He lowered the baton.

I turned to the big guard, who had just realized that things weren't going according to plan. His arms were reaching for me as though he wanted to sweep me into an embrace. I hit him as hard as I could, just below the sternum. You don't aim for the surface, the skin and flesh—you aim for the spine. He gasped, doubling over, and his sweeping arms flew down and grabbed at his belly.

I turned to the smaller guard. He was about to make a comeback, shaking his head and trying to focus as he raised the baton again. I clipped him on the jaw with a pretty good left and he took two steps backward and sat down. The baton bounced once, then thumped against the carpet.

I looked at Bigelow. He had the telephone receiver to his ear and he was quickly tapping buttons on the base unit. His florid face seemed a shade or two darker.

"Have a nice day," I told him, and left.

INSIDE THE ELEVATOR, sliding smoothly down to street level, I checked my left hand to make certain that all the knuckles were still attached to their proper fingers. They seemed to be.

There was a woman in the car with me, a gray business suit, blue rinsed hair, Joan Crawford eyebrows, Broderick Crawford jowls. She eyed me for a moment, and then edged slightly away, toward the door. Maybe I was smiling oddly.

Sometimes there's nothing quite as satisfying as taking out your aggressions in an absolutely physical way. Particularly when you're still upright and mobile afterward. I believe it was Rocky Marciano who first made this observation.

Rita, of course, has often maintained that this is a childish attitude. But, as I've often pointed out, no one ever called Rocky Marciano childish.

BACK IN THE CHEVY, the tie torn off and draped across the passenger seat, I considered my options. If Bigelow had called the police to complain about my littering his office with rent-a-cops, I probably didn't have many. I had believed Sergeant Bradley when he told me that if he heard any reports about my hassling his citizens, he would request that I vacate the City of Angels.

Not much point in worrying about it. Either Bigelow had called the cops or he hadn't. Either the cops would pick me up or they wouldn't. I might as well proceed as though everything were still hunky-dory.

I had an appointment at five with Charles Hatfield, the head of the L.A. branch of Sanctuary. It was twelve thirty now. I had time to get myself some food—maybe try one of those tofu burgers I'd read about. Afterward, I could drive to Beverly Hills and attempt to learn more about Melissa Alonzo.

BY THE TIME I reached Beverly Hills I was dyspeptic and grumpy and tired. Dyspeptic because the burrito I'd eaten was now eating me back. Grumpy and tired because the adrenaline that had gushed through me in Bigelow's office had now flushed itself from my system. And my left hand hurt.

The house was hidden behind a tall fieldstone wall, but it was one of the few houses on the sweeping, shaded street that didn't have an electrified gate at the front. I followed the winding driveway up past a rolling lawn just slightly smaller than Arlington National Cemetery, and I parked the car behind a long black diesel Mercedes that could have done duty there as a hearse. The house was stone, like the wall, and it was huge, the towering gray walls draped with green ivy so glossy it must have been waxed once a week.

I've never understood why two people need more than a few rooms to live in. A living room, a couple of bedrooms, a den for the bowling trophies, maybe a spare room to tuck the Pope away when he dropped by for the weekend. This house—which looked like it had been shipped here stone by stone from some medieval estate in France—must have held fifteen or twenty rooms. Perhaps the owner needed all that space to contain his ego. Or his house guests. And their egos.

As I padded toward the front door, I thought I saw someone move away from one of the casement windows to my right, a sudden darting movement that might have been merely the reflection of a passing bird. Perhaps it had been.

At the door, I rang the bell and after a few moments it was opened by a Hispanic woman in her fifties, plump, gray-haired, looking homey in a housedress and a floral apron. She smiled at me. "Yes?"

"My name is Joshua Croft," I told her. "I'm an investigator licensed by the state of New Mexico. If Mrs. Bigelow is free, I'd like to talk to her about her daughter."

Sadness replaced the smile. "A very terrible tragedy. Mrs. Bigelow is still very upset."

"I understand. And I apologize for disturbing her. I won't take much of her time."

She looked at me for a moment, thoughtful, and then came to a decision. "Well, okay," she said. Maybe she liked my cowboy boots. "You wait here, please, while I ask."

I waited some, and after another few moments the woman returned. She nodded to me. "Please follow," she said, and I did, through a dark foyer, around a corner, across a broad formal living room festooned with the kind of spindly antique furniture favored by former French kings and wealthy middle-aged hairdressers, down some carpeted steps, around another corner, and into a large room flooded with light.

The air was somehow denser in here, and it held a heavy floral scent, like the air in a greenhouse or a funeral home. White lace curtains were draped at the sides of the casement windows. The walls were white, the moldings Wedgwood blue, and the floors were oak, partially covered by a cream-colored Persian carpet. It would have been a spacious place, except that it was crammed with the same sort of dark, brittle furniture that filled the living room,

and every inch of surface area—bookshelves, credenzas, tables—
was occupied by small porcelain animal figurines: rabbits, pup-
pies, kittens, fawns, baby giraffes and hippos and chimpanzees, all
of them equipped with wide adorable stares and wide adorable
smiles. Individually, any one of them might have seemed pleasant, or at least harmless. En masse, they seemed like an invasion
force.

A petite woman in a black silk jumpsuit sat at the far corner of
a yellow loveseat. Her hair, styled in a gamine cut, snug against her
delicate skull, was as black and shiny as her outfit. Because she was
so tiny and fine-boned, at a distance she might have been mistaken for a small girl. Up close, however, I noticed the age freck-
les on the backs of her frail hand, and the tight glazed skin, smooth
as bone, along her cheeks. Her makeup was artfully applied, rouge,
lipstick, eyeliner, mascara, but in the bright daylight it had turned
her oval face into the mask of a younger woman. In her own way,
she was fighting time and age as desperately as Edie Carpenter. But
she had been fighting them for much longer.

She said, "How do you do, Mr. . . . Um?"

"Croft. Joshua Croft, Mrs. Bigelow. Fine, thanks. I'm sorry to
disturb you like this."

"That's quite all right," she said. "You have a job to do, after
all." She smiled a coy, girlish smile that seemed out of place in
these circumstances and on that Kewpie-doll face, and then she
indicated the Louis XIV chair opposite the loveseat. "Please sit
down."

I sat. I shifted slightly on the thin cushion. Louis XIV, despite
his reputation, must have been a stoic.

"Would you care for a drink?" she asked me brightly. "Or perhaps a coffee?"

"A glass of water would be fine."

"Annabella, would you see to it?" She lifted a glass that had
been sitting beside her on the end table and she smiled shyly, almost apologetically, at the Hispanic woman. "And could you bring
another, please?" The glass was half full, ice cubes and a pale
amber liquid that I assumed was scotch. I also assumed that for her
the glass was half empty. She moved and spoke with the exaggerated precision of the alcoholic who's had a few drinks but who
wants to, who still needs to, maintain a front of polite sobriety.

But it wasn't my place to judge her. She'd lost two daughters,
one of them only last week.

As the Hispanic woman left the room, Mrs. Bigelow took a polite sip from her drink and smiled that girlish smile again. "So. How may I help you, Mr. . . I'm so sorry, what was it again?"

"Croft. I was wondering—"

"Croft, of course, yes. My silly memory. I must be getting old." This she said with a kind of hopeful flirtatiousness, seeking a denial.

I smiled my neutral smile and said, "I was wondering, Mrs. Bigelow, whether you'd heard anything from your daughter Melissa since she disappeared last August."

The drink in her right hand wobbled as her left hand flew to her chest. Her eyelids fluttered for an instant and then she looked quickly around the room, as if for assistance. She looked back to me and said, "But I thought . . . you said, you told Annabella that this was about Cathryn."

For a moment I regretted my deliberate ambiguity at the front door. "Maybe there's been a misunderstanding, Mrs. Bigelow. I'm an investigator licensed by the state of New Mexico. I've been hired to locate Melissa."

She sipped at her scotch, less politely now. She cocked her head, a quick, birdlike movement. I wondered then if she'd been the figure I thought I'd seen behind the window as I approached the house. And, if she had been, who or what had she been expecting? And why had she darted away?

"An investigator?" she said. "Not a police investigator?"

"A private investigator."

"From New Mexico?"

"Santa Fe."

She smiled a small dreamy smile. "Melissa always said that it was so very beautiful there." Then she remembered herself, and she remembered me. "But we don't talk about Melissa," she said. "None of us. Not to anyone." She said this by rote, as though it were a lesson learned so long ago that she'd forgotten who taught it to her, and why. And then—perhaps curiosity had gotten the better of training—she asked me, "Who hired you? Roy?"

"His uncle." I explained the arrangement I'd made with Norman Montoya. "Mr. Montoya is concerned about Melissa and Winona's welfare."

"But what—oh, thank you, Annabella," she said, and gave me a quick complicitous glance. The Hispanic maid, or housekeeper, or whoever she was, had returned to the room, carrying a tray with two glasses. She held out the tray for me, and I took my water and thanked her. Mrs. Bigelow drained what was left of her drink, delicately set it on the tray, delicately lifted its replacement. She and I didn't speak to each other until after the other woman had left.

Then, delicately, she set her drink on the end table. "Mr. Croft, I'm sorry, but I'm afraid I can't tell you anything about Melissa."

I thought that she could. I thought that she wanted to, or that at least a part of her did. Why else had she given me that look, why else had she gone silent while the other woman was in the room?

But I knew that I could be wrong. Maybe complicitous glances were a part of her repertoire of flirtation, and held no meaning beyond that.

I took a sip of my water. Since there was nowhere to set down the glass without crushing some cuddly little creature, I held it in my lap. "Mrs. Bigelow," I said, "your daughter Cathryn received a post card from Melissa not too long before her death. Did you receive a card too? Or any other form of communication?"

"I . . . Mr. Croft, you're asking about personal matters, family matters. I really can't talk about them. Perhaps if you spoke to my husband." She looked down, eyelids fluttering, and again I was reminded of a little girl. Which was the idea, of course—to disarm me with her vulnerability. I suspected that it was something she had done all her life, something she did now reflexively, without thinking.

Absently, she smoothed down the fabric that lay along her thigh.

"I did talk to your husband," I said. "This morning. He wasn't very helpful."

She looked up at me. "Cal's a good man," she said defensively. "A kind man, gentle and generous. It's just that Melissa has . . . disappointed him so. We tried so hard, both of us, but she wouldn't listen to anyone. We thought that she'd change after she married Bill."

"Bill Lester?" I wasn't particularly interested in Bill Lester, but at least I'd gotten her to talk. "He was a partner in your husband's firm, wasn't he?"

She nodded. "And a wonderful man. And madly in love with Melissa. I thought at first, you know, that he might be too old for her—she was only twenty, and Bill was all of forty-five. But Cal was certain that things would work out, and for a little while it seemed he was right. They seemed to get along so well together. But it ended so quickly. In less than a year."

She lifted her drink, sipped at it, looked away. "Things would've been so different if she and Bill had worked out." She sighed. There was genuine emotion in the sigh, but there was also the high school theatricality of a young girl. She was a woman, it appeared to me, who had survived by means of her affectations, or who thought she had, and who probably had difficulty determining what was real in herself from what was artifice. So did I.

I said, "How did you feel about her marrying Roy Alonzo?"

THIRTEEN

SHE TURNED BACK TO ME. She spoke without any hesitation now—whether because of the alcohol or because of a simple need to talk. "Well, you understand that we weren't sure about it, of course. When you've lived in this town as long as we have, you tend to be a bit...wary of movie people, you know. Actors, especially. You hear so many terrible things. Drugs, infidelity. And worse. But Melissa was *so* terribly happy."

She sipped at her drink. "Even Cal had to admit she was happy. We thought, the two of us did, that Melissa had finally settled down. Finally found herself. And then when Winona came, such a beautiful little girl, it seemed that everything was perfect. A happy marriage, that beautiful, beautiful child. And then we started hearing those terrible stories..." With another quick birdlike motion, she shook her head, as though denying the truth of the stories, or that such stories could exist.

"What stories?" I asked her.

"Horrible," she said, making a little girl's face of horror. "Absolutely disgusting." She took another drink. "I really couldn't repeat them, and I'm sure you wouldn't want to hear them. They were complete fabrications, of course. *I* knew that. But they disturbed Cal, and he confronted Melissa with them. Well, Melissa lost her temper—it's possible that Cal was a bit too brusque, he can be that way sometimes. He doesn't mean to be, it's just the way he is. One thing led to another and the two of them had a terrible row. And both of them are so stubborn. Melissa is a lot like Cal that way."

She drank from her glass. "They didn't speak to each other for a year or so, until she and Roy divorced. I tried to mediate between her and Cal, tried to bring the two of them back together—we were a *family*, after all—but..." She shrugged an elaborate shrug of hopelessness: What's a woman to do?

"They spoke again after the divorce?"

"They reconciled, yes. I was so pleased. And then..." She looked down again, sadly, and without the girlish affectation.

The whiskey was beginning to affect her careful pronunciation: words slightly slurred, *s*'s turning into *sh*'s.

I prompted her, "And then Melissa accused Roy of abusing Winona."

"It was *horrible*," she said. She looked away and quickly shook her head again. *"Horrible."*

"Your husband wasn't pleased about Melissa's accusation," I said.

"Cal begged her not to take Roy to court. The scandal. The press. It had been bad enough when Melissa and Roy divorced. People calling us night and day, newspaper reporters, television reporters. He told her he'd handle it himself. But Melissa was determined. It was the only way, she said, to make sure that Roy never came near Winona again."

"Mrs. Bigelow," I said, "do you know why Melissa made the accusation? Do you know about any particular incident that might've caused it?"

She lowered her head, and for a few long moments I thought I'd lost her. Not to reticence or shame; to alcohol. But apparently she was deciding whether to tell me. I don't know why she decided what she did. The alcohol, maybe. Or the loneliness. Maybe both.

She raised her head and said, "Melissa called me one night. She was . . . she wasn't hysterical, really, but she was extremely upset. She told me she'd been putting Winona to bed that night, dressing her in her pajamas. This was a Monday night, after Winona had stayed the weekend with Roy." She sipped at her drink.

I waited.

"She said—she was dressing her, did I mention that?—she said that Winona looked up at her and told her that she'd had sex with Daddy." She took another sip from her drink, made a girlish grimace once again, and she looked away.

I waited.

She turned back to me. "Melissa said she didn't know what to think. At first, of course, she thought that Winona was confused, that she didn't know what the word meant. Children can say things sometimes without really understanding them. But then, when Melissa kissed Winona good night, Winona . . . Winona stuck her tongue in Melissa's mouth . . . And then she smiled at her. And Melissa said that the smile was absolutely diabolical. Absolutely *evil.*" Again she made that face, with more real pain in it this time, and again she looked away.

Suddenly I didn't want to be here, in this close confining room with its smell of scotch and fading flowers, its grotesque clutter of gaping animals. Didn't want to be sitting across from this wounded, painted woman, a fading flower herself; didn't want to be hearing what I was hearing. I didn't want to turn over this particular rock.

But turning over rocks was what I was paid to do.

Mrs. Bigelow said, "I told Cal when he came home. He was angry, of course, he was furious, and he left and drove over to Melissa's. When he came back, he was even more furious. Because Melissa wouldn't listen to reason. She refused to see, Cal said, that Winona was probably making it up. Winona's always been an imaginative child, like Melissa when *she* was a little girl. Cal was convinced that she'd seen something on television, or possibly heard somewhere, someone talking, and that she'd invented this."

I said, "What did you think, Mrs. Bigelow?"

"I...I honestly didn't know. I didn't know what to think. I still don't know. I liked Roy, I really did. It seemed impossible that he could do something like that. That *anyone* could do something like that. But you read the papers, you know, and you see that it happens all the time. But *Roy?*"

She drank some more scotch. "And then the doctors. At the trial. One said this, the other said that. Contradicting each other." She stared down into her glass for a moment, then looked up at me. "How can that happen, Mr. Croft? How *could* someone do something like that?"

How do you explain evil? It was a fundamental question, of religion, psychology, even politics; perhaps it was *the* fundamental question. Maybe it had an answer, but I didn't know what it was, and I told her so.

She shook her head, looked down at her glass again.

I said, "Mrs. Bigelow, Melissa has been in contact with you, hasn't she?"

Without looking up, she nodded.

"By mail?" I asked her. "Over the phone?"

"By mail," she said, still staring down at her lap. "A postcard." She looked up. "From New Mexico. The same postcard she sent...the same one she sent to Cathryn. The message, I mean. *'The flower in the desert lives.'*"

"When did you receive it?"

"September. The end of September."

"When was it postmarked?"

She shook her head. "I don't remember."

"Do you still have it?"

"No. No, I . . . I disposed of it. If Cal had found it, he would've only gotten upset."

"Have you heard from her since?"

She shook her head, looked down, gently twirled the ice in her glass. She looked up at me. Beneath the mask of cosmetics, her vulnerability seemed real now. "Do you think she's all right, Mr. Croft?"

"I don't know," I said. I wasn't going to tell her what I'd been telling everybody else, that her daughter Cathryn's death might possibly be linked to Melissa's disappearance. "I hope so. But I think it'd be better for her and Winona if I found them. Mr. Montoya will be able to help them a lot more than whoever's helping them now."

"Who is helping them now?"

"I'm not sure. Did she ever talk to you about the Underground Railroad? A network of people who help women in Melissa's position?"

She shook her head, gently twirled her ice again. "We haven't talked much. We weren't talking much, I mean, before she left. Just a phone call now and then." She set the glass on the end table, reached out for a small beige box encircled by a platoon of adorable baby animals, and pressed a button in its center.

I asked her, "The message on the postcard. Do you know what it means?"

"I assumed . . ."—she waved her hand vaguely—"I assumed it was a sort of reassurance, a way to tell me she was all right."

"Did Melissa ever mention anyone in Santa Fe she might've gone to, a close friend?"

She looked off to the window that faced the front lawn, her eyes focused on some place far beyond the grass, then she looked back at me. "There was a woman. An artist, a painter. Deirdre, I think . . . Deirdre Polk. But she didn't live in Santa Fe." She frowned, trying to remember.

Deirdre. I took out my notebook and pen. I wrote the name down. "Where does she live, Mrs. Bigelow?"

Her face was pinched in concentration. Finally, she said, with a mock desperation that threatened to become real, "Isn't that awful? I can't remember. I—" Abruptly she put on a bright, vacant smile as the Hispanic woman returned. "Thank you, Annabella." She set her empty glass on the tray, took the full one waiting for her, cocked her head, and turned the bright smile in my direction. "Are you sure I can't get you anything?"

"I'm sure. Thanks."

The Hispanic woman padded away.

"*Hartley,*" Mrs. Bigelow said suddenly. "That was the name. The name of the town."

North of Santa Fe, closer to Taos, it was a small town, locally famous for its artists' colony. I wrote the name down.

"Anyone else?" I asked her.

She shook her head, took a sip from the fresh drink. Her face was slack now, as though the effort of remembering had drained it of life. Her voice was toneless. "We never really talked, Melissa and I, about the people she knew in Santa Fe."

"Did she ever mention a woman named Juanita?"

Mrs. Bigelow canted her head to the side, thoughtful. At last she said, "We had a housekeeper named Juanita once. But she's dead now, I believe. Yes, I'm sure she is. We sent flowers."

"No other Juanita?"

"Not that I can recall."

I said, "Did she ever tell you how she met Deirdre Polk?"

She waved a hand vaguely. "Some opening or other."

"In Santa Fe?"

"I believe so."

I said, "What about the people involved in the group she worked with. Sanctuary."

"*That,*" she said, looking displeased. She shifted slightly in her seat.

I asked her, "Did she ever mention the names of anyone in the group?"

"It was something we didn't really discuss. She knew that Cal and I didn't approve of her involvement with those people." It seemed that there were a lot of things that Melissa and her mother never discussed.

"Why is that?" I asked.

She sat upright, gathering herself together. "Please don't misunderstand me. I'm sure that many of them are very well intentioned. Like Melissa is. And I suppose they see themselves as romantic figures, flouting authority, aiding the downtrodden. But it seems to me that they're no better than common criminals, some of them. They're helping illegal aliens, you know. They're breaking the law of the land. I know that Melissa would never be involved with *that* part of it. But we felt that it was dangerous, her being a member of a group like that. The law is the law, after all. If we didn't have laws, we'd be no better than animals." This she said as though it were something else she had learned many years ago, and had often repeated since then. Repetition had emptied it of any conviction it might once have had, genuine or hoped for.

"How much of her time did Melissa spend in Santa Fe? While she was married to Roy?"

She thought for a moment. She blinked. "Well, she and Roy used to go out there for the summers, when Roy wasn't making that television series. And then later, toward the end of the marriage, she spent more of her time out there, she and Winona. A week here and there."

"Did she go there after the divorce?"

"Yes. Occasionally."

"Does Sanctuary have an office in Santa Fe?"

"I really couldn't say. As I said, we didn't discuss those people."

"Did Melissa speak to you after she returned from El Salvador? Before she disappeared?"

She shook her head. "I didn't even know she *had* disappeared until Roy called me and asked if I'd heard from her."

She looked down again.

I said, "Is there anyone else you can think of, Mrs. Bigelow? Any other friend she might've gotten in contact with?"

She shook her head slowly. Then she looked up and stared out the window once more. I saw that quietly, politely, discreetly, she was crying. Tears dark with mascara rolled down her taut cheeks. Without looking at me, she said, "Lately, you know, we haven't talked that much."

It occurred to me then that if she *had* been the figure I'd glimpsed at the window, she might have been looking out across that broad sweep of lawn for Melissa. Standing there, drink in hand, waiting for her daughter to return. Since last week, the only daughter she had left.

It was not a happy thought.

I told her, "I'll find Melissa, Mrs. Bigelow." There was nothing else to say.

"Please," she said softly, still staring out the window. Then she closed her eyes and she sat there, holding her drink in her lap with both hands, as the tears made small slick trails down the mask that was her face.

FOURTEEN

"MELISSA ALONZO," Charles Hatfield told me, "is a committed woman. Absolutely dedicated. Her assistance has been invaluable to this organization."

I hadn't expected to like Charles Hatfield. After leaving Mrs. Bigelow and her grief, I hadn't expected to like anyone. But the L.A. director of Sanctuary surprised me. He didn't look like a common criminal, but then I hadn't thought he would—an organization like Sanctuary wouldn't last long if its directors resembled street thugs.

He was English and he was short and a bit overweight and his thick white hair was combed back in waves over a pair of ears that were slightly larger, and slightly redder, than ears were supposed to be. A waxed white mustache curled heroically from beneath his rounded nose. His ruddy face was friendly and sincere—a combination that often makes me uneasy, but one that in Hatfield's case I found myself buying. He wore a white oxford shirt, a club tie opened at the neck, tweed trousers, and a tweed jacket that sported leather patches on the elbow and a leather patch at the right shoulder, the kind that's designed to keep the cloth beneath from getting ruffled by the butt of your Purdy shotgun when you blast away at some wily pheasant. Or some wily peasant. I doubted that Hatfield had ever blasted away at anything.

His cordovan wingtips were perched atop his wide mahogany desk, and he was smoking a bulldog pipe that refused to stay alight. Every five minutes or so, he torched it with a jet of flame from his Dunhill lighter and puffed up a cloud of blue smoke.

I asked him, "Have you heard from her since she disappeared?"

"No. Nothing." He sucked at his pipe, then grinned engagingly around its stem. "Wish I had. We could use her right now. Work's piling up right and left."

"What exactly did Melissa do for you, Mr. Hatfield?"

"Little bit of everything," he said. "Typing, filing, general secretarial. May not sound like much, but in a place like this"—he waved his pipe to take in the office, and, by implication, the rest of Sanctuary—"absolutely essential."

The office in question was about the same size as Elizabeth Drewer's, but it was done up as an alcove in a gentlemen's private club: red carpet, black leather chairs studded with brass, framed lithographs of Irish setters on the dark hardwood walls, a glassed-in mahogany bookcase holding shelves of handsome leather-bound books that had probably never been read.

"And Melissa," he said, "was sharp as a tack. Never made a mistake. Never misfiled anything. I wanted something, some record, all I had to do was ask her, and she'd have it to me in a shot."

"She didn't work here full time."

He waved his pipe negatively. "No, no, no. Once or twice a week. Wish it'd been more. It's a completely volunteer staff here, and Lord knows they've all got their heart in the right place, splendid bunch, work like slaves. But some of them, well, *amateurs* pretty much says it. Not Melissa, though. A real professional. Had her job down cold."

"What about her trips to Central America?"

He sucked at his pipe, smiled. "What about them?"

"What were the trips for?"

The pipe had gone out again. He lifted his lighter from the desk, flicked it open, spun the wheel. He held it to the pipe and a long finger of flame tapped at the bowl. "Fact finding," he said around the pipe stem, through a billow of smoke. "Getting the scoop on those bullies down in El Salvador and Guatemala. First-person accounts." He flapped his hand, waved away the smoke.

I looked down at my notebook. "According to the press reports, there were other people on the trip with her. Bob Slavin, Terrence Courtney, and Beatrice Wocynski. I understand that Melissa was supposed to leave with them from San Salvador on August twenty-first. What was their reaction when she left on the seventeenth?"

"They didn't know she'd left the country until the twentieth, day before they left themselves. Melissa didn't show up at the Hilton, in San Salvador, like she was supposed to. They called her hotel in Santa Isabel, discovered she'd checked out on the seventeenth. Left a message for them. Flying home, personal business."

"And what was their reaction?"

"Surprise." He grinned around the pipe. "Mystification."

"And what was your reaction?"

He frowned slightly. "Well, surprise, too, naturally. But I know Melissa a bit better than they do. She's...mercurial." He liked the sound of the word. Nodding, he repeated it: "Mercurial. She's done things like that before, you know. Gone off on her own, without a word to anyone. Not that she isn't a responsible person, fundamentally. She is. Like I say, when she worked here at the office, she had her job down cold."

"What was your reaction when you learned that she'd disappeared from L.A. with her daughter?"

"Now that worried me, got to confess. Leaving Salvador was one thing, but leaving town like that..." He shook his head sadly. "And with Winona. Something else again. Not like her." He puffed at the pipe.

"Do you know why she left?"

He shrugged. "Under a lot of pressure, wasn't she? Lot of stress. The court case, that cretinous judge awarding visitation to that swine of a husband."

"You think that Roy was guilty of child abuse?"

"Course he was. Melissa would never've accused him otherwise. Would never've put Winona through all that sordid business. The court, the press. Horrible. She loves that little girl. Crazy about her."

I nodded. "Do you know Roy Alonzo?"

He snorted into his mustache. "Thought I did. Saw him fairly often. Drinks, dinner. He was our spokesperson, you know. Typical actor. All smiles and charm outside, pit viper inside."

"He's not the spokesperson now?"

He looked affronted. "Course not. Last thing we need is a bloody bent swine for a figurehead. I took it up with the board myself, straightaway. Got to get rid of this pig, I said. A total liability. Got to dump him."

"But what if Roy was innocent? What if Melissa misunderstood something Winona said?"

"Rubbish. I told you, Melissa wouldn't have gone ahead with this thing if she hadn't been sure. And there was the doctor's reports. Roy was no innocent." He shrugged. "Besides, didn't matter in the end. Image. That's what's important in this town. Image. Caesar's wife. We couldn't have him representing us. Simple as that."

I nodded. "One thing I'm a little unclear about."

His eyebrows—both of them—arched expectantly.

"What was Melissa doing in Santa Isabel?" I asked him.

"Bit of R and R," he said. "It's on the coast, Santa Isabel. Quiet little place, palm trees, sand, grass huts. The four of them had pretty much finished with their business down there. Interview, whatnot. Terry and Bob flew off to Costa Rica, Melissa rented a car and drove to Santa Isabel. Beatrice stayed in San Salvador."

"Did anything happen in Santa Isabel while Melissa was there? Anything that might've put her in jeopardy?"

Below the elaborate mustache, his mouth widened in a grin. "Sand in the margaritas. That's probably the worst thing that could happen in Santa Isabel. Tiny little place. Very pretty. Very quiet, like I say. Quaint. Miles and miles from the fighting."

So much for Rita's theory that Melissa was running from some unknown event that had occurred down there.

I said, "Could you give me addresses for the three people who went with her?"

"Bob and Terry are in Guatemala right now." He grinned. "Suckers for punishment, the two of 'em. Beatrice is around, though. Give you hers, if you like."

"I'd appreciate it."

"Want it now? That it? We finished?"

"First," I said, "could you tell me what it is that Sanctuary does, exactly?"

He shrugged. "Bit of everything. PR for the cause. Legal aid for the people in the camps, posting bonds, finding sponsors—"

"The camps?" I interrupted him.

"The INS, the Immigration and Naturalization Service, calls 'em service processing centers. But concentration camps is more like it. We've got a couple here in California. The men's camp at El Centro, the SPAN women's facility in Pasadena. Between three and four hundred men at El Centro, all treated like animals. Overcrowding, slop for food. Half of them are OTMs—"

"OTMs?"

"Sorry. Border Patrol lingo." His pipe had gone out again. "Other than Mexican. Salvadorans, Guatemalans, Hondurans." He thumbed his lighter, sucked at the flame. "No problem with the Mexicans. Border Patrol just VR's them—VR, that's voluntary return." He puffed, waved away the smoke. "Gets them to sign an I-274, waive their right to an immigration appearance, and then ships 'em back across the border. A farce. Most of 'em slip over the fence again an hour later. They know they're going to, and so does the Border Patrol."

"What about the rest? The other than Mexican?"

"Bit more trouble there. They do *not* want to go back. Who could blame them? Salvador, give you an example, has a wretched track record when it comes to handling returned emigrants. Some of these poor people are arrested. Disappear, never heard from again. Some are simply shot on arrival. Simpler that way. Sets a nice example for the others, as well."

"The INS knows that?"

"Course they do. Thing is, the INS likes to call these people illegal aliens. They're not. The Geneva Convention of 1948 forbids signatories—and the U.S. is a signatory—from returning refugees to a war zone. And if any country qualifies as a war zone, it's El Salvador. But of course this government, the United States government, has gone on record as saying that the government there is a fine, upstanding, peaceful democracy."

He puffed at his pipe. "Which it isn't, of course. Basic fascist oligarchy. Fourteen families own everything, including the police and the army. Official government policy for dealing with the unruly countryside is *pacification*. Means the same thing there it used to mean in Vietnam."

He puffed some more. "Fact is, under international law, all these refugees have a legal right to come here, and a legal right to stay here, until hostilities cease. The INS, by denying them that right, is the party that's acting illegally."

"Does Sanctuary provide shelter for the kind of refugees you're talking about?"

He smiled. "Safe houses, you mean?"

I nodded.

"Official policy is to operate entirely within the law. And we do. As I say, legal aid, sponsorship, educating the public. But that's not to say that individuals within the organization mightn't stretch the law a bit. We discourage it, naturally, but—" He shrugged. "Some people see it as a matter of saving lives. Simple as that."

"Was Melissa Alonzo," I asked him, "ever involved in the movement of illegals?"

His eyebrows lowered and his lips frowned around the pipe stem. "Been talking to the FBI, have we?"

"Yeah. They talked to you?"

He nodded. "Fellow named Stamworth. Very smooth, very polite. Bit too smooth, I thought. He wanted to know the same thing."

"When was he here?"

"End of September."

"And what did you tell him?"

"Absolutely not. Too visible. A celebrity's wife. Our spokes-person's wife." He shook his head, frowning against the pipe stem. "Wouldn't do, you know."

"Would she know people within the organization who might've been involved in sheltering illegals?"

He puffed thoughtfully. "Perhaps. But she wasn't involved herself. I'd swear to it."

I nodded. "Does Sanctuary have an office in Santa Fe?"

He nodded. "Want the address?"

"Yeah. Thanks. Did Melissa do any work for the Santa Fe office?"

"Don't think so. If she did, it was on an unofficial basis. What I gathered, she used Santa Fe as a kind of . . . sanctuary." He grinned. "No pun intended. But that was where she went to relax. Recharge. You follow? I shouldn't think she involved herself in anything with our people out there."

"Did Melissa ever mention a woman named Deirdre Polk to you?"

He thought for a moment, then shook his head. "Can't say she did."

"What about a woman named Juanita?"

Again he thought, again he shook his head. "Doesn't ring any bells. Sorry."

"Did you ever meet Melissa's sister, Cathryn?"

"She stopped by the office a few times, when Melissa was here. Nice girl, she seemed to be. Retiring type. Shy. Shame about her death. Makes you wonder what this town's coming to." He frowned suddenly. "You don't think her death's got anything to do with Melissa?"

"I don't know. I hope not."

He stared off at an unpleasant distance. "Good Lord," he said. "How awful."

"The phrase *'The flower in the desert lives.'* Does that mean anything to you?"

He thought for a moment, then shook his head again. "Can't say that it does."

"Did Cathryn ever contact you, to tell you that she'd heard from Melissa?"

"No. Why would she?"

"You have no idea where Melissa might be?"

He shook his head. "No," he said. "Not a one. Sorry."

AFTER LEAVING Hatfield's office, I drove back to the hotel. I called Beatrice Wocynski, one of the three people who had accompanied Melissa Alonzo to El Salvador. She was polite and concerned, but she was unable to give me anything I didn't already have. Melissa's disappearance from Los Angeles had been as much of a surprise to her as Melissa's disappearance from El Salvador. Like Hatfield—but less intimately, I suspected—she had known Roy Alonzo. And like Hatfield, she had no trouble seeing him as a child molester. She liked Melissa, thought she was a "wonderful person," but, again like Hatfield, she had no idea where Melissa might be now.

I had dinner in the restaurant downstairs—some fish and some brightly colored vegetables artfully arranged around an expanse of white porcelain plate, like bits of sculpture on a skating rink—then I went back to my room and packed.

PART TWO

FIFTEEN

RITA SIPPED at her coffee. "If Stamworth isn't FBI," she said, "then who or what do you think he is?"

"No idea," I said. Sitting at the opposite end of the sofa, I was drinking hot cocoa. A bright rectangle of morning sun lay across the Persian carpet. Rita wore a white silk blouse and a pleated black skirt. Her hair, thick and black, was pulled loosely behind her neck, folded like wings along her Indian cheekbones. The stainless steel walker stood upright beside her.

"It's the INS," I said, "who handles illegal aliens, not the FBI, but I can't see him as INS either. He's something federal, though. He has to be. The FBI is backing his story, or the L.A. cops wouldn't be buying it. Which must mean he's got some kind of federal juice."

I shrugged. "Maybe he's a mailman."

"He was on the scene before Cathryn was killed."

"Yeah. And he says there's no connection between her death and Melissa."

"But you think there is."

"I think it's a possibility."

"I think you're right," she said. "And I think you're right to worry about the phone," she said. Her large dark eyes were thoughtful. "I'll have Leroy put an indicator on the line." Leroy, a distant relative of Rita's, was an electronics expert. "And you and I will have to be discreet for a while. Not say anything over the phone we'd prefer that Stamworth not hear."

"I'm always discreet, Rita."

"Obviously there isn't much point in our getting scramblers."

"Not unless we issue one to everybody who might be calling us."

"It's possible that I can learn something about him on the computer."

I sipped at my cocoa. "About Stamworth? You can do that? Hook into the government's computer files?"

"*I* can't, no. But I know someone who could, possibly."

"Who? Captain Crunch?"

She smiled. As usual, her smile created a constriction in my chest. "A young hacker on CompuServe," she said. "He's helped me out before."

Still another item she hadn't shared with me. My early-morning high spirits—my pleasure at being back in New Mexico, at the shining sun-splashed October day, at the elegant curve of Rita's throat—I could feel all of that beginning to unravel.

I said, "That doesn't sound especially legal."

"It isn't. We'll wait to see if Stamworth makes another appearance." She sipped at her coffee and she smiled again. "I know I'm going to regret this, but how was Los Angeles?"

"I'm thinking about moving out there," I said. "Get myself a couple of silk shirts, a bunch of bean sprouts, start working on my tan and my screenplay."

Another smile. "I do hope that when you become famous, you won't forget all of us little people."

"Who?"

She laughed. It was a very gratifying sound. "Enough," she said. "You talked to Melissa's parents."

"Yeah." Without mentioning my rent-a-cop experience at Bigelow's office, I explained what I'd learned and what I hadn't.

"That poor woman," Rita said. "She's caught in the middle, between her husband and her daughter."

"I think the sister was, too. Cathryn. Apparently she wasn't supposed to see Melissa. Daddy didn't like the idea. But she saw her anyway. I keep thinking that I should've stayed out there longer, tried to find out more about her. She's as much of a cipher as Melissa is. More so."

"Joshua, her death was either connected to Melissa's disappearance or it wasn't. If it wasn't, there's probably nothing you could learn about her that would help us locate Melissa. If it was, the police will probably determine that. They wouldn't want you interfering in an open case, anyway."

"I know."

"The last anyone heard from Melissa, she was somewhere here in the Southwest. This is where you should be looking right now. If it's necessary, you can always go back to Los Angeles."

"Swell."

She smiled. "Tell me about Elizabeth Drewer."

I told her about Elizabeth Drewer.

She said, "The two of you got along very well, evidently."

"Like peaches and cream. She thinks that convicted child molesters should be castrated. And I got the feeling that she wouldn't mind if that practice were extended to a large percentage of the male population. Maybe all of it."

"Her compassion, evidently, has a narrow focus."

"What there is of it."

"Well, she certainly seems compassionate enough about the children." She sipped her coffee, returned the cup to the saucer on her lap. "But she seems to be forgetting that by her own account the victimizers were often victims themselves."

"I don't think she allows much room for subtle nuances of motivation."

"Nor should she. It's a terrible thing. But there are other approaches."

"Besides. 'Off with his balls,' you mean?"

She smiled faintly. "Do you remember Norma Hermann?"

"The shrink? Her brother-in-law disappeared with her case histories?"

"Yes. I spoke with her yesterday. She's working at St. Vincent's now, with abused children. Her thinking, which makes sense to me, is that when an accusation of sexual abuse has been made, the legalistic approach is basically mistaken. What these people need, the parents and the children, is some kind of therapeutic help that deals with the entire family, all of them, as members of a single unit. And that's true, she thinks, even when the accusation is false."

"It may be a little late for that here."

"Probably. But I can't help worrying about that little girl."

"Neither can I." I sipped some cocoa. "But I'm not a shrink, Rita. All I can do, if I'm lucky, is find her. I can't heal her."

"Finding her would be a start. What else happened out there? Did you talk to Charles Hatfield?"

"Yeah. He's one of those Brits who haven't really existed since *The Charge of the Light Brigade*. The movie, I mean, not the poem. Tweeds, a pipe, a guardsman's mustache. Very pukka. I liked him. But he didn't know anything about Melissa's whereabouts. No one does. The thing is, I can't get a handle on her, on what she's really like. On the one hand, she's a dedicated volunteer for a group that aids political refugees. On the other, she's a loving mother. On the *other,* she's involved in S and M orgies. This is a life riddled with contradictions, Rita."

"That's three hands," she smiled.

"Yeah. What is the sound of three hands clapping?"

"Joshua, only idiots and saints live without contradictions. The idea is to find out what the contradictions have in common."

I shrugged. "Like I said, I'm not a shrink. I'm beginning to dislike this woman."

"Obviously she's never realized how much her life would inconvenience you."

"Obviously. I did find out who Deirdre is."

"Who?"

"An artist. Deirdre Polk. She lives up in Hartley. I tried calling her, but I got her machine. If I can't get through to her, and if there's time, I'll drive up there later today."

"I told you you'd find her. Have you located Juanita yet?"

"Nope."

"You will. Did you ask Hatfield about Santa Isabel?"

"Yeah. Nothing happened there."

"Not in Santa Isabel, no."

I sighed. "Rita, Rita. You're about to sandbag me again, aren't you?"

"About thirty miles northeast of Santa Isabel," she said, "there's a small farming village called Cureiro. On August sixteenth, sometime during the night, the village's Catholic priest and a woman friend were murdered. He was Father Manuel Cisneros. She was Maria Vasquez. They were apparently dragged from inside the house and shoved into a car that drove them a few miles away, into the countryside. They were made to kneel down and they were shot in the head with automatic weapons. The bodies weren't found until a week later."

"You got that off the database?"

"Yes."

Apparently there was something to be said for the database. "But this place is thirty miles, you said, from Santa Isabel."

"Thirty miles isn't that far. And the timing is right. If Melissa saw something while she was in Santa Isabel, or heard something that concerned the murders, it might explain why she left the country when she did."

I swallowed some cocoa. "Sounds like kind of a long shot to me, Rita."

"Have you discovered any other reason for her leaving so suddenly?"

"No, but that doesn't mean that one doesn't exist."

"And it still leaves this one open as a possibility."

"Remote."

"Suppose that before she left for El Salvador, Melissa *had* been in touch with Elizabeth Drewer. Suppose that she'd been seriously considering disappearing along the Underground Railway, taking Winona with her. And suppose that she saw or heard something down there about these killings. Suppose that she *knew* who was responsible, and suppose she felt that the knowledge put her life in jeopardy." She sipped her coffee.

I said, "So she runs back to L.A., grabs Winona, and the two of them jump on the Underground Railroad, which is already waiting for them at the station."

Rita nodded.

"A lot of supposing," I said. "And I don't see how we can follow it up. Do the police down there have any suspects?"

"The police down there *are* the suspects. Have you talked to Hector about any of this?" Our friend Hector Ramirez worked in the Violent Crimes Division of the Santa Fe Police Department.

I said, "I was out in Lotusland, remember?"

"I'll call him and ask him if he knows anything about Railroad safe houses here in town."

"Hector won't know anything about safe houses, Rita. That's federal business. And you know, there's another possibility here."

"The Sanctuary group."

"Yeah. They've got an office in Santa Fe, which probably means they've got a fair amount of members here. From what Charles Hatfield tells me, some of those members might be helping illegals move around."

"And some of them might be helping Melissa."

"Right."

"Your friend Montoya. Would he know anything about the movement of illegal aliens?"

"Maybe. But I don't want to bring him into this. I can hardly act as a go-between if he's the one who locates her."

"So you *don't* trust him."

"I think I do. But I could be wrong. And I don't want to do anything that might jeopardize Melissa and Winona."

She nodded. "Who will you be talking to at the Sanctuary office?"

"A woman named Rebecca Carlson. Got her name from Hatfield. She's the honcho there. I've already called her, made an appointment for this afternoon."

"All right, Joshua. Let me know what happens."

"Don't I always?"

She smiled. "Sometimes you tend to gloss over an incident or two."

"I? Gloss?"

"You neglected to mention, for example, the two security guards you assaulted at Calvin Bigelow's office."

"You found *that* on the database?"

She laughed. "Bigelow called me last night." We have call-forwarding on the office phone; after five o'clock, anyone telephoning there will be routed to Rita's home number. I had left my business card, with the office number on it, on Bigelow's desk. "He was not pleased," she said.

"Really? He seemed happy enough the last time I saw him."

"Something about sneaking around his back to harass his wife. And, of course, the assault in his office."

"Not an assault. A minor dispute."

"I see. Well, it might be in your best interests not to dispute with anyone today."

"Yes dear."

"And don't forget to pick up the fax from Arthur at the fax service."

"Yes dear."

"Go away, Joshua."

"Yes dear."

I DROVE DOWNTOWN. There's a pay phone just outside the entrance to our office building, and I used it to call Deirdre Polk. She still wasn't home. I called the fax service and learned that no fax from Arthur had arrived. I went to the office, where I worked on reports until twelve, then I walked down the stairs, out into the garden courtyard, and out through the archway that opened onto the territorial-style portico facing Palace Avenue. I called Deirdre Polk again, and this time she was in. She told me, with just a hint of asperity in her voice, that she didn't have any information about Melissa Alonzo, but she agreed to speak with me that afternoon at five thirty, at her house in Hartley. I didn't mind the asperity. I get a lot of it.

I walked down to Washington, bought a carnitas-filled tortilla and a glass of lemonade at Rogue and Mona's stand, beside the museum, and ferried them across the street to the Plaza. I found a shaded bench not far from the Memorial, sat down, and ate my lunch.

It was a beautiful day. Overhead, the sky was a canopy of cobalt silk. The sweet smell of freshly mowed grass swayed in the air like a drapery. The bright clear sunlight angled through the yellowing leaves; the bright clear carol of children's laughter floated across the lawn.

Most of the tourists were gone now. I saw only one couple from Out of Town. Standing at the corner of San Francisco and the Old Santa Fe Trail, she was squinting extravagantly as she peered down at a street map, while he stood rock steady and used a bulky VHS camcorder to take an extremely protracted snapshot of the La Fonda Hotel's rock-steady facade. On the low stone wall that circled the Memorial, two long-haired young boys and a long-haired girl sat sunning themselves, eyes shut, backs curled against the green wrought iron fence, heads uptilted, all of them looking as though they had slipped here through some time warp from 1968 Haight-Ashbury. A few feet away, a red-haired teenage girl, a man's bulky black work shirt hanging loose over black spandex tights, sat hunched over a paperback book. Two small giggling children, boy and girl, played tag around the trunk of an oak tree. Down the leafy sidewalks walked a pair of Hispanic grandmothers, a fat businessman boxed in gray worsted, two slender businesswomen, one wearing a black miniskirt and a red plaid blazer, the other more formal in gray tweeds. Here and there around the square, in small flocks of five and ten, pigeons strutted with enormous self-importance, as though they were sporting dinner jackets. Occasionally, attacked by a whooping child, they took sudden fright, and flight.

I sipped at my lemonade and watched a young woman and her daughter enter the square from the east side, at the Trail. The woman, tall and slim, in her late twenties, wore long brown western boots outside her tight stone-washed jeans, and a bulky white cotton turtleneck sweater whose hem reached to her thighs. Her long hair was brown and fine and it was shiny in the sun. The young girl, probably Winona's age, wore a thin white cotton sweater over a lemon yellow jumper, white anklet socks, and black patent leather shoes. Her hair was blond and loose and it was as shiny as her mother's. Her left hand clutched at her mother's right, and she moved in that pigeon-toed, determined march of childhood, her right arm swinging in exaggerated arcs at her side.

As they passed by me, and I caught the faint fragrance of their soaps and shampoos, the girl said something. Her mother laughed, tossing back her head, and sunlight flashed along her hair. It was a good strong laugh, free and easy, unrestrained, filled with a gladness that seemed suddenly to define the moment, the day, and their entire lives.

I wondered if, somewhere, Melissa Alonzo was still able to laugh like that.

I wondered if, sometime, I would ever be able to laugh like that.

Sitting there, watching the woman and her daughter walk away, I felt abruptly old and battered and solitary.

I had never been close to children. Had never had any, had never really spent time with any. Had never been in a relationship where children, the having of them, had seemed part of an inevitable progression.

Cowardice, perhaps, on my part. They made demands, they needed food and clothes and shelter, they needed love and time. And they needed protection. Their vulnerability was absolute. This world was filled with jagged edges, sudden drops, explosions, with machinery and malice and very real monsters. Things that could pummel and tear tender flesh, shatter fragile bones, poison a small heart, smash a budding universe of thought and feeling. Perhaps Winona, right now, was facing some of these.

It was cowardice, certainly. I simply had not ever possessed the bravery required to protect and cherish another life. Not another adult's, not a child's. And I wondered now whether my recent unease with Rita was related in some way to the cowardice. Rita was no longer imprisoned in her chair. Soon she would be walking. Soon, the kind of involvement between the two of us that I had fantasized for years, that I had convinced myself I wanted—soon that might actually be possible. The notion of children was just one among many that we might have to confront.

That I might have to confront. Maybe I wasn't afraid that Rita would be walking out of my life. Maybe I was afraid that I'd be walking out of hers. Maybe, now that she was suddenly attainable, Rita was suddenly a threat.

I caught myself. Hold on there, scout. Who said that she was attainable? Aren't you maybe rushing things a bit? The woman has never suggested children, never suggested an involvement, never suggested a date at the malt shop. Perhaps panic is a tiny bit premature.

Enough, as Rita would put it. Forget the angst. Next week you can join a men's group, head up into the mountains with a bunch of accountants, pound drums and yodel and roll in the mud. In the meantime, you can do your job. You can use your old, battered, solitary skills to find a lost child and a lost mother, root them out from whatever underground they were hiding in, and bring them back into the sunshine. Give both of them a chance to laugh again.

You can do it. It's what you do. You ask questions, you get answers, and you find people.

So get started. Now.

SIXTEEN

"DON'T YOU THINK he's a wonderful man?" Rebecca Carlson asked me.

"I certainly do," I told her. "And a terrific actor."

"I've got every episode of 'Valdez!' he ever made. On tape, at home. I think he's just so... *distinguished*. Do you know what I mean?"

"I certainly do."

"And yet, when you get to know him, he's really just a regular person. Very down to earth."

"It's amazing, isn't it."

"And you say you're working for him?"

"For his family. They're concerned about Winona, his daughter."

"How *is* Roy?"

"It's been difficult for him, naturally. But you know how he is. The show must go on, is the way he puts it."

She smiled, shook her head in admiration. "Isn't that just like him."

"He's a trouper, all right."

Rebecca Carlson was a short woman in her fifties wearing a floral print dress and a battleship gray permanent that looked as if it would slice off your fingers if you were brave enough to touch it. Her mouth was fleshy, her nose was slightly bulbous, and her pale blue eyes, beneath the thick lenses of her spectacles, were small and shiny and they had an excitement in them, or a hunger, whenever she mentioned Roy Alonzo.

Her office was on Marcy Street, not far from mine, in a building that, like a lot of downtown buildings, hadn't been there five years ago. It was a two-room affair, the main room for her and an anteroom for her secretary, a young Hispanic woman. It was the sort of office, functional, nondescript, that might have been leased by an insurance company or a financial consultant. The only indication that the business conducted there had anything to do with aliens, illegal or otherwise, was a framed painting on the wall behind Rebecca Carlson's desk. It showed a spectacularly handsome Mexican farmer standing in front of a rising sun with his brown hands fisted on his slim hips, his serape thrown back over his broad manly shoulder, his jaw firm, his eyes steely. It was inspiring.

"I think it's just terrible," she said, "what that awful woman put him through."

"It certainly was," I said. "But at least the courts finally straightened everything out."

"Yes, but only after she said all those terrible things and dragged his good name through the mud. Only after he lost his job and they canceled his show. And then to go and kidnap his daughter! Why, the woman is deranged!"

"You knew both of them?" I asked her. "Roy and Mrs. Alonzo both?"

"Of course," she said from behind her desk. "He was our spokesperson, did you know that?"

I nodded. "I think I read about it in *People* magazine."

"They had a big article a few years ago. They didn't say much about us, our little operation here in Santa Fe, but they did talk about Roy and how dedicated he was." She shook her head. "I feel so sorry for him. The poor, poor man. To have everything the way he did, and then have it all stolen away from him by that mean, spiteful woman. It's a tragedy, pure and simple. Honestly, it would've been better for him if he'd never even met her. I saw it coming, you know. I remember, I said to a friend of mine, I said, Silvia, you mark my words, but Roy Alonzo will rue the day he ever married that horrible woman." She smiled a small conspiratorial smile. "I admit that the language I used at the time was a *lot* stronger than that. You know how it is when the girls get together and let their hair down."

I had a sudden mental image of Rebecca Carlson letting down her hair. I suppressed it. "When was this, Mrs. Carlson?"

"Oh, years ago. Long before the divorce. Like I say, I saw it all coming. Anyone could have, if they had a pair of eyes in their head."

"What made you think there were problems with the marriage?"

She smiled comfortably. "Some of us can sense these things, you know."

"Certainly. I envy you. I wish I could. But was there any particular incident you can think of, something that indicated a problem?"

"Oh, yes. More than one. They had a big cocktail party out at their house once, out in La Tierra, and naturally I was invited. This was three or four years ago. It was a lovely party, all the best people in town, the real hoi polloi, the mayor, everybody. Even some actor friends of Roy's. Skip Peterson was there."

"Skip Peterson?"

"'Aloha'? He's a retired spy who keeps getting involved in all these wild adventures? He lives in Hawaii?"

"Lately I haven't been able to watch as much TV as I'd like."

She frowned, disappointed. I had failed her. "It's been on for over three years."

I smiled, shrugged. "This detecting business can really take up your time."

She looked at me, curious. "Is it dangerous work?"

I smiled. Self-deprecating, dauntless, hinting at damsels delivered, dragons slain. Wild adventures. "Not usually," I said. "You were talking about a party?"

"Yes. Roy's party," she said. She began to regain her momentum. "It was a beautiful affair. The food, the drinks, all of that must've cost *thousands*. And such a lovely setting. Have you been out to La Tierra? Then you know how spectacular it is, all those lovely rolling hills, the vistas and all. The party was out on their patio, and everyone was having a wonderful time—in a very cultivated way, I mean. It was all very dignified—but not stuffy, not at all. Refined. They were all very nice people, very cultured. Do you know what I mean?"

"Certainly."

"*Except* for Melissa Alonzo. *She* was as drunk as a sailor. At the beginning she was just sitting off by herself, sulking. Poor Roy had to do all the hosting by himself. But later, after she'd had a few more drinks, she started to get more and more noisy. Laughing—screeching, more like it. And using *terrible* language at the top of her lungs, just like a fisherwoman. You could've heard her a mile away. I'm no prude, not at all, but this was in *public*. It was terribly embarrassing. I felt so bad for Roy. And then later, Roy was talking to some poor young girl, and Melissa just stormed up to them and threw her drink at Roy. *Threw* it at him, glass and all. And then stalked off into the house. Poor Roy was soaking wet. He tried to put a good face on it, laughing and joking about it, being gracious, the way he always is. But you could see he was mortified. And it just *ruined* the party. Everyone left fairly soon after that."

"Where was Winona when all this happened?"

"In her bedroom, with the nanny. Thank goodness."

"So you'd say that Melissa Alonzo was a jealous woman?"

"*Insanely* jealous. An absolute *witch*. Why, one time, right here in my office, she hit him, slapped him right across the face, just because he was talking to my secretary. I was sitting here when she came in, and the door was open, and I saw it all. Roy and I had finished our meeting, and he stopped to talk with Patty about some Sanctuary business, and that woman came in. She called him an awful name, for no reason at all, out of the clear blue sky, and then she hit him. Slapped him. And then, just like before, she stormed off."

"When was this, Mrs. Carlson?"

"About three years ago. They got divorced about six months later. I thought at the time that it was the best thing that could've happened to Roy. The divorce, I mean. But that was before that awful woman started spreading those terrible lies about him. I'll tell you right now, Roy Alonzo would *never* do those disgusting things to his daughter. He's a perfect gentleman, and he loved that little girl. She was the apple of his eye."

I nodded. "Why do you suppose she made the accusation?"

"Spite, pure and simple. Roy was getting on with his life and she just couldn't stand that. She's a vicious woman. Vindictive."

I nodded. "Did Mrs. Alonzo have anything to do with this office? Did she do volunteer work here?"

"None. She was too good for the likes of us, don't you know. She stayed away from here, except for a time or two, like the time she went crazy and attacked poor Roy. And to tell you the truth, I was perfectly happy with that arrangement. Not having her here, I mean. I'm a forgiving person, see no evil, hear no evil, but Melissa Alonzo was a terrible woman, and honestly, the less I saw of her, the better. I just couldn't stand the way she treated that poor man."

"Did she have any friends or close acquaintances among the local membership?"

"No. Like I say, she was too good for the likes of us. Sometimes my secretary met her for lunch. Melissa Alonzo was her sponsor, and I could hardly *forbid* Juanita to meet with her."

"Juanita?"

"Juanita, yes. Patty, my first secretary, left us quite a while ago. Juanita was here for almost two years. And now Juanita's gone, too. She called up last week and told me she was sick. *Sick*. She never called in again, and she didn't answer her phone. And when I sent Bill Theodore, he's one of our volunteers, a wonderful man, when I sent him out to check on her, he found out she wasn't even at home."

"When did she call in sick?"

"Thursday."

"And she's left home?"

"Probably setting up house with some gas service attendant." She frowned, as though she'd heard herself. "Oh, I know that's a terrible thing to say, but honestly, you do what you can for these people, you bend over backwards to help them, and then they turn around and do something like this to you. They have no gratitude."

"When you say 'these people,' Mrs. Carlson, whom do you mean?"

"Our refugees. Some of them are very nice people, of course, very polite. But a lot of them think the world owes *them* a living. You give them an inch and they take a mile."

"Juanita was a refugee?"

"From El Salvador. And one of the lucky ones. She knew English, not perfectly, of course, but fairly well. She's supposed to come from a good family down there, but of course you couldn't prove that by *me*. And she did have some secretarial skills, I'll give her that. We went all out for her, managed to get her a sponsor, paid her legal bills, even gave her a very good job. And this is the way she repays us. Disappears without even a thank-you. I had to spend all day Thursday on the telephone, trying to find a temporary girl." She let out a long-suffering sigh. "It sometimes makes me wonder whether all of this is worth it. All the effort, all the work."

"It must be hard for you."

"It is, Mr. Croft, it is. You don't know the half of it."

"I wonder, Mrs. Carlson, if you could tell me Juanita's last name?"

"Carrera." She frowned. "And I suppose you want her address, just like the others."

"The others?"

"Two of them. One of them was a man from the FBI. He was a real gentleman, like yourself. Very nicely spoken."

"Was his name Stamworth?"

"That's right, yes. Do you know him?"

"We've met. When did you talk to him?"

"A few weeks ago, and then again last week. Thursday. I remember because I was just so frantic, trying to find a temp to do all the work Juanita left behind."

"Did he say why he wanted to talk to Juanita?"

"He said it was a routine matter. Nothing important. He seemed a very nice man."

Why had Stamworth been in Santa Fe last Thursday, asking about Juanita? And why had he been back in L.A. this week?

I asked her, "Had you talked to Stamworth before?"

"No. There was another FBI man here, asking about Melissa Alonzo, but that was months ago, when she ran off with the child."

"Did that agent talk to Juanita?"

"You know, I believe he did. I asked Juanita about it back then, and she got all flustered and nervous and wouldn't give me a straight answer. So I assumed he had. But she's been moody for the past month or two. They're very high-strung, these girls."

I didn't ask her whether she meant secretaries or Hispanic women. "You said there was another man?"

She made a face. "Him I didn't like at all. He was very greasy-looking. His hair was all slicked back and he had these dark little eyes that looked like they were dead. Do you know what I mean?"

I nodded. "What was his name?"

"I forget. Something Spanish. I didn't pay much attention because he lied through his teeth. He told me he was Juanita's cousin and he was trying to locate her. Well, I know for a fact that Juanita doesn't have any relatives. He was probably some old boyfriend. So I told him he was insulting my intelligence and I asked him to leave."

"What did he say to that?"

"Nothing. He just stared at me for a minute with this nasty little smile, and then he got up and left."

"And this was when?"

"Last Friday."

"What did he look like, Mrs. Carlson?"

"Greasy, like I say. Like Rudolph Valentino. He had one of those thin little mustaches."

"Was he tall?"

"Medium, I'd say."

"Thin? Fat?"

"Medium. I don't really remember much, except for those eyes of his and that nasty little smile. And the mustache." She frowned. "Why is Juanita so important all of a sudden?" There was a hint of resentment in her voice, the star peevish at the attention paid to the understudy.

"I don't know. But could I trouble you for her address and phone number? Roy and his family want me to track down any lead I can find."

"Of course," she said. "Anything I can do to help." She leafed through a Rolodex on her desktop, found what she wanted, wrote it down on a memo pad, tore off the memo, and handed it to me.

"Thank you," I told her.

"She's long gone, though," she said. "Just like I told Mr. Stamworth. These people can disappear in the blink of an eye."

"Probably," I said, "but I have to try. Mrs. Carlson, when I spoke with Charles Hatfield out in Los Angeles, he told me that sometimes the members of the organization provide not only legal assistance, they also provide shelter. Safe houses."

She shook her head. "Not here, Mr. Croft, not in Santa Fe. Not anyone from this organization. They might run things differently out in California—I'm not saying that they do, of course—but here in Santa Fe we stay within the official Sanctuary guidelines. We stay within the law."

"Good. I'm glad to hear it. Just one more question, Mrs. Carlson, and I'll be out of your way."

"Oh, not at all. I'm enjoying our little chat." Her eyelids fluttered.

I smiled. It took some effort. "Can you think of anyone besides Juanita, in or out of Sanctuary, who might've kept in contact with Melissa Alonzo?"

"No. Like I say, she kept very much to herself."

"All right. Well, thanks very much for your time."

"Not at all. And you tell Roy that if I can do anything else to help, all he has to do is let me know."

"I'll do that," I told her. "And keep up the good work."

THE PIÑON COURT Apartments were way out on Cerrillos, past Siler, not far from Airport Road. The attached, single-story units were arranged in the shape of an L around a cheerless gravel parking lot, the top of the L facing the street. There were no trees, there was no grass. None of the cars in the lot was less than ten years old. The building was cinderblock, stuccoed and painted beige to make it look like adobe. The plaster was cracked and starred, and here and there irregular chunks had slid away and fallen to the base of the wall, where they lay crumbling like dreams and hopes in the stark sunlight. It was the kind of place the occupants tolerated because they were beginning their lives with hopes of better things, or ending their lives without them.

Apartment 14, Juanita Carrera's, was at the end of the base of the L. There was no car in front of her unit. I parked the Subaru, walked to the front door, pushed the buzzer at the door. Black paint had chipped from the buzzer's metal frame.

No one answered. I wasn't surprised; no one had answered the phone when I called. I moved to the window, tried to peer in. The curtains were drawn. I walked back along the gravel driveway to Cerrillos Road, to the line of faded black mailboxes numbered with stick-on-gold numerals. Cerrillos is one of the main drags into and out of town, and the usual swarm of cars were whizzing down its length, most of them breaking the speed limit, some breaking the sound barrier. Their noise rattled against my ears, their backdraft slapped against my face. I opened the box labeled 14 and pulled out a stack of mail.

It was mostly junk, coupons and fliers. A copy of *Cosmopolitan*. No postcard from Melissa Alonzo. No personal mail at all.

"Help you, Bub?"

I turned. He stood about seven feet away, hands on his hips. He was big, my height but heavier. Late thirties or early forties. His black hair was rumpled and his jowls were unshaven. He wore an opened wool suit vest over a T-shirt that had been white before someone used it to clean the floor. It strained against his pudgy breasts and his round stomach. He wore stained green work pants that had probably never seen any actual work, held up by a thin black leather belt whose tip dangled in a loose curl from the buckle. He wore battered running shoes that had probably never seen any actual running. The shoes and the Cerrillos traffic had prevented my hearing his approach atop the gravel. But I should have been warned by other indications. I was downwind of him, and now I could smell stale beer and the sharp bitter smell of clothes that had been sweated in, allowed to dry, then sweated in again.

"I'm looking for Juanita Carrera," I said. "Have you seen her lately?"

He nodded to the mail I held. "That's a federal offense, what we got here. Tampering with the U.S. mails."

"I can see you know your law."

"A wisenheimer, huh?"

"You'd be the manager."

"I already know who *I* am, Bub. Question is, who the hell're you?"

"My name is Croft. I'm a private detective. We can do this a couple of ways. I can put the mail back, and then you and I can have a friendly conversation. Maybe both of us will get something out of it. A mutual exchange. Or we can duke it out like a couple of kids. Somebody might get hurt. Nobody would benefit. You decide."

He looked me up and down. He said, "You probably go what, about a hundred and ninety, hundred ninety-five?"

"About."

"Keep in shape, huh?"

"The Jane Fonda tapes."

"A private detective, that what you said?"

"That's what I said."

He shrugged, let his hands fall from his hips. "What the fuck. Who needs a hassle, right?"

SEVENTEEN

WE SAT IN HIS apartment and we drank Budweiser from the can, the way real men drink it. The apartment was cluttered with secondhand furniture, all of it draped with dirty clothes—shirts, pants, socks, underwear. I practiced an ancient Oriental breathing technique in which you only exhale.

The manager's name was Bill Arnstead. He was a philosopher.

"These chiquitas," he opined, "they're cute as a button when they're young. Nice headlights, nice tight butts. Good in the sack, too, once you get 'em away from their mamas. But they're over the hill at thirty. They turn into cows." He grinned. His teeth needed work. "All them tacos they eat, prob'ly."

This I found curious, coming as it did from someone who looked as though he were on the critical list at Weight Watchers.

"How old was Juanita Carrera?" I asked him.

"I dunno. Twenties somewhere. A good-looking piece. Wouldna kicked her outta bed for eatin' crackers, that's for damn sure. Nice setta jugs on her. And nice long stems. You don't see that too much on your chiquitas, they tend to run stubby. But she was snooty. Wouldn't give ya the time o'day. They're like that sometimes. They got some kinda burr up their ass and they don't like white people."

He reminded me—although she would've been horrified to learn it—of Rebecca Carlson. They possessed the same sort of small, cramped, bitter minds, trapped behind the same cramped walls of cliché and ignorance. Occasionally we like to believe that these people, no matter how offensive, are basically harmless, because their hatreds are so obvious and so transparent. But unfortunately, and unlikely as it seems, some of them can actually breed. Down through generations they can reproduce and multiply their poisons and their poverty of spirit.

He said, "How come she's so popular all of sudden, anyway?"

"Who else has been asking about her, Bill?" I was sitting back in a yellow padded chair. Arnstead was slouched at the end of a brown Naugahyde sofa, his feet propped upon a matching ottoman. Between his feet and the ottoman lay a denim work shirt, artfully folded into a lump.

He smiled slyly. "Dint you say somethin' about a mutual benefit? Like if you're askin' questions, and I'm givin' you answers, don't you think we got a situation here calls for some renumeration? I mean, hey, no offense, but this beer don't exactly grow on trees."

I tugged my wallet from my back pocket, opened it, slipped out a twenty. I put back the wallet and laid the bill on the end table, beside an empty beer can.

"A twenty is all?" he said. "You got an expense account, right?"

"Think of it as a down payment, Bill. Who else was asking about her?"

"Couple guys. One of 'em was FBI. Showed me his card. A real slick operator." He swallowed some beer.

"What was his name?"

"Stamford, somethin' like that. I got a card he left, somewhere around."

"Did he say why he wanted to talk to her?"

"Routine, he says. Those FBI guys are like cops. They won't tell ya shit."

"When was he here?"

"Thursday. Day after she left."

"What time Thursday?"

"Afternoon."

"Who was the other guy?"

"Some greaser. Mean-lookin' motherfucker. Said he was her cousin. I figured that was bullshit, 'cause of the FBI guy, day before, but I wasn't gonna argue with him. Sonofabitch was *mean*. Little slitty eyes, looked like they could see right through ya. And your greasers, lotta them carry blades. I can take care of myself, but who wants to fuck with a blade."

"And when was he here?"

"Friday. Afternoon again."

"And what did you tell them, Bill?"

He smiled another sly smile. "What I knew. Same thing I could tell you if I wanted."

I slipped out my wallet, removed another twenty, put it beside the first, put the wallet back in my pocket, sat back against the chair, waited.

He grinned. "That didn't hurt so bad, right?"

I said, "Why don't we start with how long she lived here."

"'Bout two years. Be two years in January. Didn't have a thing to her name when she showed up, just one of them cheap plastic suitcases. No furniture, nothing. The apartments are all furnished, see."

And regally, if they were all furnished like this one. "Did she have many visitors?"

"None. She was snooty, like I said. Kept to herself." He finished off the beer, crumpled the can in his fist. "Want another brewski?"

"I'm fine."

"Be right back." He swung his legs off the ottoman, lumbered out of the sofa, thumped his way into the kitchenette. Over the Formica counter I watched him open the refrigerator door and reach in. He slammed the door shut, then came thumping back, carrying two beers in his big right hand. He eased down into the sofa, grunted, put one beer on the table to his left, swung his feet back up onto the ottoman. "Case you change your mind." He popped the other beer open. "What was it you wanted to know?"

"You said she didn't have visitors. Did she go out often?"

He shrugged. "She went to work." He drank some beer.

"Besides that?"

"Once in a while, yeah. Sundays, she went to church. I know it was church 'cause I asked her one Sunday where she was comin' from. She told me it was none of my business, but just for my information she went to church every Sunday." He shrugged. "Snooty. Like I said."

"Did she go out any other times?"

"Sometimes. Like on the weekend. At night. For a couple hours, maybe. I got to watch out for the place, see, so I check out the cars come into the lot. She goes out sometimes on a Saturday night, maybe at seven, and usually she comes back ten, ten thirty. Went to a movie, I figure. I don't think she was gettin' any. Dint have that look they get when they're gettin' pumped steady."

"So no men friends."

"Nah. She dint have that look. And I never saw none."

"Woman friends?"

"Uh-uh."

"She came back from work at the same time every day?"

"Uh-uh. Other guys asked the same question. She came back late on Tuesdays and Thursdays. Around ten, ten thirty. Had to work late, prob'ly."

"What kind of car did she drive?" I could've learned that from Motor Vehicles, but Bill was available now.

"A Honda. One of them Civics. With the hatchback."

"Color?"

"Yellow. Real beat-up. A junker."

"You know what year it was?"

"Nah. All them Jap cars, you can't tell years. It was old."

"You said she left on Wednesday. What time?"

He drank from the can. "Wednesday night. Ten o'clock, maybe."

"Anyone with her?"

"Uh-uh."

"She have a suitcase?"

He shrugged. "Maybe. Couldn't tell."

"You have a passkey to her apartment, Bill?"

He drank some more beer. "Well now," he said, and the sly smile reappeared. "Me lettin' you in there, that'd be against the law, right? And what happens you break somethin'? I'm the one responsible."

"You've already made forty dollars, Bill. In less than half an hour. Pretty good wages."

He grinned. "Yeah. But you're sittin' there wonderin' what's inside her apartment, and I'm the boy can get you in."

"That's not what I'm wondering."

"Yeah?" He grinned again. "Whatta ya wonderin?"

"I'm wondering how much damage I'll do to my boot when I kick your fat ass out the window."

He sat up. "Hey." His grin was gone. His mouth was open.

"I'm wondering what your nose would look like coming out the back of your head. I'm wondering what the cops'll think when they find out you haven't reported Juanita Carrera missing."

"Hey, I got no obligation—"

"She's been gone for over a week. Two people have come looking for her. No one knows where she is. Missing Persons would be interested. And I'm wondering what kind of code violations the cops will find when they come out to this dump. That's what I'm wondering, Bill."

"Listen, you got no call to talk to me like that. I been answerin' all your questions. I been cooperatin'."

"Bill?"

He swallowed a quick gulp of beer. "What?"

"Get the passkey."

His eyes dipped downward, then looked back up at me. "I got to come along. It's the rules."

He was breaking the rules even by letting me enter the apartment, but I'd already drawn enough blood. "Fine," I said.

THE LAYOUT OF Juanita Carrera's apartment was identical to Arnstead's. A small living room, a smaller dining alcove, a kitchenette, a tiny bathroom, a bedroom in the back. But Arnstead's apartment looked like it had been lived in by the three little pigs, and Carrera's was spotless. The cheap furniture was clean and polished, and nothing seemed out of place, except for a few books lying on the dining table. There was a faint smell in the air of dust, and of some sweet floral scent.

Arnstead stood at the door, leaning against the jamb, his arms folded above his belly. I asked him, "Did the FBI agent check this place out?"

"Yeah," he said. Still sulky.

"What about the other guy?"

He shrugged. "Yeah, sure."

"Were you here while they did it?"

His glance shifted slightly, came back to mine. "Sure."

"Bill. Code violations?"

He looked blank for a moment, and then, frowning, he shrugged. "I was here with the FBI guy."

"The other guy slipped you some cash, did he?"

He frowned again, and then said defensively, "Guy's gotta make a living."

"Did the FBI man find anything?"

"Uh-uh. So what's the deal here, anyway? If I may be so bold to ask." This was accompanied by a weak, tentative smile.

"You don't want to know, Bill."

He nodded, frowning sourly. "Yeah, right. That's how come I asked."

I started searching. Stamworth had slipped up before, by not checking the tape on Melissa's answering machine, and it was possible that he had slipped up here, while he searched the place. It was possible that the other man had, as well. But I didn't really expect to find anything in Juanita Carrera's apartment that would help me locate her, and I didn't.

I came back from the bedroom into the living room, walked over to the dining room table. The three books on its top were textbooks, two of them psychology texts, and one was opened. The third was a study of American literature. On the flyleaf of each was written, in neat cursive script, *Property of Juanita Carrera*. Below that, in the same script, was her apartment number and the Cerrillos Road address. Beside the books, standing upright on its base, was a yellow Magic Marker. I flipped through the books and saw that, here and there, paragraphs had been highlighted in yellow.

So Juanita had been taking classes somewhere. That would explain why she returned to her apartment later in the evening on Tuesday and Thursdays.

I looked around. She was tidy, Juanita Carrera. The inexpensive clothes hanging in the bedroom closet were conservative and subdued, the dresses and skirts and sweaters of a person who wanted to be presentable but not necessarily memorable. She had a subscription to *Cosmo*, which suggested she was at least curious about the Modern American Single Woman, and that perhaps she might aspire to that pinnacle herself. She was apparently taking college-level courses, which suggested she was trying for a degree. I didn't know the woman, but I was inclined, on the evidence, to like her. I would feel sympathetic, anyway, toward anyone who had to put up with both Rebecca Carlson and Bill Arnstead in the same lifetime.

And now, like Melissa Alonzo, she had vanished.

She had vanished last Wednesday, October the second. Cathryn Bigelow had been killed last Wednesday, October the second.

Coincidence?

I didn't think so. Cathryn Bigelow and Juanita Carrera did have one thing in common. Melissa Alonzo.

"HELLO." The male voice had a faint Spanish lilt to it.

"Hello. Could I speak to Norman Montoya, please."

"Who's this calling?"

"Joshua Croft."

"Hold on a sec."

I waited. I was in the lobby of the public library, using one of the two pay phones.

Montoya's voice came on the line: "Yes, Mr. Croft. How may I help you?"

"Is your phone line clear?" I asked him.

After a brief pause, he answered, "I am assured that it is. This is a serious consideration?"

"Maybe. Things are getting complicated."

"That, of course, is in the nature of things, Mr. Croft."

Wonderful. A Zen telephone conversation. "Mr. Montoya, do you know anyone with connections to people who might be aiding illegal aliens?"

Another brief pause. "May I inquire as to why you ask?"

"There's a woman missing. She worked for a group called Sanctuary. You know them?"

"Yes, of course."

"She knew Melissa Alonzo. Melissa was her sponsor. She disappeared last week, the same day that Melissa's sister, Cathryn, was murdered in Los Angeles. I think she's running scared. I need to find her and find out why."

Another pause. "You have become convinced that the sister's death is related to Melissa's flight?"

"I'm becoming more and more convinced that it's likely."

"This woman. The one who disappeared last week. You are aware, of course, that she could have left the area entirely."

"She could have, yeah. But she worked for Sanctuary. Maybe she knew people who provided safe houses. Her boss says otherwise, but I have a feeling that her boss may not know everything that's going on. And the woman had at least some kind of attachments to Santa Fe. She was probably going to college here. I think there's at least a chance she's still around."

"You do realize, Mr. Croft, that from everything you have told me, it will now be possible for me to identify this woman without any further assistance from you." I thought, but couldn't be certain, that I detected a smile in the voice. "And you realize that having identified her, and assuming that she is still in the area, I could proceed to locate and question her on my own. Without you being any the wiser."

"Yeah. I realize. But as I recall, you gave me your word you wouldn't interfere."

A soft chuckle came over the line. "Ah, Mr. Croft. If you truly had no doubts about the value of my word, you would hardly remind me of my having given it."

"The other thing," I said, "is I can't afford to screw around right now. Melissa and her daughter might be in serious trouble. There's some clown from the federal government looking for this woman. And another man, too, a Hispanic. I don't like the sound of him. I don't want to go to the cops with any of this because the cops would probably scare the woman. She's Salvadoran, a refugee, and I doubt that she has any real fondness for people in uniform."

"Who is this other man you mention?"

"I don't know. But the consensus seems to be that he's not a nice guy."

Another pause. "Very well, Mr. Croft. Give me the woman's particulars. If she is still in the area, my people will be able to uncover her. If they do so, they will approach her, discreetly, and make arrangements with her to contact you. Without themselves questioning the woman. Is that satisfactory?"

"Yeah." I didn't see that I had much choice. I gave him Juanita Carrera's name, and everything I'd just learned from a call to Motor Vehicles. Age, twenty-seven; height, five feet eight; weight, 120 pounds. No eyeglasses. And a description of her car, including the license plate number.

"She's probably very skittish," I told Montoya.

"I understand. My people will exercise caution. The federal agent you mentioned. What is the nature of his involvement?"

"I don't know yet."

"With with agency might he be associated?"

"I don't know. He says FBI, but I have my doubts."

"I see. Is there anything else in which I might help you? Money, perhaps? Perhaps an assistant?"

"Muscle?"

The chuckle floated down the line again. "Such a colorful vocabulary. Yes, muscle, Mr. Croft, if you like."

"No thanks. But I'll bear the offer in mind."

"Please do so. You asked about the phone lines. Have you reason to believe that your own might be unsafe?"

"It's a possibility. I'll find out later." Rita's cousin, Leroy, had a key to the office and by now Rita had given him a key to my house. He had probably already installed tap indicators on both lines.

"An excellent idea. But in the meantime, perhaps we should make arrangements now for your meeting the woman, in the event that my people succeed in finding her." Norman Montoya was a man who thought ahead.

"Okay. If you find her, have her meet me in the parking lot opposite the state capitol building. You give me the time."

"Very well. And please do not hesitate to contact me again if I may be of further help."

"Thanks."

"Good day, Mr. Croft."

After hanging up on Montoya, I looked at my watch. Quarter to four. About half an hour free before I had to head up to Hartley to see Deirdre Polk. I went into the Library and looked through the catalogues for the three colleges located here in town: St. John's, the Santa Fe Community College, and the College of Santa Fe. Juanita might have been taking courses in Albuquerque, at UNM or at one of the other schools down there; but Albuquerque, down and back, was a three-hour drive. That didn't leave her much time to attend classes and get back to her apartment by ten.

The College of Santa Fe was the only school that offered the right courses at the right time. The Intermediate American Literature class met on Tuesday night, from seven until nine thirty. Abnormal Psychology met on Thursday at the same hours. Assuming that it had been Juanita Carrera who left the psychology book open on the table last Wednesday night, and not any of the people who'd been tramping through her apartment since then, that fit. I wrote down the phone number for the college, and the names of the professors who taught the courses, then went out into the parking lot and climbed into the Subaru.

I STOPPED AT the fax service on my way out of town. The fax from Chuck Arthur had arrived.

In the car, I glanced down the list of long-distance calls that Melissa had made in July and August. There weren't that many, and there were no calls dated after August 2, the day she'd left for El Salvador. She might've cleared the messages from her machine when she returned to the house on the seventeenth, the day she got back to L.A., but she hadn't used her home telephone to make any out-of-state calls.

There were two numbers I recognized on the list. On three separate occasions in July, and again on August 1, the day before she left, she had called Juanita Carrera.

EIGHTEEN

THE WEATHER WAS changing as I drove north. Up ahead, black clouds were crowding out the span of blue. Great shafts of sunlight from the west poked aslant beneath their bulky billowing shapes.

An impressive spectacle, but I couldn't enjoy it. I was worried. As I'd told Norman Montoya, I didn't like the sound of the Hispanic man who'd spoken with Rebecca Carlson and Bill Arnstead. I didn't know who he was or where he fit in.

Or where Stamworth fit in. He, too, had been questioning both people last week.

Juanita Carrera was apparently the key. She knew something, something that had to do with Melissa Alonzo.

It had to be. I knew, from the phone bills and from the message on Melissa's machine, that Melissa and Juanita Carrera were connected. Melissa's sister, Cathryn Bigelow, had been killed last Wednesday morning. On Wednesday night, Juanita Carrera had disappeared. Suddenly, as though something had frightened her. On Thursday, Stamworth had talked to Carlson and Arnstead, trying to locate Carrera. On Friday, the Hispanic man had done the same.

On Tuesday night, two days ago, Stamworth had been in Los Angeles. Why? I hadn't believed his Shining Path story then and I didn't believe it now. So who was he?

Who was the Hispanic man?

What did the two of them want with Juanita Carrera? And what did they want with Melissa Alonzo?

And how had Stamworth known about me? How had he known that I was in Los Angeles looking for Melissa?

Whoever they were, Stamworth and the Hispanic man were a week ahead of me. They had known about, and tried to locate, Juanita long before I'd known that she existed.

Where *was* Juanita Carrera?

And where were Melissa and Winona Alonzo?

I was worried. The countryside around me, ragged high desert, gullied and brown, spotted with piñon and juniper, seemed more bleak and barren and vast than I could remember it being. Wilder, emptier, easier to get lost in. The black clouds up ahead seemed ominous, foreboding.

The pathetic fallacy. Projection.

So I told myself. But after I passed the bright orange explosion of cottonwoods down in the valley at Velarde, after I slipped into the canyon of the Rio Grande and the sunlight guttered out and there were only the weathered black cliffs climbing up on either side, and the gray roof of sky, and the dark river sliding silently along to my left, I felt a sudden physical chill.

BY THE TIME I reached Hartley, a small mountain town of frame houses huddled among the oaks and elms, a storm was about to hit. The homes were lit up within, promising a warmth and security that, in my business anyway, is more often remembered than experienced. Overhead, huge black clouds were piled one atop the other, their swollen bellies streaked a sickly gray. Now and then, lightning flashed, bright jagged bolts snapping across the sky. A few seconds later, thunder slammed against the earth, sudden ear-splitting booms that tapered off, rattling, into long low resentful growls. Any moment now, the rain would start.

Deirdre Polk had given me directions. I turned left past the general store, followed a tree-lined dirt road down the hill and over a narrow concrete bridge, then down a tunnel formed by arching black branches. The road twisted among the trees. Windblown leaves flapped through the headlight beams like flocks of pale startled bats. I passed a small shivering meadow, its tall gray grasses flailing as gusts ripped across them. I passed a few houses to the right, a few to the left, each separated from the next by black thickets of shuddering brush or by black clusters of trees drunkenly swaying.

Her house was the last one on the road, a small shingled structure set back among the trembling oaks, with a roofed wooden porch that ran along its front. The porch light was on. I parked the Subaru in the dirt driveway, behind an old Volvo station wagon. When I stepped out of the car, the wind clawed at me. Trees hissed and moaned. Hunching my shoulders against the cold, I jogged up the wooden steps to the front door. No doorbell. I was about to knock when the door suddenly opened.

"Mr. Croft?" she said. "I heard your car. Come in."

I stepped in and she closed the door behind me, muffling the wail of the wind.

She was tall, close to six feet tall. Her shining black hair was cut short, nearly as short as a man's, lying lightly over her ears and parted on the left. Somehow it suited her strong cheekbones, her aquiline nose, her large brown eyes, her wide mouth. She wore a pale blue cotton turtleneck sweater, a pair of faded jeans, a pair of brown lizardskin cowboy boots. Her shoulders were square, her breasts were large and firm. Big-boned and well proportioned, she held herself upright, unashamed of her height, her size, and she moved easily, gracefully—a woman comfortable with herself, her body, her life. She was handsome rather than beautiful, but she was very handsome.

She smiled. "It'll be pouring out there in a minute. Have a seat." Her voice was low, musical, and sounded of Eastern universities.

I turned, and something growled.

To the left, sitting on its haunches on the hardwood floor, was an extremely large male German shepherd. His head lowered, his ears flat against his big skull, he eyed me as though I were a pork chop with pretensions.

"Friend," said Deirdre Polk, and abruptly the dog's ears relaxed. He stood up, panting happily, and lumbered over to me, claws clicking at the floor. I offered him my hand to lick. Or to eat. Whatever he wanted. He licked it and I squatted down in front of him, scratched at his ears. A rough wet tongue the size of a bath towel reached out and thwacked my face.

"Enough, Marcel," she said, and the dog looked at her, trying to determine whether she was absolutely certain about this.

"Enough," she said.

The dog sighed and turned and padded over into the corner, lay down beside a black potbellied wood stove, looked up at me from beneath a furrowed brow.

I grinned and stood up. "Marcel?"

"Duchamp," she smiled.

I grinned again. "Of course."

"Please. Have a seat."

After the wind and the cold and the darkness of outside, the modest living room seemed almost impossibly cozy. Like the floor, the walls were wood, hung here and there with small, carefully wrought paintings like the ones I'd seen in Melissa Alonzo's house. Below two of them, on the wall to my left, stood a low oak bookcase filled with oversized hardcover books. The curtains on the windows were a festive red. The furniture was Early American, an oak sofa frame supporting embroidered white cushions, and, facing this across a brightly patterned red Navajo rug, a pair of matching oak rocking chairs, also cushioned. There were two brass Aladdin kerosene lamps, one on the end table beside the sofa, the other on the antique cherrywood table that separated the rockers. Through their ivory-colored shades, both gave off a clear, white, gentle light. The air was warm and it smelled of piñon logs burning and of apples and cinnamon.

I sat down on the sofa. Deirdre Polk, standing there with her hands in her back pockets, said to me, "I've got some mulled cider on the stove. And there's some Calvados. I like to put a shot of it in the cider. Would that be all right?"

She was being much more pleasant than she had sounded on the telephone. "That," I said, "would be perfect."

She smiled and left. I looked at Marcel. As soon as Deirdre Polk disappeared around the corner, he clambered to his feet, clicked across the floor, sat down beside my foot, and put his head on my knee. It weighed about the same as a bowling ball. I scratched his ears. He looked up at me with shiny tragic eyes. We communed.

Deirdre Polk returned to the room carrying two white ceramic mugs. "He's such a baby. If he's bothering you, just tell him to lie down." She handed me one of the mugs. Outside, suddenly, thunder crashed.

The dog looked at me as though he expected me to do something about all this noise. "He's okay," I said.

She crossed the Navajo rug, sat down in one of the rockers, crossed her long right leg over her left. Before I could speak, she said, "I want to apologize for the way I must've sounded on the phone. People have been pestering me about Mel now for months. After I talked to you, I called some people I know in Santa Fe. Bonita DeMarco knows you. She's a friend of mine."

Bonita DeMarco owned a gallery on Canyon Road. I'd helped her out with something once, a small something, and I'd been receiving invitations to openings at her gallery ever since. She was a fat, Falstaffian woman with a ribald sense of humor and a loud infectious laugh. She was also a lesbian. Deirdre Polk's friendship with her didn't necessarily mean that Deirdre was a lesbian herself, but it was suggestive. I felt a small flicker of regret.

Typical male chauvinist response. The implication being that if Deirdre Polk were straight, she'd have gone belly up in my stunning presence.

"I like Bonita," I said.

She smiled. "She's very fond of you. She says that you don't lie."

I smiled. "I've been known to exaggerate."

"Are you working for Roy Alonzo?"

"No. I'm working for his uncle." Once again, I explained my arrangement with Norman Montoya.

"And he really means it?" she said. "He's really only concerned about Melissa and Winona's safety?"

"I think so, yeah."

Her dark eyebrows moved toward each other. "You're not sure?"

"I'm as sure as I can be. But I could be wrong." I shrugged. "I'm not a mind reader. Unfortunately."

She frowned, sipped at her drink.

I sipped at mine. It was good. Apples and spices and the mellowness of the Calvados. It went down warm and it stayed warm when it reached bottom. I said the same thing I'd said to Melissa's mother. "Melissa's been in contact with you, hasn't she?"

She lowered the mug to her lap, lifted her head slightly. "Yes."

"A postcard?"

She shook her head. "She was here. Last month."

DEIRDRE POLK told me that on September 23 she had returned from Taos, where she'd been shopping. She had parked the car, carried her bags into the house. Fifteen minutes later, someone had knocked at the door. It had been Melissa. For an instant, Deirdre hadn't recognized her: Melissa was wearing dark glasses and her long blond hair had been cut, permed into curls, and dyed brown.

"How did she look otherwise?" I asked. I was feeling a certain sense of unreality. Despite my determination to find Melissa Alonzo, I realized now that I'd begun to think of her as a will-o'-the-wisp, a figure forever on the distant horizon, forever unattainable. Probably because I had talked to so many people who hadn't seen her for so long. Here was someone who had actually seen her, spoken with her, a few weeks ago.

"Tired," Deirdre Polk said. "She looked tired. She'd lost some weight. But she was happy, or she seemed to be. We laughed a lot.

I made fun of her hair.'' She smiled. ''It was so strange to see her with hair like that. She'd always kept it long. Long, straight blond hair. I used to call her Alice. Alice in Wonderland.'' She smiled again, looking off, remembering, then turned to me. ''It was wonderful to see her again. Really wonderful. I hadn't heard anything from her since the beginning of August.''

''Was Winona with her?''

''No. Winona was back in Santa Fe, at the house of the people they were staying with. A young couple. She wouldn't tell me their names. They were part of a group that helps out women and children like Melissa and Winona.''

''The Underground Railroad.''

She nodded. ''She said they were really very special people. They had a daughter of their own, Winona's age, and the two girls had become friends. But she said there were problems. These people had decided they couldn't keep harboring Mel. Their daughter had just started school for the first time, kindergarten, and they felt it wasn't fair to her, all the secrecy, all the precautions everyone had to take. They were miserable about it, Mel said. About asking her to leave. They felt guilty. But guilty was something that Mel understood. She probably felt more guilty about the situation than they did. She'd made arrangements to take Winona somewhere else.''

''Where?''

''She wouldn't say. She wouldn't tell me. But it was somewhere nearby. Here in New Mexico. She told me she'd be getting in touch with me soon.''

''Has she?''

''No. That's why I'm telling you all this. I thought about it for hours, after I spoke to Bonita. She says I can trust you. So I'm trusting you, Mr. Croft. I don't really have a choice. I'm worried. I'm really very worried. It's not like Mel. If she says she's going to do something, she does it. She would've contacted me somehow, unless . . .'' She frowned as the possibilities presented themselves, and then she chose to bury them beneath a generality. ''Unless something were wrong.''

Outside, with nice timing, the rain began to fall, rattling against the leaves, clattering against the rooftop.

''The place she was going to,'' I said. ''You're certain that it was somewhere in New Mexico?''

She nodded. ''She told me that much. And she said it'd be good for Winona. That there were a lot of children there. Boys and girls

Winona's age. It's been hard on Winona, she said. The hiding, the moving from place to place. She felt terrible about that. I don't think she realized, when she started all this, how hard it would be on Winona. She realized it intellectually, of course, but that's always different from actually *seeing* it.''

"Did she mention any of the places she'd stayed?"

"No. She wouldn't tell me anything about the Railroad at all."

Once again, thunder crashed and rumbled outside. The big German shepherd raised his head from my knee and looked at me, disappointed. I scratched his ear. He laid his head back down and closed his eyes.

I said, "You said that people have been pestering you about Mel for months. Who did you mean?"

"Back in August, toward the end of the month, two men came here from the FBI. They wanted to know if I'd seen her or heard from her."

"And you hadn't."

She shook her head. "She called me before she went down to El Salvador. And that was the last I heard until she showed up at my door."

"Who else asked?"

"There was another FBI man. He was here twice, once in September, and then again last week. He said he was following up on the earlier investigation."

"What was his name?"

"Stamworth. Jim Stamworth."

I sipped my cider. "When was he here last week?"

"Thursday night."

"Did you tell him you'd seen Melissa?"

"No. When she was here, Mel begged me not to tell anyone that I'd seen her. She was deadly serious about it. She made me promise." She frowned. "I'm not sure I'm doing the right thing now. Telling you."

"I think you are. Has anyone else been asking you about Melissa?"

"I got a phone call from Los Angeles some time ago. A private detective who said he was working for Roy Alonzo. Back in August, this was. He asked me, like the others, if I'd seen or heard from her. And at the time, I hadn't."

The Hispanic man, whoever he was, evidently hadn't learned about Deirdre Polk. Yet. "When Stamworth was here, did he mention Melissa's sister, Cathryn?"

She frowned. "Cathryn? Why would he mention Cathryn?"

She apparently hadn't heard of Cathryn's death. "Were Melissa and Cathryn close?"

She frowned again. "Close? Well, they're sisters. Mel's fond of her, naturally, but in a kind of distant way. The impression I always got was that Mel likes her, loves her, but that in a way she feels sorry for her, too. Whenever she mentioned her, she called her 'poor Cathryn,' as though Cathryn . . ." She shrugged. "I don't know. As though Cathryn hadn't lived up to her full potential, maybe."

My face must have shown something because she frowned at me. "What is it?" she asked. "What's wrong?"

"Cathryn is dead," I said. "She was killed last week."

It took a moment to register. Then the muscles of her face went slack with shock. "Killed? Murdered? But . . . my God. That's horrible. That's *horrible*. Does Melissa know?"

"I don't know."

"But *why*? Who killed her?"

"I don't know. The Los Angeles police don't know."

"But . . ." Her eyes opened in alarm. "This doesn't have anything to do with Melissa, does it?"

"The police don't think so."

"But what do *you* think?"

"I honestly don't know. I know I want to find Melissa."

"But *murdered*? How was she killed?"

"She was strangled." There was no reason to elaborate.

Deirdre Polk winced and her hand went protectively to her throat, fingers spread. "How awful!"

"Ms. Polk. You said before that guilt was something Melissa understood. What did you mean?"

She was looking off. She turned to me. "I'm sorry. What?"

I repeated myself.

She frowned. She removed her hand from her throat, placed it atop the arm of the rocker, closed it, opened it. She took a breath. "I meant it's something she's lived with all her life. Her father's a very domineering person. He always has been. Everything has to be done *his* way, or not at all. From what she's said, I don't think he's ever told her that he was proud of her, that he's ever once given her a sense of worth. A sense that she was valuable. As herself. As Melissa. Her mother, from what Mel said, is kind of a nonentity. Well intentioned, but basically ineffectual. No match for her father. I think Mel grew up with a feeling of guilt, a sense that she didn't quite measure up, didn't meet the expected standards."

I said, "I apologize for asking personal questions. I need to learn as much as I can about Melissa. Your relationship with her. You were close friends?"

She smiled a small bleak smile. "Close, yes. Friends, yes. We weren't lovers."

"I'm not trying to pry," I said. "Well, yeah, I am trying to pry. I have to."

She nodded. "I'm not ashamed of who I am. I'm gay. It's a part of me. It's an important part, but it doesn't define me, any more than my hair or my clothes or the kind of food I eat. Melissa isn't gay, and being straight doesn't define her. You're not one of those sad, sorry men who can't believe that a close friendship is possible between a gay woman and a straight woman?"

"I don't think so, no." I smiled. "But some of my best friends are sad, sorry men."

She sipped at her cider. "She told me once that she'd tried it in college. A roommate. It didn't work for her, she said."

"When did you meet her?"

"About two years ago. Just after her divorce. I had a show down in Santa Fe, with two other women, and Mel came to the opening. We talked, and she asked me if I wanted to meet her for lunch the next day. We became friends. She liked my work, but I think she liked me mostly because I knew what I wanted to do, and I was doing it. In a way, Mel was still trying to figure out who she was. What she wanted to do. Sometimes she seemed to be playing at her life. Acting a part rather than living it."

"When I was out in Los Angeles," I said, "I heard a story about Melissa. According to the story, Melissa and Roy were occasionally involved in S and M parties. Would you know anything about that?"

She frowned. "Is that important?"

"At this point, I don't know what's important. All I can do is keep accumulating information every way I can. And hope that some piece of it, sooner or later, leads me to Melissa."

She sipped at her cider. "She told me it was something that she and Roy did occasionally. Scenes. They did them out in Los Angeles, and here, in New Mexico. There's a group down in Albuquerque, apparently. The two of them went down there once or twice."

It surprised me to learn that an S and M group existed in Albuquerque. I've never considered Albuquerque a hotbed of kinky sex. "Did she ever give you any names for anyone down in the Albuquerque group?"

"No. I never asked. It was something I wasn't particularly interested in. It all struck me as sort of...lost and unhappy." Her smile now contained both sadness and irony. "Mel used to tease me about how straight I was. Despite being gay."

"Okay. Let's go back a bit. She called you, you said, before she went to El Salvador. What was her mood like then?"

She frowned. "It was funny. Strange funny. I expected her to be frantic. She *had* been frantic a few weeks before, when the judge announced his decision. And she was still angry. But she seemed almost excited about going down there. She made it all sound very mysterious, as though she were on some secret mission. That's what I mean, about her playing a part. She said that while she was down there, she was going to be doing something for Juanita."

NINETEEN

"JUANITA," I SAID. "Juanita Carrera?"

Deirdre Polk nodded. "Yes. Have you met her?"

"Not yet. Have you?"

"No, but Mel's talked about her a lot. Mel'd been Juanita's sponsor, with a group called Sanctuary, and the two of them had become friends. What Mel told me was that she was going to do something for Juanita down there, in El Salvador."

"Did she say what it might be?"

"No." Another faint, sad smile. "Mel can be awfully stubborn when she wants to. If she doesn't want to tell you something, she won't."

"This thing she was going to do for Juanita. Did it sound to you like she was talking about something important?"

"Important to Juanita, yes. It had to be something important. Because Mel told me, when she was here three weeks ago, that the reason she was back in Santa Fe was to see Juanita. She said there were things she had to tell her."

"She didn't say what they were?"

"No. It had something to do with El Salvador. Something had happened down there. She wouldn't tell me what it was."

So Rita had been right. As usual. "Why not?" I asked her.

"She said it was better that I didn't know. At first I thought she was playacting again." She frowned, shook her head. "Maybe I'm giving you the wrong impression about Mel." She sipped at her cider, frowned again. "All right," she said, "she playacts from time to time. Sometimes she dramatizes herself, her life. In a lot of ways, she's still a little girl, looking for approval. But maybe most of us are still little girls and boys, still carrying around our private wounds, still looking for the approval that'll make them all better. It doesn't mean she's a trivial person. She isn't. She really cares about the people she was helping in Sanctuary. She really loves Juanita, and she'd do anything she can to help her. There may be all sorts of complicated psychological reasons why she feels that way. Maybe because she's been neglected all her life, maybe because she has a cold, distant father. Probably that's all true. I'm not a psychologist, I don't know. But I don't think it matters, really. She's got a good heart, a really compassionate heart, and she can be absolutely fearless when she's protecting the things and the people she cares about.''

I nodded. ''You said that she wasn't playacting when she refused to tell you what had happened down in El Salvador.''

''No. No, she frightened me.'' She took a breath. ''I'm still frightened.''

''Before she left for El Salvador, had she spoken to you about the Underground Railroad?''

She nodded. ''We talked about it on the telephone once. Just after the court ruled against her. She said she'd talked to a woman named Elizabeth Drewer. She's a lawyer in Los Angeles and she's connected to the Railroad, apparently. Mel said that Drewer had explained how the Railroad worked, and what Mel would have to do if she decided to use it.''

''Did she sound inclined to use it, back then?''

Deirdre Polk frowned. ''She was torn up about it. Undecided. It was a huge step, she knew that. It was enormous. It meant giving up everything. Her house, her friends, her entire life. Running, hiding, for who knows how long. Forever, maybe. But on the other hand, if she stayed in Los Angeles, Roy would have access to Melissa. He'd have unrestricted visitation. And that idea terrified her.''

''What are your feelings about Roy Alonzo?''

She shrugged again. ''I've never met him. But he needs help, obviously. You can't do something like that if you're not a deeply troubled person.''

''You've got no doubts that he abused Winona.''

She shook her head. ''Melissa would never have put herself, she'd never have put Winona, through that terrible mess of a trial if she wasn't completely convinced that Roy was guilty. We talked about it, before she decided to take Roy to court. I asked her if she was absolutely positive that Roy had done it. She said that if he hadn't done it, then Winona was lying about it, for no reason at all, and that all the doctors were wrong, all the psychologists and the MDs who examined Winona, all of them.''

''Did she ever mention a woman named Shana Eberle?''

She frowned. ''The name is familiar.''

''Roy Alonzo was involved with her when the sexual abuse case came up.''

She nodded. "Mel did mention her. She said the woman was famous for sleeping around with everyone in Hollywood." She smiled another sad smile. "She said that Roy had finally gotten exactly what he deserved."

"Was Melissa jealous of her?"

"Jealous? Why should she be?"

I shrugged. "I've heard that Melissa was a jealous woman."

"While she and Roy were married, yes, probably. Jealousy has a lot to do with a need for approval, I think. But Roy encouraged her. Deliberately. He was a terrible womanizer, and he used to flirt with women right in front of Mel. He did it intentionally. He used to laugh about it, she said. Brag about the women he'd had. But after the divorce, after she got away from the situation, Melissa really didn't care what Roy did." She smiled faintly. "Or who."

"She made the shift that quickly?"

"It wasn't made quickly. She spent a year getting over the divorce. And she had some rough moments. It was her second divorce, and this time there was a child to consider. But by the time Roy got involved with Shana Eberle, Mel was over the worst of it."

"Were there any men in her life?"

"I don't think so. She told me that her lawyer—the man who represented her in the divorce and the custody trials—she said that he had a kind of crush on her. I don't remember his name."

"Chuck Arthur."

"Yes. She liked him. And it pleased her, knowing that someone like him would find her attractive. He was younger, and smart, and good at what he did. But so far as I know nothing ever came of it."

"Okay," I said. "Does the phrase *'The flower in the desert lives'* mean anything to you?"

She frowned. "No. Is it supposed to?"

"I don't know. It was on some postcards Melissa sent."

She shook her head. "I never heard her use it."

I finished off the rest of my cider, set the glass on the end table. "All right. Thank you. I appreciate your being so open with me."

She leaned slightly forward, over her cider mug. "Do you think you'll find her?"

"I'll find her." I said this with more real conviction than I'd felt when I said it before. I knew now that Melissa was somewhere along the Underground Railroad. She had been here, in this house, less than three weeks ago. She had been in Santa Fe, and she had been about to leave for somewhere nearby. Sooner or later, I would find her.

I scratched the dog's head one final time, and then stood. The dog yawned, lay down at my feet, and went immediately to sleep. I had evidently made a strong impression.

Deirdre Polk set aside her mug and stood up, put her hands in her front pockets. Concern showed on her face. "This thing about Cathryn. The murder. That really frightens me."

"It frightens me, too," I said. "But it may have nothing to do with Melissa. The cops don't think it does, and they're usually right about these things."

The concern was still there.

I said, "I wish there was something more comforting that I could tell you. There may be something soon. As soon as I know anything definite, I'll get in touch with you."

She nodded, smiled sadly. "Thank you."

Changing the subject, I turned to the paintings on the wall. "By the way, I like your work. Melissa has a couple of your paintings in her bedroom, out in California."

Another sad smile. "She bought one at the opening, when I first met her. I gave her the other for her birthday, last year." She nodded to the paintings. "Those are old. My first efforts. I keep them to remind me how far I've come. And how much farther I've got to go."

I stepped forward and looked more closely at the paintings. One was a view of the living room in which we stood, painted from the corridor that led into the kitchen. The other showed a view through a bedroom door of a rumpled bed, a lace-curtained window, a patch of shiny wooden floor. Both displayed the same fine detail, the same polished, sensual surfaces as the two paintings in Malibu, and both possessed the same curious sense of ghostly occupancy. But the bedroom scene, because the light was more subdued, the colors darker, seemed melancholy. As though the ghosts skulking around the corner were lonely and morose.

"They're both very fine," I said. "But I think I like this one better." I pointed to the bedroom scene.

She had crossed the room to stand beside me. She nodded. "That's a sad painting. I was going through a pretty rough time when I did it."

"I like it."

She stepped forward, lifted it off its support, and held it out to me. "Here."

"I can't take that."

"Things should belong to the people who enjoy them the most. Please. Take it. I really want you to have it."

"I can't. Do you give your paintings away to everybody who likes them?"

"Not everybody. But I'd like you to have this. Please, Mr. Croft."

I smiled, embarrassed. "If you're going to be giving me gifts, you'll have to call me Joshua."

She smiled. "Joshua, then."

"Why don't you hold on to it until I find Melissa. I'll take it then."

"Take it now. Please?"

It would have been rude to continue refusing. I took it. "All right. Thank you."

"I'm glad you like it."

I looked down at it. "Thank you. It's a beautiful painting." I remembered something, looked up at her. "Listen. There's some other man involved in all this, asking questions, looking for people. He's Hispanic. I don't know who he is or what he wants. But he might be trouble. If he gets in touch with you, could you let me know?" I reached into my pocket, brought out a card, handed it to her.

The concern was back. "What does he have to do with Melissa?"

"I don't know," I said. "Maybe nothing." I didn't believe that, but I didn't want her to worry about it. "But if he shows up, let me know?"

She nodded. "And you'll let me know if you hear anything about her?"

"I will," I said.

I LEFT Deirdre Polk's house at seven thirty. As I drove back to Santa Fe, the rain turned to snow, the first real storm of the season, and the snow turned to slush along the bottom of the windshield, packed there by the wipers. Big fat flakes, streaks of blinding white, came shooting down the headlight beams. The wind lurched at the sides of the station wagon. I put the car into four-wheel drive and slowed down to fifty.

By the time I reached town, around ten o'clock, the wind had died down. The snow was still falling, but softly now, silently. Three or four inches of the stuff lay on the ground.

When I got back to my house, I found a note from Leroy, Rita's distant relative, atop a small black plastic box that had been attached to my telephone.

"Green light means the line is clear," the note read. *"No light means a tap. Leroy."*

I lifted the telephone receiver off its cradle. The green light went on.

It was annoying, having to worry about a tap on the line. And probably the worry was only paranoia. But paranoia, as I'd often concluded before, can be a useful social skill.

I lighted a fire in the fireplace, poured myself a drink, and sat down on the couch with the names of the two College of Santa Fe professors I'd gotten from the catalogue in the library. Raymond Gallegos taught abnormal psychology, Paul Cavanaugh taught American literature.

I knew one person at the College—Larry Morgan, who taught anthropology. I picked up the phone. Green light. I called Morgan and asked him about the two professors. He said that Gallegos was crazy. I said that most professors were. He said that he didn't know Cavanaugh all that well, but that he'd heard he was competent. He wanted to know why I was asking, and I told him it had to do with a job. He agreed to call up both men, explain who I was, and ask them to call me.

Over the next hour, they both did, Cavanaugh first. Each told me that Juanita Carrera had been his student. Both said that she was quiet, reserved, and intelligent. So far as they knew, she didn't have any friends among the other students. Both told me that Stamworth had talked to them at the college, last Friday. Both were curious, wanting to know what all this interest in Juanita Carrera might signify. I told both of them that I didn't know. Cavanaugh had been out of town from Friday until Wednesday, yesterday, and hadn't seen the Hispanic man.

Gallegos had, on Monday. The man had claimed, once again, to be Juanita's cousin.

"It's possible, of course, that he was telling the truth," Gallegos told me.

"Why?" I asked him.

"Well, we were speaking Spanish, and from his accent and a few of the words he used, I'd say he was Salvadoran. So was Juanita. But it's also possible that he was lying. He was a pretty unsavory character, I thought. Not someone I'd like to meet in a dark alley."

"What did you tell him?"

"There was nothing I *could* tell him. As I said, Juanita didn't socialize, not with the other students, and certainly not with me. Is she in trouble?"

"I don't know. I hope not."

"Is this something political?"

"Political?"

"There's a paramilitary organization in El Salvador called OR-DEN. A pretty ruthless bunch of right-wing cutthroats. I'm not saying that this fellow is connected to them, mind you. I don't know. But he did have those lifeless gestapo eyes. Was Juanita involved in Salvadoran politics?"

"I don't know."

"Well, look, let me know what you find out, would you? I like her. I'd hate to think she was somehow involved in that mess down there."

I thanked him for his help.

Pretty much a dead end. Except that now I had more reason than ever to worry about Juanita Carrera.

I called Norman Montoya. He told me that, so far, his people had been "unable to locate the item in question." I thanked him.

Forget Juanita Carrera for the time being, I told myself. You can't do anything more than you've done. Concentrate on Melissa and Roy Alonzo.

I got out the press clippings that Ed Norman had given me in Los Angeles. Until now, I'd only glanced through them. Most concerned the child abuse trials. The reporters had covered them as though they were soccer matches. Melissa Alonzo's doctors testify: one point to Melissa. Roy Alonzo's doctors testify: one point to Roy

In his battle with Melissa, Roy Alonzo had finally won. He had obtained the right to have his daughter visit him for the weekends, with no supervision. The reporters who followed the trial seemed to think that this was the end of it. Since only the good guys *can* win, he who wins is by definition a good guy.

I wasn't so sure. Granted, most of the people with whom I'd spoken had been friends of Melissa's. Granted, the medical evidence in the case was ambiguous, as it usually is in such cases. But in the accounts of the conflicting testimonies, Melissa's doctors seemed to me humane, concerned, and shocked at the horrors they believed Winona had undergone. Roy Alonzo's doctors seemed sleek pompous, and dismissive.

Maybe I was letting myself become biased. Talking to Deirdre Polk today, I'd finally begun to get a sense of Melissa as a living, breathing human being, and I found now that I was beginning to believe the story she'd told the court. If Norman Montoya had asked me, that night, for my advice, I would've told him to keep Roy Alonzo away from Winona.

After I finished reading, I got up, made myself another drink, picked up the painting Deirdre Polk had given me, returned with it to the couch.

It was, I thought, a remarkable piece of work. Serene and yet somehow infinitely sad. The surface of the things it depicted seemed to resonate with a wrenching sense of emptiness and loss. Looking into the painting, I found myself imagining that Melissa Alonzo and her daughter were hiding somewhere in that precisely detailed bedroom, locked in each other's arms and shivering, both of them, with grief.

She was a talented woman, Deirdre Polk. I had liked her. I had admired her skill, her honesty, her affection for Melissa. She seemed solid, whole. It seemed to me that she had made her accommodation with solitude, which is perhaps the most important thing that any of us can do, and usually the most difficult.

At eleven thirty, the state police came to tell me that she was dead.

TWENTY

I COULD SEE TWO OF THEM through the peephole in the door, standing out there under the lamplight in the softly swirling snow. Neither matched the description of the Hispanic man who was looking for Juanita Carrera. One was slightly shorter than the other but both were tall and both wore dark overcoats pulled shut against the cold. Knotted ties showed at their necks. Their faces had that absolute lack of expression that came from too many years of seeing and hearing too much. They didn't have to wear badges on their chests for me to know they were cops.

"Who is it?" I called through the door.

"State police, Mr. Croft," said the taller one. "We need to ask you a few questions."

I opened the door, and they stamped their feet, wiped snow from the shoulders of their topcoats with gloved hands, and stepped in, the taller one leading. I closed the door. The taller one said, "I'm Agent Hernandez. This is Agent Green."

Hernandez was about thirty. A black crew cut, a square red face, broad shoulders. Green was probably younger but looked older because he was balding. A broad forehead, a round face, gray jowls, unreadable brown eyes that were glancing casually around my living room. Twenty years from now he would be able to describe the kachina doll that stood atop my bookcase.

As they peeled off their gloves, I said, "Could I see some identification?"

Still expressionless, they reached into their suitcoat pockets. I examined their IDs. "Thank you," I told them. I gestured toward the couch. "Have a seat."

I sat down opposite them in the leather chair.

They were sitting forward, their weight on their feet. Green took from his topcoat pocket a small spiral notebook and a Cross pen.

I said, "How can I help you?"

"You were up in Hartley this evening, talking to a woman named Deirdre Polk."

"What's happened?" I asked him. I think I already knew. There was a sudden coldness in my chest.

"She's dead," Hernandez said. Green said nothing. Both watched me.

"Jesus," I said. I sat back and shut my eyes. In the darkness I saw Deirdre Polk's face. It was concerned, worried, her brows furrowed, her wide lower lip lightly caught between her white teeth. "Jesus," I said.

Hernandez said, "How well did you know her, Mr. Croft?"

I opened my eyes. "How was she killed?"

Green's dark brown eyes flicked to Hernandez, flicked back to me. Hernandez said, "Could you please answer my question, Mr. Croft."

I took a breath. "Yeah, I will. I'll be happy to cooperate. But I need to get some bearings here. I hadn't expected this. I liked the woman. How was she killed?"

Hernandez watched me. "She was strangled," he said.

"Shit." I took another breath. Suddenly the air in the room was too thin. "Was she tortured?" My voice seemed to be coming from someone else. I wished it had been.

Green's eyes flicked again to Hernandez. Hernandez frowned slightly. "Maybe you'd better start answering our questions, Mr. Croft."

I rubbed my forehead. It was cold and wet. I said, "You'll want to talk to a Sergeant Bradley, out in Los Angeles. He's Homicide, and he's got the same kind of case on his hands. Same M.O. I'm not certain, but I think the man you're looking for is a Hispanic male, probably a Salvadoran. Medium height, medium build. He has a small, thin mustache. Slicked-back black hair. He's in his thirties."

Green snorted lightly and produced an almost infinitesimal sneer, as though his contempt were so deep that he couldn't work up enough energy to express it more fully. He looked at Hernandez and spoke for the first time. "I guess we can go home now, huh?"

Hernandez never stopped looking at me. He said, "How well did you know Deirdre Polk, Mr. Croft?"

"I met her for the first time today. You found my card at her house?"

Hernandez said, "What was the nature of your relationship with her?"

"There was no relationship. I was asking her some questions. About a case I was working on."

"What case is that?" Hernandez asked me.

I told them. Everything. Told them about Roy Alonzo, Melissa, Cathryn Bigelow and her murder, all the people I'd spoken to out in Los Angeles, all the people I'd spoken to since I returned to Santa Fe. I told them about Juanita Carrera. If the Hispanic man had killed Deirdre Polk, then Juanita was in danger. Someone had to find her before he did. The police, as I'd told Chuck Arthur, had more resources than I would ever have.

The only person I left out was Norman Montoya.

When I finished, Hernandez said, "So you think there's some connection between this Carrera, Melissa Alonzo, and Deirdre Polk?"

"I know there is," I said. "I just don't know what kind of connection. Listen. Deirdre Polk had a dog. A big German shepherd. Is the dog okay?" I knew, even as I asked, that it was a foolish question.

"The dog is dead," Hernandez told me. "Shot."

He would have had to kill the dog to get to Deirdre.

"Okay," said Hernandez. "Let's go through it one more time."

"What was the time of death?" I asked him.

Hernandez frowned slightly. He was supposed to be asking the questions. But I'd been cooperating, and he bent. "Body was still warm, from what we have. We haven't been to the scene. We're out of the Santa Fe station. Hartley comes under the Española substation. Taos County sheriff's department called them at eleven. Española didn't have anyone free to come down here, so they called us. Friend of Polk's, a woman, found her at ten thirty. According to you, she was still alive at seven thirty."

"I was here getting phone calls at ten thirty."

Hernandez nodded. "From Gallegos and..." He glanced at Green. Without looking at his notebook, his eyes steady on me. Green said, "Cavanaugh."

"Cavanaugh, yeah," said Hernandez. "Take you a couple of hours to get here from there, this weather." He shrugged. "So maybe you've got an alibi. Depends on what the M.E. tells us, after the autopsy."

I had a sudden quick image of Deirdre Polk's long body sprawled naked atop a stainless steel table. I said, "It was pretty smart of me to leave my business card there after I killed her."

Hernandez shrugged again. "People do funny things."

"I could've left the card there last week. Last month."

"Neighbor saw a dark Subaru wagon driving into Polk's drive-way just before the storm hit. You own a dark Subaru wagon. You changing your mind? You saying you weren't there tonight?"

"I was there."

Hernandez nodded. "Let's start from the top. Roy Alonzo came to your office."

THEY LEFT AT a quarter to two. I walked into the kitchen, poured myself another drink. I walked back into the living room, stood staring down for a long time at the painting Deirdre Polk had given me. It was propped against the lamp on the end table. I took a sip of the bourbon and then, making a low growl in my throat that I heard only vaguely, as though from a distance, I hurled the glass at the wall. It trailed a comet's tail of whiskey through the air and then shattered loudly against the plaster.

How had he found Deirdre Polk? If he'd had access to Melissa's phone bills, he would've located her months ago. The FBI had. How had he found her?

I stood there for a minute or two. Then I went back to the kitchen, ripped the roll of paper towels out of the plastic holder, carried it into the living room. I cleaned up the mess. I noticed that some of the whiskey had spattered Deirdre Polk's painting. A few droplets were very slowly rolling down its smooth surface, like tears down a face.

One of those chance junctions of the commonplace that momentarily seem filled with significance. We're creatures of meaning, acute to signs and portents. And we get them. The solitary raven circling the graveyard. The No Sale on the 7-Eleven cash register after some febrile moron blows away, in an instant of rabid excitement, a harmless clerk. Like a bad movie, life is happy to provide us with symbols that hint, briefly, at import. But they're empty, cheap and tawdry, meretricious, and all they finally signify is the random association of lifeless objects in what must be, with all its casual cruelties, a random universe.

Or so I felt then, without any conscious thought. And for an instant, once again, I was enraged. I very nearly reached out and smashed the painting against the wall.

Instead, I took a breath, and then, carefully, gently, I patted the painting dry. If we can't discover meaning, we can provide it.

When I finished cleaning, I made another drink, carried it back into the bedroom, set it on the nightstand. I undressed, climbed into bed.

I didn't sleep well that night.

LEROY'S SHOP on Cerrillos Road didn't open until eight thirty, but I was up and dressed by seven. Steel-toed insulated waffle-stompers, tan cords, denim shirt, crew-neck sweater. I knew I should eat but I wasn't hungry. I forced down some toast and coffee. I cleaned the Smith & Wesson. I sat for a while watching smiling people on the television trade snappy patter. I cleaned the Smith again, and reloaded it. At eight I put on the sheepskin jacket, picked up the .38, put it in my right-hand jacket pocket, slipped on my gloves, and left.

I walked out into a world of glare. Sunshine, blue skies, brilliant white snow. The neighboring houses looked like ancient pueblos, lying abandoned beneath the drifts. Snow fell in soft clumps from the trees and blew like smoke from the rooftops, glittered through the air like tiny sequins. It was a beautiful morning. Deirdre Polk wouldn't be seeing it.

In the station wagon, I opened the glove compartment and got out my sunglasses, put them on. I drove in four-wheel down to Acequia Madre, took a left, followed the narrow road until it met Paseo de Peralta, took another left, shifted into two-wheel, drove down to Cerrillos. The snow was already gone from the major streets and they were black with moisture and gritty with the sand laid down by the early morning work crews.

Cerrillos Road, as usual, was busy, cars splashing at speed through today's slush and sand as though it didn't exist.

Leroy wasn't at the shop when I arrived. I waited in the car.

He showed up at eight thirty-five and I told him what I wanted him to do. I drove the Subaru around back and into his garage, turned off the ignition, got out.

Leroy was short and squat and he moved in a perpetual stoop. His hairy arms were too long and his heavy forehead was too low. He was a genius. Rita had once said that he was the sort of person who could make you rethink your position on evolution, whatever your position might be. But he wasn't genius enough, this morning, to know that I was in no mood for chatter. As he stalked slowly around the Subaru, holding a small black box that looked like an oscilloscope, he would not stop yammering.

"So I'm out with this chick, right, she's Anglo, a honey, awesome body, dynamite legs, very *bonita,* and we're gonna go to dinner, then maybe for drinks someplace nice, maybe Vanessie's or that new place on Palace, whaddya call it, Armand's, next to the gallery there, so I say to her, I say, So whaddya feel like eating, you know, and she tells me tofu. Tofu, she says. I say to her, *Tofu?* And she says to me, Tofu, yeah, it's like made from soybeans, and I say to her, Yeah, I know what it's made from, I ate it once, it tastes like spit only it's solid. It's very healthy, she tells me. It's *natural,* she says. I say to her, It's *natural?* Like it what, it grows on trees? You ever see a field with chunks of tofu growing all over? I'll tell you what's natural. You know what's natural? You know what they eat in the rain forests, I tell her, those little guys with the blow guns and the leather jock straps, climbing trees all the time, you know what they eat? You know what's natural for those guys? Sure, of course, they eat a lotta weeds and stuff when they don't have any choice, rocks and dirt too, probably, who knows, but what really turns 'em on, what really floats their boat, is nice fresh monkeys. That's what they really like. They shoot down a monkey with one of those darts they got and they're happy as clams. Okay," he said, and pushed a button on the machine. "Nothing."

"What does that mean?" I asked him.

"Means we eliminate the second string. Now we see about the first." He stalked, long arms swinging, over to a locked metal cabinet. "So anyway, I say to her, I say, maybe, you want natural, we should go someplace they got monkeys...."

I let his voice fade out and I glanced around the garage. Tape decks and CB radios, some used, some still in their boxes, arranged in stacks along the plywood shelves. Speakers, too, and amplifiers and graphics equalizers, and piles of complicated equipment that probably I would never be able to identify.

"... solutely *gross,* she says." He was circling the car again, holding this time a red metal box, larger than the first. "I can't believe you'd say that, she says. Are you some kind of—hold *on,* man, we are *hot* here." Excited now, holding the box before him as though it were a treasure chest, he was approaching the rear of the wagon.

"Something?" I said.

"*Something,* man, Jesus Christ, you have got a goddamn *honey* in here." He was at the tailgate. "You got the keys to the gate?"

I took them from my pocket, walked over, handed them to him. He unlocked the top gate, lifted it, swung the box inside. "Sonofabitch, man, you got the *mother* of honeys." I moved closer as he turned and set the metal box on the floor. He reached into his pocket, fished out a small flashlight, lowered the bottom gate, leaned into the cargo space. He threw back a flap of the carpeting and tugged off the stiff sheet of plastic that concealed the spare tire well. "*There* you are, sweetie," he said, his voice hushed. "Oh, Jesus, you are just one beautiful little honey, aren't you now?" He looked back to me over his shoulder. "C'mere. Take a look."

I DROVE UP NORTH on St. Francis past the Old Taos Highway, turned left on Camino La Tierra. This used to be called Buckman Road, back before the developers put in La Tierra, a community of expensive adobe homes tucked between the juniper and piñon on ten-acre lots. It was paved, and some traffic had already passed over it this morning—the snow was gray and rutted. Roy Alonzo's house was somewhere back in here, among the rolling hills, but I wasn't going to Roy Alonzo's house.

Two or three miles in, the road went from pavement to dirt beneath the snow, and the station wagon began to fishtail. I slowed down and shifted into four-wheel. There were fewer tire tracks here, and after another mile or so there were none at all. I drove on for half a mile, found a space to turn around, angled the car to block the road, put the stick into neutral, left the engine running, and got out. Arms crossed, I leaned back against the right front fender. Once again, I waited.

The air was cold but the sun was bright. Snow was melting off the scrub pines, and above the huge silence of empty space I could hear the drip of meltwater patting against the drifts, and an occasional soft thump as clusters toppled off the branches, and puffed against the smooth white banks.

About fifty yards ahead of me, back toward town, the road rose slightly and angled to the right, out of sight. Behind me, a thin unsullied swatch of snow led off through the trees. Farther along, another mile or two beyond the hills, was the river and Diablo Canyon.

Time passed, maybe fifteen minutes. Except for the melting snow, nothing moved. If there were any animals out there, they were in hiding.

Cold started to seep into my boots. I stomped my feet.

I heard the car before I saw it. A big engine snarling low in its throat as it shifted. At least six cylinders, probably eight. I took the

Smith from my jacket pocket, bent down over the fender of the wagon, sighted at the rise in the road, and waited some more.

The car came more quickly than I had expected, a big black Bronco bouncing over the rise, and it had two men sitting up front. I had believed there would be only one, and I thought for a moment that thcsc two were a couple of cowboys out for some winter fun, and then the man on the passenger side rolled down his window and started shooting at me.

He couldn't hit anything with a handgun, no one could, not at that distance, and not with the Bronco skidding in a slide to a stop, then kicking up snow and dirt as it spun, turning, into reverse. But it gave me pause for thought. And then, for just a second, the Bronco was broadside to me and I poked up my head to take a shot, but the man on the passenger side didn't care for that at all and he had a gun with a lot of cartridges in it, and he used some of them. I heard a loud brittle pop as a headlight on the wagon went, and then a high-pitched buzz, like a wasp, as a slug zipped by my ear. And then the big Ford's rear end was slamming left and right across the road as the car raced up the rise and over it, gone.

I jumped into the Subaru, banged the door shut, threw the stick into first, and jammed my foot against the pedal. Tires hissing, the car vaulted forward.

TWENTY-ONE

"IT WAS FUCKING STUPID, Josh," said Hector Ramirez.

"I know, Hector."

"What were you gonna do? Make a citizen's arrest?"

"That's probably what I told myself. Something like that. I wasn't thinking very clearly."

"You weren't thinking at all."

"Yeah. Right."

We were in Hector's cubicle at the Santa Fe Police Station, on Airport Road. Hector sat behind his desk in rolled-up shirt sleeves, his tie loosened. The taupe-colored tie was silk. The neatly pressed shirt was cotton, off white, patterned with thin vertical taupe stripes. Hector dressed well, but it must've cost him some money to find shirts with a nineteen-inch neck and enough room in the sleeves for twenty-five-inch biceps.

"So you lost them," he said.

"I lost them. Couldn't keep up. By the time I reached St. Francis, they were gone."

"You get the number of the tag?"

"Covered with mud. But the Bronco had to be either stolen or a rental. They didn't drive it up here from El Salvador."

"You don't know they came here from El Salvador."

"It makes sense to me."

"Lot of dumb things make sense to you."

"Like coming here, to talk to you."

Hector said nothing. He leaned forward, picked up the object on his desk. Covered with a shiny yellow epoxy, it was about the length of a cigar and about the width of two double-A batteries placed side by side. Idly, he turned it over in his fingers. "What do you want me to do with this?"

"One notion does spring immediately to mind."

Below his bandito mustache he smiled bleakly. "Fifteen years a cop and I gotta take insults from some cowboy PI."

"You could have someone take a look at it. You must have experts somewhere, or access to them. According to Leroy, it's state of the art. It runs on lithium batteries that last for three months, and it's got a range of over five miles. He couldn't find it with a standard RF sweep. He had to use a wide-band receiver. It's a frequency hopper—it jumps all over the band, between a hundred and sixty to five hundred megahertz. He says there's something better, but it's something only the feds have, some Captain Marvel transponder that can bounce signals off a satellite."

"You don't think the feds planted this thing?"

"No. The only fed involved in all this, that I know about, is Stamworth. Maybe there's some other bunch of whiz kids floating around, but I haven't turned them. And Stamworth had already talked to Deirdre Polk. He probably got her off Melissa's phone bill, like the FBI people who talked to her in August. If he wanted to kill her, he could've killed her last month. Besides, what's the motive?"

"What's the motive for your Salvadoran?"

"I told you. He wants to get to Melissa Alonzo. He's not particular how he asks his questions. Afterwards, he has to clean up the mess."

"He wants to get to Alonzo because of something that happened down in El Salvador."

"Yeah."

He shrugged. "It's a stretch."

"I thought so too. But Deirdre Polk told me that Melissa had seen something down there. Melissa's sister was killed last week. Deirdre was killed last night, the same way."

"Alonzo took off in August. Why'd this guy wait so long to start whacking people?"

"I don't know. And I don't know why Stamworth started hanging around last week either."

"There's a lot you don't know."

"No shit."

He turned the oblong device over in his hand. "Why not give this to the state boys? Deirdre Polk is their case."

"I give it to them and that'll be the last I hear of it. Far as they're concerned, I'm still a suspect."

"Withholding evidence."

"I'm not withholding anything. I'm giving it to you. And who's to say that this thing is connected to Deirdre Polk?"

"You are."

"But I can't prove it."

Hector lightly tapped the device against his desktop. He looked up at me. "No PI in New Mexico has a concealed carry permit."

"I know that, Hector. Maybe I carted the gun out there in my glove compartment."

"That what you did?"

"I was wearing it on my watch chain, next to my Phi Beta Kappa key."

"Not funny, Josh. You should've come to us. Or gone to the state police. We could've set something up."

"Listen, Hector—"

"No, you listen. I know you're pissed off because someone planted this thing on you, this homer. And maybe you're right, maybe that's what led them to Deirdre Polk. So you feel like shit. You feel guilty. I understand that. But that doesn't give you the right to start acting like Dirty Harry. A stupid Dirty Harry. If you'd come to us, we could've arranged something. Some cars, some backup. Those two assholes wouldn't still be out on the street."

"I know that, Hector. That's why I'm here now. You're not telling me anything I haven't already told myself."

"A little late for it, isn't it?"

"Yeah."

"They could've whacked *you,* you know."

"They didn't."

He nodded. Bleakly. "Fucking funeral would really screw up my month."

"Good thing I didn't get whacked."

He smiled faintly. "I didn't say that."

I smiled faintly myself. "So are you going to check that thing out?" I nodded to the transponder.

He shrugged. "Only people I can give it to are the feds. They're the ones with all the shiny equipment."

"So give it to the feds."

"And what happens if it's one of theirs?"

"They'll try to smoke you, and then you'll know it's one of theirs. But like I said, I don't think it is. They've got better stuff, Leroy says. But he also says that the government, the federal government, has dumped a lot of second-string technology in third world countries. Maybe that's how that thing ended up in El Salvador."

"You're really pushing this El Salvador business."

"Because it fits."

"For you it fits."

"Okay. For me it fits. What about Juanita Carrera?" If the state police believed my story, they would already be looking for her. Juanita Carrera might be afraid of the police, state or otherwise, but right now, it seemed to me, the more people who were looking for her, the better.

He nodded. "I'll talk to Missing Persons."

"And you'll have someone check the car rental places?"

"It's an amazing coincidence."

"What is?"

"How I was just sitting here hoping you'd come in and ask me to run some little errands for you."

"These guys broke the law, Hector. Attempted murder."

"Murdering a PI is considered a public service in some circles. Mine, sometimes."

"They discharged a firearm within the city limits. They discharged it a lot. One of those big nine-mil jobs. Fourteen rounds in the clip."

"Only your word for that."

"And a busted headlight on the station wagon."

"Time you got a new car anyway."

"Fine. I'll check them myself."

"I wouldn't want you to do that. You're too busy buzzing around playing Cowboys and Indians. Takes it out of a guy."

"So we're talking yes?"

He sighed. "Yeah, yeah. Won't hear anything for a day or two. Besides, they've probably dumped the Bronco already."

"Probably. But if they used plastic to rent it, maybe you can trace them through the card. I appreciate it, Hector."

"I see it as an honor."

"You're a prince."

"And you're an asshole." He tossed the homer to the desk. "Listen to me. Hear me good. Don't fuck up again."

"Right."

I PICKED UP the local newspaper on my way to the office. Deirdre Polk had made the first page. My name wasn't mentioned in the article.

When I got back to the office, there were a bunch of messages on the machine. The first, the third, the sixth and seventh were from Roy Alonzo. He seemed anxious to talk to me. The second call was from Norman Montoya, the fourth from Rita, and the fifth from Bob Neiman, a reporter I knew who worked for the same newspaper I had just tossed into the wastebasket.

I picked up the telephone receiver and the green light on Leroy's box suddenly started glowing. I called Norman Montoya.

He answered the phone himself. Maybe the hired help was off negotiating a merger with General Motors.

"This is Croft," I said.

"Ah, Mr. Croft. Good of you to return my call. I understand that you had visitors last night."

Norman Montoya evidently possessed sources of information other than the newspaper.

"State police," I said. "You know about Deirdre Polk?"

"Your telephone line is clear?"

"Supposed to be."

"I know that you are alleged to have visited her on the evening of her death. Presumably she is connected in some way to Melissa and Winona."

"A friend of Melissa's."

"I find that very disturbing."

"So do I."

"Whom do you believe responsible?"

"Right now I'm leaning toward the Salvadoran."

"Yes. I understand that the state police are searching for the man."

"Good." Among other things, that meant that Hernandez and Green had believed my story. Provisionally, anyway. "The state police keep you informed of their progress, do they?"

"I learn what is in my interests to learn. Mr. Croft, once again I make you an offer of assistance. Perhaps it would be wiser of you not to continue with this project on your own."

"Thanks. If it looks like I need someone, I'll call you."

"I do hope, Mr. Croft, that you will not let your pride lead to your downfall."

"So do I. By the way, the Salvadoran's not alone. He has a friend."

"Mr. Croft, please. Allow me to send my nephew, George, to assist you. You know him, and I assure you that he is quite capable."

"I only mentioned the other guy so that you and your people will know what they're up against. I'm all right. And I'll call you if things start looking grim."

"Please do so, Mr. Croft."

"What about Juanita Carrera? Have you found anything?"

"Ah. Some good news, I believe. It seems that she may still be somewhere nearby. I should be learning more later today and, naturally, I shall keep you informed. But in view of recent events, and, of course, assuming that you are willing, I should like to make some small changes in our arrangement."

"What changes?"

"If my people succeed in locating the woman, I should like them to bring her here, to my home, where I can guarantee her safety. The remainder of our agreement will remain unchanged. I will make no attempt to learn from her the whereabouts of my great-niece and her mother."

Juanita would most likely be safer in Norman Montoya's house than she would be anywhere else. Maybe Montoya would keep his word and maybe he wouldn't, but enough things had happened lately for me to start thinking that his word might not matter any longer. Montoya wasn't the danger; the Salvadoran was. Even if Montoya were lying, I didn't believe that he wanted to kill Juanita Carrera and Melissa Alonzo. And I believed the Salvadoran probably did.

"All right," I said. "But only if she agrees. And if your people find her, have them tread gently. She's probably terrified."

"Yes, Mr. Croft. My people have been so instructed." A gentle reminder that we had already discussed this.

"All right," I said. "Thanks."

"Oh, one thing more."

"Yes?"

"I understand that in the account you gave to your visitors last night, you were kind enough not to mention my name. I sincerely appreciate your discretion, but I wanted to tell you that it was in this case unnecessary. Please feel no hesitation whatever about providing my name, should you be asked it."

"Fine."

"I suspect that I shall be able to withstand any scrutiny offered to me by the state police."

Why not. He'd been withstanding that, and worse, for most of his adult life.

I CALLED RITA NEXT.

"All right, Joshua, this idiotic little light of Leroy's is on, so I'm assuming it's safe to talk. I tried to reach you at home as soon as I read the newspaper, but you'd already left. What on earth is going on?"

I told her about my interview with Deirdre Polk, and what Deirdre had told me about Juanita Carrera. "It looks like you were right," I said. "Something happened down there, in El Salvador. Probably something that involved Carrera in some way."

"What have you done about locating her?"

I told her that the state police, Missing Persons, and Norman Montoya's troops were all out looking for her.

She said, "Tell me about the state police."

I did, and then I told her about finding the transponder in the Subaru.

"And you think it was planted by the Salvadoran," she said. "And you think that was how he found Deirdre Polk."

"I know it was planted by the Salvadoran. But there's more than one of them. I saw them both this morning. We compared hardware. Theirs was better."

There was a brief silence on the line. Then Rita said, "Do I want to hear about this?"

"Probably not."

"Tell me anyway."

When I finished, she said, "And you're all right?"

"I'm fine. They blew out a headlight on the station wagon. I brought it in to Ernie's, on St. Francis. I'm driving a loaner, a Jeep."

"Joshua, I don't care what you're driving."

"It's a pretty neat car, Rita."

"It was foolish, leading those two men out there."

"Yeah, I know. Hector's already explained it to me."

Another silence. "Deirdre Polk's death wasn't your fault, Joshua."

"I know that, Rita. I'm okay now."

"You're okay because you let someone shoot at you. If he'd hit you, you'd probably feel wonderful."

"Right, Rita." There was some truth in what she said.

She was silent for a moment, and then she said, "What did you do with the transponder?"

"Gave it to Hector."

"You'll have to be careful, Joshua. They know now that you know about them. And they know that you're looking for the same thing they are. They may decide that you're a liability."

"I intend to be a very big liability."

"This isn't a game, Joshua. Concentrate on Melissa Alonzo."

"Yes dear."

"Stop it."

"There is one thing we could try. Deirdre Polk told me that Melissa occasionally visited an S and M group down in Albuquerque. Maybe if we could locate it, someone in the group could tell us something about Melissa."

"I've already located it. It's called the New Mexico Power Exchange."

"How'd you do that? Not the computer."

"The computer. When you told me that Melissa had been involved in S and M in Los Angeles, it occurred to me that she might've been involved out here. I left a message on the CompuServe bulletin board asking for information about S and M groups in the Southwest. I got an answer last night, and a phone number. I called it and talked to the woman who runs the group."

"And? Does she know Melissa Alonzo?"

"Yes, but she didn't want to talk over the phone."

"So I'll go down to Albuquerque."

"You won't have to. She's coming to Santa Fe today. She'll be at my house at three o'clock this afternoon."

"I'll be there."

"Good. Call me if anything else happens. And be careful."

"Yes dear."

She hung up.

I WAS JUST ABOUT to dial the number of the local newspaper when the telephone rang. I picked it up.

"Croft, what the fuck is going on? Where've you been all morning?"

Roy Alonzo.

"Gathering rosebuds. Get off my back, Alonzo. I told you, I'm not working for you. I'm working for your uncle." There was more anger in my voice than I generally liked to hear.

He hesitated a moment, and then he said, "All right, look. I apologize. But I'm fucking frantic. The state police came to see me this morning. I hadn't even finished my goddamn coffee." Me they bother in the middle of the night. With Roy Alonzo, they wait until morning. Fame has its advantages. He said, "This woman that was killed, Deirdre Polk, she was a friend of Melissa's?"

"Yeah. The PI you hired back in August knew that. He talked to her."

"He mentioned her name. I got the impression she was just a casual acquaintance, an artist whose paintings Melissa liked. And now the police are telling me she's dead, killed the same way that Cathryn was. What's going on here, Croft? Is Melissa in danger?"

"That matters to you?"

"Of course it matters. Melissa has her problems, she's fairly screwed up, obviously, and I've got good reasons to be angry with her, but I certainly wouldn't want her to get hurt. And my daughter's with her, remember?"

"I remember."

"So what's the story here? Who killed Deirdre Polk?"

"I don't know. The police are working on it."

"Look, could we meet sometime today? I've got a business thing at one o'clock, but I'm clear after two thirty. I'd really appreciate it, Croft. I won't take much of your time."

I didn't want to meet with the man. Probably because I'd come to believe that the appellate court had made a mistake. I was more or less persuaded now that Alonzo had been guilty of molesting his daughter. But I knew that I could be wrong. And he sounded genuinely distressed.

I said, "Do you know the Fort Marcy complex? Mager's Field?"

"Off Washington? Across from the Ski Basin Road?"

"Yeah. I'll be there around five thirty."

"Great. Thank you. I'll be there."

"I'll be at the pool."

"Terrific. See you then. And thanks again, Croft."

As I SET THE telephone receiver back in its cradle, it rang in my hand. I picked it up.

"Mondragón Investigations," I said.

"Mr. Croft? Do you recognize my voice?" I did, and I was surprised to hear it. It belonged to Elizabeth Drewer, the Railroad lawyer in Los Angeles.

"Yes," I told her.

"Are you free at the moment? This is very important."

"I'm free."

"What time does your watch read?"

I looked. "Twelve forty-four. Thirty seconds."

"I'll call you back in two minutes." She hung up.

I waited, wondering what this was all about. Had she decided to give me Melissa Alonzo? And if so, why? Had she heard about the death of Deirdre Polk?

Exactly two minutes after she'd hung up, the telephone rang. I snatched the receiver from the cradle. "Hello?"

"Mr. Croft, leave your office as soon as you hang up. Go to the Palace Avenue entrance to your building. Someone will meet you there."

"What's going on?"

"Hang up now, Mr. Croft. The Palace Avenue entrance."

I hung up.

TWENTY-TWO

THE CAR WAS a Ford Taurus wagon, pale blue, and its front door swung open as it veered toward the curb where I stood. I stepped in, pulled the door shut. The car took off, not quickly, but not slowly either.

The driver was in his late twenties. He had brown hair that hung in bangs across his forehead, brown eyes, a strong nose, a small mouth, a chin that in profile was somewhat less strong than the nose. He wore an unzipped dark blue down jacket, a red chamois shirt, jeans, and expensive moccasin-toed work boots. The yuppie lumberjack look. He glanced at me. "Mr. Croft?"

"Yeah."

"I'm Larry Cooper." He swung the car right onto Washington. "I just want to make sure we're okay, and then I'll take you where we're going."

"Fine."

He looked in his rearview mirror.

We drove up Washington to Paseo, turned right, took Paseo past Marcy and Palace, past the PERA building and the state capitol, riding on a long arc as the street circled the downtown area. From time to time Cooper glanced in the rearview mirror.

The air was warming up, the world was melting. Silver dripped from the trees, the black streets glistened. Cars passed us, their roofs still frosted with snow. No one in any of the cars seemed the least bit interested in the pale blue Taurus.

At St. Francis, Cooper turned north. "I think we're all right."

"Swell," I said.

It came out more curtly than I intended. Sudden mysterious phone calls, sudden mysterious automobile rides dodging potential surveillance—I was getting a small taste, a very small taste, of the kind of life that Melissa Alonzo and her daughter had been living for the past few months. I didn't like it.

He looked at me. "I'm sorry about all this. All this cloak and dagger stuff. But we've got to be careful."

I didn't know what he meant by *we*—him and me, or him and someone else—but whoever he meant, he was probably right. I was the one, after all, who'd just had tap detectors installed on my telephones. "Sure," I said. "I'm in a bad mood today. Ignore me."

"We'll be there soon," he said.

I nodded.

We stayed on St. Francis as it climbed up past the Picacho Hotel. Cooper eased the car into the right lane and then turned right onto the Old Taos Highway, heading back into town. I looked back over my shoulder.

No cars behind us.

So long as no one had planted a transponder in Cooper's car, he was right. We were clean.

We drove for a quarter of a mile and then he turned left, onto a narrow winding road that led downhill into a small valley wooded with the usual junipers and piñons. The road was dirt beneath the snow and the ride was bumpy. Adobe homes were scattered along the slopes. Some of them were small and modest, looking warm and snug beneath their thin layers of melting white icing. Others were large and imposing, massive buttresses and sheets of double-glazed glass swaggering through the trees.

At the bottom of the hill, we crossed a snow-filled arroyo, and then he turned onto a thin white ribbon of driveway that ran between the trees for a hundred feet. The house we reached was a large square adobe, gingerbread brown. At the right side, a coyote fence enclosed a small courtyard. The shades were drawn at the two broad windows that flanked the front door. Below the window on the left was a long stack of firewood, half a cord or so, covered with a black plastic tarp that dripped meltwater. In front of the stack was a gray Dodge pickup, five or six years old. The house was invisible from the road.

We got out of the Ford and I followed Cooper around the Dodge and up the front steps. More meltwater fell in a thin shiny trickle from a canali on the roof and spattered onto a patch of brown mud in the snow.

The door was unlocked and he opened it and signaled me to enter.

As I did, a woman stood up from a sofa opposite me. Short and pretty, she wore dark brown boots and a long stonewashed denim dress. The color of the dress matched her pale blue eyes. Her long hair was blond and pulled back into a ponytail.

"Sarah," said Cooper, taking off his down jacket, "this is Mr. Croft. Mr. Croft, my wife, Sarah."

She crossed the room and offered me her hand. I shook it. Her grip was firm but her eyes were uncertain. She hadn't spoken since I'd arrived. She was a few years younger than her husband and she looked worried.

"Take your coat?" Cooper asked me.

"Thanks." I slipped the jacket off my shoulders. He accepted it and hung it beside his coat on a tall wooden rack.

"Have a seat, Mr. Croft," he said, and nodded to a heavily padded fabric chair.

I sat down. The two of them sat on the sofa.

It was an airy space, high ceilinged, divided by a wooden counter into a roomy kitchen and the big living area in which we sat. Large framed black and white photographs of stark desert scenes decorated the walls. Some children's toys—a doll, a red plastic wagon—decorated the floor. The furniture had been lived in, but didn't resent it much. Heat radiated softly from a gray rectangular wood-burning stove along the east wall, beside a doorway that led to the rest of the house. Classical music, one of the Brandenburg Concertos, floated from the stereo to my left.

Sarah Cooper had been watching me. Now, finally, she spoke. "Are you recording this conversation, Mr. Croft?"

Her husband looked at her and frowned slightly. It seemed to me that her caution, and his own, made him uncomfortable. He would rather have assumed that the world was filled with decent, upright people who always played fair. She clearly assumed otherwise. She would be right, of course, more often than he was.

"Nope," I told her.

She said, "If you deny you're recording this, and you're lying, and we admit to violating the law, wouldn't that be entrapment on your part?"

"It only works that way for law enforcement officers," I told her. "So far as the law is concerned, I'm not much different from a private citizen. And a private citizen can't be charged with entrapment."

She frowned.

"But I'm not recording this," I told her. "Later on, if there is a later on, it'll be your word against mine. Two against one. You're the couple that Melissa and Winona stayed with, aren't you?" No great intuitive leap here. A phone call from Elizabeth Drewer, a young couple and their mutual paranoia.

Sarah Cooper glanced at her husband. He said to me, "We read this morning about that woman up in Hartley. Deirdre Polk. She was a friend of Melissa's."

It wasn't really a question, but I answered it anyway. "Yes, she was. And if you think that her death is connected in some way to Melissa, you're most likely right."

He looked at his wife, who sat there watching me.

"Listen," I said. "You're worried. I'm worried, too. We wouldn't all be here if we weren't worried. What did Elizabeth Drewer tell you about me?"

"That you were a private investigator," Larry said. "Looking for Melissa. She said she'd made some phone calls to some people here in town. You're supposed to be honest."

"I'm supposed to be, but I don't always pull it off."

He smiled slightly. "She also said you were kind of a wiseass."

I smiled. "That, I can usually pull off."

His wife spoke. "Did Melissa's ex-husband have anything to do with that woman's death?"

The idea had never occurred to me, and I took a look at it for a moment. Roy Alonzo hires me to track down Melissa, or he tries to, because he wants to kill her. He's the one who slips the transponder into my car. He follows me to Deirdre Polk's house, tortures her for information, strangles her.

But why would he want to kill Melissa? Revenge? To pay her back for ruining his career?

Maybe, but how would Roy come by a sophisticated tracking device like the transponder?

And Deirdre Polk had probably been killed by the same person who killed Cathryn Bigelow. And Roy had been in New York when Cathryn was killed.

According to him.

I reminded myself to ask Roy where he'd been last night.

Finally I said, "It's possible, but I doubt it."

She told me, "From what Melissa said, he was a monster."

"He may be. But there are all kinds of monsters. I don't think he's that kind." Not the kind who strangled women in cold blood. It would be bad for his image.

She frowned. "Who did kill her, then?"

"I'm not sure. But I think that whoever he was, he wants to find Melissa. I want to find her first. You wanted to talk to someone about this. I'd like to hear what you have to say. I'm not going to go to the police with anything you tell me, unless I believe the information might keep Melissa and her daughter out of jeopardy. And I won't give them your names."

Larry Cooper glanced at his wife and then he said to me, "We've been worried about Melissa since she left us, worried about her and Winona."

"Why?" I asked him.

"After she left here, she never got to where she was going."

His wife spoke again. "We didn't know that, not for sure. But she was supposed to call us. She was going to call person to person, collect, and ask for Linda. And we'd say she had the wrong number and then hang up. We'd know she was all right." She crossed her arms. "But she never called." She shrugged sadly.

I said, "Why don't we start at the beginning. You're part of the Underground Railroad."

He said, "Yes." She nodded.

"I don't really know how this works," I told them. "Would that be standard procedure, for her to call and let you know she was all right?"

"No," said Larry Cooper. "Once people leave here, they're not supposed to contact us at all. It's safer that way, or it's supposed to be."

"It was my fault," said Sarah. "I asked her to. I'd gotten really fond of her and Winona. The times before, when people stayed here, I never really got close to them. But with Melissa, it was different."

Her husband said, "We've been on and off the phone for hours, ever since we read about Deirdre Polk. We talked to... someone in California, and then Elizabeth Drewer called us. We've been going back and forth with this all morning."

I asked them, "When did Melissa arrive here?"

"Last month," Larry Cooper said. "On the twentieth."

"And how long did she stay?"

Sarah said, "She was going to stay until the first of October. But we had a situation with Julia, our daughter. She just started school this year. She's a really intelligent little girl, really open and friendly, and we were afraid she'd say something to someone without meaning to. We tried to explain to her that Melissa and Winona were a secret, that she wasn't supposed to tell anyone. But secrets are difficult for children. And really, they shouldn't have to worry about them. It's not fair."

Her husband said, "They were going to be the last people we helped. Melissa and Winona. We would've liked to keep on with it, the helping. These people deserve all the help they can get. Not just Melissa and Winona, all of them. But it's been rough. It was rough even before Julia started school."

"It's been nerve-racking," Sarah Cooper said. "Keeping it hidden from the neighbors, jumping when the telephone rang. And Julia. Once when she and I were in Kaune's, shopping, I ran into a friend of mine, and Julia, without ever really intending to, she mentioned something about the people who were staying here at the time. I had to cover it up, say it was my cousin visiting. And then afterward I had to explain to Julia why I lied." She frowned. "That was the worst part." She looked at Larry, looked back at me. "It's my fault. I was the one who got both of us into this."

"That's not true, babe," Larry said. "We both agreed."

"It was my idea," she said with mournful resignation.

I asked them, "How *did* you get into this?"

Larry ran his fingers back through his hair, pushing it away from his forehead. "Do you really need to know that?"

"No," I said. "I'm just nosy. Sorry."

Sarah still wanted to accept the blame. She said, "Someone from my incest survivor group mentioned the Underground Railroad. I'd read about it, and I thought they were doing good work, important work, and I said so. In group, in front of all the others. Afterward, she came up to me and asked if I'd really like to help. When I said I would, she told me to talk it over with Larry and get back to her. We talked it over and we agreed we wanted to do something."

"We both agreed," he told her.

She smiled sadly at him, then turned back to me. "I was sexually abused when I was a child. By my adoptive father. I used to think it happened because I was an orphan, because I was damaged goods. That it was my fault. That it wouldn't have happened if I'd been with my natural parents." She shrugged. "I found out, from group, that none of that was true. It can happen to anyone."

Larry put his arm protectively around her shoulder. She leaned slightly toward him and reached out to lay her hand on his thigh.

I liked them and I admired their closeness, maybe even envied it, but I needed to know about Melissa. "You said that Melissa visited Deirdre Polk while she was here. Did she visit anyone else?"

"A woman named Juanita," she said. "Melissa didn't want to talk about it—she acted very mysterious whenever I tried to ask her. I only asked because it might've been dangerous, being seen in town. Someone might've recognized her. She told me that no one could possibly do that. She *did* look different from pictures I'd seen of her, in magazines, during the trial, but I still didn't think it was safe. But Melissa was determined to see her. She could be so damn stubborn sometimes.''

"When did she see her?" I asked.

"The twenty-third of September," she said. "The same day she saw Deirdre. I remember because it was the first day of fall and it was such a beautiful day, like a day in the middle of June."

The twenty-third was also the day Melissa had posted the card to her sister, Cathryn. And perhaps posted the card to her mother. "How long was she gone?"

"For most of the day. She left at nine in the morning and she came back around six. She seemed less tense when she came back, less worried."

"She'd seemed worried before?"

She frowned. "Not worried, exactly. More like she was carrying a terrible burden. Something really painful, oppressive. Something that had nothing to do with her own position, I mean. And God knows, that was burden enough. But when she came back from meeting Juanita, she seemed much better."

"Did she ever mention El Salvador?" I asked her.

She shook her head, turned to her husband. "No," he told me. "But I really didn't spend much time with her. I've been busy for the past few months."

"Larry's a photographer," Sarah told me.

"I had an assignment and I spent most of September in the darkroom," he said. "I didn't have much of a chance to talk to her."

I indicated the photographs on the wall. "Yours?"

"Yes."

I nodded. "Okay," I said. "*The flower in the desert lives.*' Does that mean anything to either of you?"

They looked at each other. She shrugged. He told me, "No."

I asked them, "Did Melissa make any phone calls while she was here?"

"No," Sarah said. "The only person she called was Juanita and she drove her car into town, to a phone booth, to make the call."

"She had a car?"

"She bought one when she got here. That was something else I didn't think was a very good idea. But Melissa said she was sick and tired of buses. She said she wanted a car, even if she only had it for a little while, a few weeks. I drove her out there to get it. It was a little Honda. She paid cash for it. Nine hundred dollars.''

"What color was the car? What year?''

"White? It was a little two-door. I don't know the year." She turned to Larry. "Eighty-two?''

He shrugged. "Eighty-two, eighty-three,'' he told me. "Something like that.''

I could find out from the dealer. "Where'd she buy it?''

She gave me the name of a used-car place on Cerrillos.

I said, "She needed a driver's license to get the car.''

Sarah said, "She had a California license made out to another name. It was her photograph, though.''

"What was the name?''

She looked at her husband. He nodded.

"Linda Lattimore,'' she said. "That was why we were going to use *Linda* when she called to let us know she was all right.''

"Did she register the car? Get plates for it?''

"No. It had temporary plates, good for thirty days, and she said she wouldn't be using it any longer than that." For the first time, she smiled. Faintly, sadly. "She called it her 'disposable dream.' It was part of her last fling, she said. I remember, she laughed out loud when she got into the front seat. Like a little girl. She was really incredibly happy.''

Melissa was a California Girl. Being without a car had probably felt like being without legs. "Okay," I said. "Tell me about her leaving here.''

"Well,'' Sarah said, "she knew how difficult it was for us. The problem we were having with Julia. It was really her idea to leave. In a way, of course, we were relieved, but we also felt terribly guilty about it. It was like we were throwing her out on the street. But Melissa said it was only right that she go. She's the one who persuaded *us*. So we called, so *I* called a number in California—I used a pay phone—and I explained the situation. Melissa wanted to stay in town until the first of October—''

"Why?''

"She wouldn't say." Sarah frowned. "She'd get like that sometimes. Not coy, really, but sort of...secretive. Mysterious. As though she were a spy or something." Frowning again, she thought for a moment. "It was like she sort of had to dramatize herself, do you know what I mean?''

I nodded.

"It was just a way she had sometimes," she said. "It wasn't really any big deal. It wasn't annoying or anything. Especially since five minutes later she'd be laughing about it, making fun of herself. And I guess she did have her reasons for not talking about it, whatever *it* was. Anyway, the people in California weren't happy with her wanting to stay here. They weren't happy with her coming here in the first place."

"Because someone might've recognized her," I said.

"Exactly. But they made arrangements for her to go somewhere else nearby, until after the first."

"Where?"

She hesitated.

Larry said, "The people in California want you to promise something."

I said, "What?" The question was a formality; I already knew.

Larry nodded. "We're supposed to use our own judgment. If we think it's the right thing to do, we're supposed to tell you. But they want you to promise that you won't go to the police with this."

"I can't promise that. Right now, what I need to do is find Melissa and her daughter, make sure they're all right, and then make sure they stay that way. Protecting the Underground Railroad doesn't enter it for me. And, the way I see it, protecting Melissa from kidnapping charges is less important than protecting her life. The police have the numbers. There are more of them than there are of me. I may have to go to them. But I can promise that whatever happens, I'll keep names out of it."

He took a breath, breathed out a long sigh. "Elizabeth Drewer's not very happy about this. But I told her this morning that I had to talk to someone. When I heard about the Polk woman, I almost went to the police myself. I mean, Melissa disappears, and then a few weeks later one of her best friends is killed. There has to be a connection."

Evidently, they didn't know about Melissa's sister. I didn't tell them. They had enough to worry about.

"There is a connection," I said. "So where was Melissa going?"

He looked at his wife. She nodded.

He told me.

I said, "And when did she leave from here?"

Sarah said, "On the twenty-seventh. But she wasn't going directly there. She wanted a break, she said. She was going to take Winona to a motel somewhere, just the two of them. For a day or two, she said. So the two of them could be alone together and watch cable TV. Just hang out, she said. It was part of the last fling she wanted to have."

"Did she say which motel?"

"No. She didn't know herself. But it had to be one of the places in Taos. She wanted to go to Taos. She said she'd only been there once, just driving through. And Winona had never seen it. Nobody up there knew either one of them."

I said, "When did you find out that she hadn't shown up at the other place?"

"Just today," Larry said bitterly. "This morning. When we called California." Anger ran along his voice, rasping it. "It's a monumental screw-up."

Sarah said, "We never called and asked them. About Melissa. We weren't supposed to. We weren't supposed to have anything to do with anyone after they left here. Weren't supposed to ask about them. Maybe we should have, I think now that we should have, but we didn't. We were worried when we didn't hear from her, but we thought there wasn't anything we could do. And we told ourselves that maybe she just couldn't get to a phone. There's no phone up there, and we thought that maybe she couldn't get away."

"How do they communicate with the people in California?"

"I don't know," she said. "Pay phones, probably." She frowned and said, "The woman up in Hartley. Deirdre Polk. Why was she killed?"

"I'm not sure," I told her.

"Are you going to be able to find Melissa?" she asked me.

"I'll find her," I said.

TWENTY-THREE

IT WAS NEARLY three o'clock when I finished with the Coopers. Larry Cooper drove me back into town and dropped me off on Palace and I walked across the street and up to the office. There were no messages on the answering machine. I picked up the phone, saw that the green light was still working, and called Hector. I gave him what I had on Melissa: the name on her license, a description of her car, the name of the dealer she'd bought it from. He asked me where I'd obtained the information. I said that I couldn't tell him. He said that was noble of me.

I didn't tell him, either, where she'd been going when she disappeared. That, I wanted to look into myself.

I called Rita and told her that I had a lead on Melissa, and that I wouldn't be able to get to her house by three. She would have to interview the Albuquerque woman on her own, I said. She said she thought she could handle that.

I called Roy Alonzo and got his machine. I left a message saying that I wouldn't be able to meet him at the Fort Marcy complex and that I'd call him later today.

Then I walked out of the office and over to the lot where I'd parked the loaner Jeep. I'd left it beside the attendant's narrow wooden shack, and Gerry, the attendant, told me that no one had gone near it all day.

Driving north again, I considered what the Coopers had given me. Useful information, perhaps, all of it. But what I still didn't have was Melissa Alonzo.

According to the Coopers, she had probably disappeared from some motel in Taos. That bothered me. Why hadn't she gone on to the next station on the Underground Railroad? Had she somehow learned about the Salvadoran? Had she learned about Cathryn's death?

But Cathryn hadn't been killed until the second of October. Melissa had left the Coopers on the twenty-seventh of September, and planned to spend only a day or two in Taos. So, assuming she'd kept to her schedule, it hadn't been the death of her sister that made her change her mind.

What had?

Had she decided, for some reason about which I knew nothing, to leave New Mexico, go someplace where no one knew her?

If she had, the trail I was following would dead-end in Taos.

I'd told the Coopers, as I'd told everyone else, that I would find Melissa. But it seemed that the closer I got to her, the more elusive she became.

Once again, I was worried. It seemed like I'd been worried for a long time now.

South of Española, just a few hundred yards beyond the turn-off for Los Alamos, I turned right, heading for the High Road to Taos. No one was following me.

The High Road was empty when I reached it. No cars coming at me, none behind. Just the blue sky above and the glaring sun and the fierce, absolute clarity of the light. Peaks and bluffs and valleys marched off to either side of me, their ragged edges only slightly softened by the blanket of snow. Despite its beauty, it was desolate country, lonely country.

I put a Tina Turner cassette into the tape player. Tina asked me what love had to do with it.

Beats me, I told her. But it was a damn good question.

I PASSED THROUGH Las Mujeras, the tiny Spanish mountain town where Norman Montoya lived, and for a minute or two I thought about stopping to talk to him. But Palo Verde, where I was going, lay only another twenty miles north, and I wanted to check that out. Afterward, I would go on to Taos, ask about Melissa at the motels, then head back south. If I had the time, I could talk to Montoya on the way back to Santa Fe.

Palo Verde was smaller even than Las Mujeras. A gas station, a general store, a post office, two or three dusty homes, all draped with snow and huddled at the bottom of a broad, snow-covered basin about five miles wide, encircled by white hills. I passed the store and drove for another two miles. There was no sign posted at the turn-off the Coopers had described, but tire tracks rutted the snow. I stopped the Jeep, locked the front hubs.

The road skirted some fields fenced with barbed wire, then wound off into the wooded hills. Up here, the trees were ponderosas, and the snow still lay heavily atop them and made them look like old men standing stooped and worn beneath tattered shrouds.

After going nowhere for a while, aimlessly ambling left and right among the towering trees, the road sloped down and ran along the north side of a wide white valley. Up ahead, on my right, I could see the place I wanted, a handful of wooden buildings crouched at the base of the southern hills, below the looming pines. Before them, small dark figures moved in the snow.

The road crossed a narrow creek that darkly swirled around snow-capped rocks, and then it ran another hundred yards between two more barbed wire fences and finally stopped before one of the largest of the buildings. This was a ramshackle two-story frame house running east and west, its siding weathered to a dull gray. There were four cars parked in front: a dented black Volkswagen Beetle, an old lemon-yellow Ford pickup, a boxy Dodge delivery van that had been painted long ago with psychedelic flowers, and a fairly new black Suzuki four-wheel drive. The tire tracks I'd been following stopped at the Suzuki, and its shiny hood was clear of snow. The other cars were still covered.

I parked the Jeep and got out. The air was colder here than it had been in Santa Fe.

The small dark figures I'd seen from afar were children. They played to my left in a kind of courtyard formed by three newer-looking, single-story buildings. Even painted a cheerful yellow, the buildings had the glum, institutional look of dormitories. But the children didn't seem to care. There were six of them, and although two stood warily watching me, the others were dashing around the snow, hurling handfuls of it at each other, laughing and howling. The stuff was too dry to pack well, and their snowballs disintegrated as soon as they threw them, leaving streamers of white dust drifting through the air.

Further to the left, and beyond the dormitories, stood a massive unfinished structure, its raw wood frame looking like exposed ribs. Men worked inside it, carrying lumber, hammering nails, sawing planks. None of them seemed remotely interested in my arrival.

To my right stood a large barn, as weathered as the house, its roof swaybacked from decades of ice and snow. In front of it, in an area enclosed by a tall chicken-wire fence, three brown goats, two females and a male, stood watching me with infinite patience and, like the workmen, an utter lack of curiosity.

Also watching me, but with curiosity, were two small boys standing by the fence. Maybe six or seven years old, both wore bulky winter coats and jeans and black rubber zip-up boots. The taller of the two held a long piece of wooden doweling; the other awkwardly clutched, under his arm, a stuffed panda.

I was suddenly reminded of the menagerie of stuffed animals in Winona Alonzo's room back in Malibu. And I wondered, once again, where Winona was playing right now, and how she was bearing up beneath the weight of secrecy and stealth.

A long-haired man in a gray anorak came out of the dark shadows beyond the open door of the barn and called out, "Kids?"

The two boys turned to him.

"Come on," he yelled. "Give me a hand here."

The taller boy glanced back at me, muttered something to the other, and then the two of them trudged off through the snow, to the gate in the fence.

I felt abruptly like an interloper, felt that the man had called the children to him in order to protect them from my alien presence.

Perhaps he sensed this, for when he called out to me, his voice was cheerful. "Hi. Go on up to the house. They're waiting for you."

"Thanks," I shouted.

Snow crunching beneath my feet, I walked up to the rambling front porch, and then up its wooden steps. I knocked on the door.

A few moments later it was opened by a short woman wearing wooden clogs, black tights, a long polka-dotted black granny dress, and a white wool shawl-collared pullover, limp and loose, its too-long sleeves folded back over her wrists. Her thick hair hung in wild curls about her shoulders and it was threaded through with gray. The gray had to be premature, because her round and attractive face was unlined and she looked no older than twenty. She wore no makeup. With her shining brown eyes and rosy cheeks she seemed very alive and very healthy.

She grinned at me. "Hi. Are you the private detective?"

I smiled. She had that kind of grin. "I'm one of them," I said.

She laughed. "Hey, pretty good. I'm Freddy." There was some Texas in her voice. She held out a small warm hand and I shook it.

"Joshua Croft," I said.

"Come on in."

I walked into the broad living room. A threadbare red Oriental carpet. William Morris-style curtains open at the double-hung windows. Victorian furniture, bulky and tasseled, that had possibly come with the house. Like the furniture at the Coopers, it had all been lived in. But this stuff was beginning to take offense. One chair cushion canted slightly to the left. Along the sofa's arms, padding had begun to work its way through the fabric. Still, the room had a homey quality to it. It was bright with the white light bounding off the snow outside, and it was spotlessly clean. A fire flapped in the fieldstone fireplace, and the air was scented with cooking smells. And also with the smell of patchouli oil, something I hadn't run across since the early seventies. The woman was wearing it.

She said, "I sent Bilbo to get Sam. He should be here in a few minutes."

"Bilbo?"

She grinned. "Corny, isn't it? Poor guy never got over Tolkien. Come on into the kitchen. There're some things I've got to do."

I followed her down a narrow hallway into an enormous kitchen. A door to my right, lace curtains at the window, led outside. A long trestle table ran down the center of the room, and there were enough chairs arranged around it to seat fourteen people. Salad vegetables were piled up at one end of it, beside a thick butcher's block cutting board, a gigantic wooden salad bowl, and a chef's knife. There were several acres of counter space and a throng of cabinets, all of them painted with red enamel. Along one wall hung a collection of stew pots and saucepans and frying pans and griddles. The floor was linoleum, checkered with red and white squares. Squatting atop the huge gas stove were two large pots, one of them battered aluminum, the other black cast iron. The cooking smells were stronger in here, and I remembered that I hadn't eaten lunch.

Freddy swept over to the stove and plucked the lid from the cast iron pot. A cloud of steam billowed to the high ceiling. Still holding the lid, she tilted her hip slightly, comfortably, then picked up a wooden spoon and dipped it into the pot, stirring. She turned to me over her shoulder and she grinned. "Hey, I'm sorry, my mind is scattered today. As usual. What's your name again?"

"Joshua. Joshua Croft."

"Well, Joshua Croft, you hungry? The rice isn't done yet, but this is." She peered into the pot. "It's kind of a soup, I think. Or maybe it's a stew." She turned back to me. "Are you a carnivore?"

"I'm afraid so."

"Me too," she confided. "But only secretly. My secret vice. Everyone else around here is a grazer. I've gotta sneak off to the

Burger King in Taos every couple of weeks or I start to thinking I'm chewing my cud." She nodded to the pot. "This is pretty good stuff, though. Got just about everything in it. Tomatoes, carrots, potatoes, celery, onions. Even parsnips." She grinned. "Are private detectives allowed to eat parsnips?"

"They're our secret vice."

She laughed. "So you want some? Hey, c'mon, don't start being polite. If you're hungry, eat. Warm you up."

"Sure," I said. "Thanks."

"Great." She opened a cabinet, stood on tiptoes, took down a heavy china soup bowl. She opened a drawer, took out a stainless steel soup spoon. A ladle hung on the wall to her right, beside some long metal spoons and spatulas, and she lifted it, scooped up some of the stew, and carefully poured it into the bowl. She set the ladle alongside the wooden spoon, then opened another drawer, snagged a folded cloth napkin. She carried everything over to the table.

"Sit," she said. "I hope you don't mind, I've gotta get the salad ready." She glanced at the outside door. "Bilbo better get back here pretty quick and set the table. The wolves'll be showing up soon. Want a beer?"

"No thanks," I told her. I sat down where she'd set the bowl, and she sat down at the table's end, in front of the salad vegetables. "Eat," she said, and picked up a head of Boston lettuce.

I tasted the stew.

She leaned slightly forward. "So how is it?"

"Good," I said. It was. "Very good. It's got some oregano in it."

"Not too much?"

"Perfect."

"Good," she said. "The Mediterranean touch," she said, and began tearing leaves off the lettuce. "You don't look like a private detective."

"What do private detectives look like?"

"Oh, I dunno." She tore each leaf in half along its width, then tossed the halves lightly into the bowl. "Kind of sleazy and sad. Except on TV, where they're all hunky dreamboats."

"Have you met many private detectives?"

She looked over at me and grinned. "Hey. Cool. Am I being interrogated?"

"No. We private detectives call this a conversation."

She grinned. "Technical term, huh? Y'know, you eat too fast. You should chew your food more. Sam said you're looking for that Alonzo woman?"

"Cool," I said. "Am I being interrogated?"

She laughed again and then she looked at me gravely. "Seriously. She got lost?"

"I don't know what happened to her. I know she was supposed to show up here."

She nodded. "Yeah. She never did. We thought she'd just changed her mind or something."

"Has that ever happened before?"

She shook her head, not in negation but in refusal. "Sorry. Sam says we're not supposed to talk about that." And then, as though to make up for the refusal: "You sure you don't want a beer or something? I could make some tea?"

"No, I—"

The door opened and two men came in. The first was in his forties and he was big, taller than I, and wider, and he wore an open red mackinaw over a gray plaid flannel shirt and denim overalls. A weathered, clean-shaven, craggy face. A broad forehead, bristling black eyebrows, pale blue eyes, a hooked nose, a wide friendly mouth. His long gray hair hung between his shoulders in a ponytail.

The second man was shorter and younger, in his late twenties, and he wore work boots, jeans, a black turtleneck sweater, and a leather bomber jacket. Close-cropped curly black hair, two or three weeks' worth of black beard. His eyes, set back in their sockets, were dark and intense.

"This is Joshua," Freddy said. "The big guy is Sam and the other one there is Bilbo."

Sam smiled and crossed the floor, his right hand outstretched, his left waving me back into my chair. "No, man, don't get up," he told. "Finish your food."

"I shook his hand. Bilbo, hands in his jacket pockets, silently watched me.

"He's finished," Freddy said. "He's almost as big a pig as you are. And you're getting snow all over the floor. Why don't the two of you get out of here, so Bilbo can set the table. Bilbo, stop standing there looking like Rasputin. Get the plates."

Sam grinned at me. "Jesus, man, I can't stand a bossy woman. Come on. I'll show you around the spread."

I stood up and turned to Freddy. "Thanks for the food."

She grinned. "Hey. Glad you liked it. Bilbo, the plates."

Bilbo had unzipped his jacket. Now he took it off and hung it on a hook by the door. Something heavy in the pocket thumped against the wall.

It didn't have to be a gun. And even if it was, it was none of my business, so long as he wasn't pointing it at me.

But just the possibility that it was a gun made the kitchen suddenly seem less cozy and domestic, and suddenly made me feel again like what I was, an outsider.

"Come on," Sam said to me, still grinning.

I followed him and nodded to Bilbo, whose intense dark eyes shifted away from my glance.

Outside, Sam pushed the door shut, turned, and slipped his hands into the pockets of his mackinaw. "This way," he said, lifting his chin toward the east. We crunched through the snow, circling the house.

"Bilbo's a little weird," he told me. "Used to be a junkie and he's still not real housebroken. But he's good people."

We walked along the east side of the house. The children were gone now and, except for their rumpled tracks in the snow, they might never have been here. Sam nodded toward the low yellow buildings. "One on the right there is a dorm for the kids. Boys on one side, girls on the other. Thing in the center is the school. We've got a guy here, Bennett, he's a certified teacher, so we're okay with the state. Third building's for the folks can't fit in the big house."

"The kids are raised communally?"

He grinned at me. "Right, man, that's what a commune's all about. Name of the game. Name of the game. Nuclear family just doesn't cut it. Mom and dad lay all their sad little trips on the sprouts. Guilt. Neurosis. Sexual hangups. And how can two people meet all the needs that a sprout's got? This way, the grownups balance each other out. And there's like a pool of emotional and psychological resources the sprouts can draw on." He took his hands from his pockets, held them before him as though he were shaping a ball of dough. "And the sprouts get a sense of community. They're part of a large, interconnected group. It's all organic." He slipped his hands together, fingers interlocking, to show me what *organic* looked like.

He put his hands back into his pockets and we walked on. We were walking toward the unfinished wooden structure, and six or seven people were walking toward us. I had thought that all the people working on the building were men, but I saw now that two

were women, one a blonde in her thirties, the other a young brunette who could have been a teenager. Like the men, they wore
jeans and bulky winter coats. The men looked to be in their late
twenties or early thirties and most of them had long hair and
beards and, like the young people back in the Plaza at Santa Fe,
seemed to have suddenly materialized here from some earlier and
less complicated era. But everyone looked as healthy as Freddy,
and most of them smiled and nodded at me as they passed. Only
one or two—the young brunette among them—eyed the interloper suspiciously.

"How many kids do you have here?" I asked him.

"Fifteen right now," he said, and put his hands back in his
pockets. "Ten adults."

"Have most of the kids been here long?"

"Born here, some of them. But people come, people go. Part of
the process, man. Change, movement. Nothing stands still. Ruth—
that's Freddy's little sprout—she and Freddy only came here last
year."

"Freddy's married?"

He smiled at me. "Like her, huh? No, man, Freddy's on her
own." The smile became a grin. "Watch out. She's one tough lady.
A pistol."

"What about you? Any of the kids yours?"

He shook his head. "I got a son, nearly grown now, but he's
back in Portland with his mom." He grinned again and shook his
head, as though embarrassed by this failure. "Like I said, man.
Nuclear family doesn't cut it."

We had reached the wooden structure. Two wooden steps led to
a wood flooring supported all around by a two-foot foundation of
cinder block. Sam stopped walking and looked up at the building.
"This is our new project. Meditation hall. We'll rent it out to
groups from Santa Fe and Taos. Retreats." He turned to me.
"Makes for good vibes, man, people on the property meditating.
Lots of energy." He grinned. "The extra bread won't hurt, either." He waved a hand at the flooring. "Take a load off."

I walked across the snow and sat down on the unfinished wood.
Sam sat down beside me.

"What can you tell me," I asked him, "about Melissa Alonzo?"

He shook his head. "Not a thing, man. She was supposed to be
here at the end of September. She never showed."

"That didn't bother you?"

He shrugged. "We offer a place to stay, man. Someone doesn't want it, that's *their* decision."

"You didn't notify anyone that she hadn't turned up?"

He nodded. "Yeah, well, I probably screwed up there. I admit it. See, the thing of it is, I was never too big on the idea anyway, being part of this Underground Railroad deal. I was afraid it was gonna bring the heat down on us. Some of these people, it's the feds lookin' for 'em. FBI, man. That's heavy. That we don't need. We got a real good relationship with the local fuzz right now. Well, shit, man, we should. We been here almost twenty years. Anyway, sheriff knows we don't take runaways—minors, I mean—and we keep our noses clean. No drugs, no booze except for a beer now and then. I didn't want to jeopardize that."

"Why did you?"

He grinned, shrugged. "I was outvoted, man. It's a democracy. Everyone else was hot on the idea. Gotta go with the majority. Anyway, when the chick and her sprout didn't show, I just figured she'd changed her mind. People do that. But looks like I screwed up. If anyone should've called the people in California, it was me."

"Has it ever happened before, that someone just didn't show up?"

He looked off for a moment and then he looked back at me. "Shit, man, you're puttin' me on the spot. The people out in California, the ones I talked to this morning, they told me to go ahead and talk to you about the missing chick. But they don't want me talking about anything else. I got to honor that." He shrugged. "Thing of it is, this place is blown now anyway."

"Because I know about it."

"Right. They can't take any chances." He shrugged again. "So maybe it all worked out for the best."

"It hasn't worked out that way for Melissa Alonzo."

He frowned, looked down. "No. No, man, it hasn't." He turned to me. "You think she's okay?"

"No. I think she's in trouble."

"Shit," he said sadly. "Bummer. If I can do anything, man, to help, you know, you tell me."

"When was she supposed to show up here?"

"On the thirtieth. Of September."

"How long was she supposed to stay?"

"A week. And then she was gonna move on to the next place. And I can't tell you where that is, man. I'm sorry, but I can't. I don't even *know* where it is. But she hasn't been there. The people in California told me to tell you that. She hasn't been there."

"I still don't understand why you never let them know that she didn't arrive here."

"Okay, man, I fucked up. No question. But, shit you got to realize that I got other things on my mind. Right now, here, this is the first time since sunup I'm able to sit down and shoot the shit. I got the plumbing to worry about, and work crews for the Hall, and food supplies, and we got someone sick over at the hospital in Taos. If it's not one thing, man, it's another. Twenty-five people here, man."

"I'll explain all that to Melissa Alonzo, when I find her."

"Hey, man, come on. I didn't tell her not to come here. That was her decision."

"I hope so."

He frowned again. "What's that mean?"

"It means I don't know that it was her decision. I won't know anything until I find her."

"Shit, man, it hasn't even been two weeks. She'll show up. She's probably, like, taking a little vacation. Maybe it got too much for her, hiding out and all."

"Maybe," I said. "I hope you're right. Bilbo's carrying a gun, isn't he?"

"Huh? Oh. Yeah. I thought you glommed on to that. It's empty, man. I got the bullets. He only carries it 'cause like I say he's not housebroken yet. It's like a pacifier for him, man. Guy's gone through some rough times. I could tell you stories, make your hair stand on end. But basically he's good people. Wouldn't hurt a fly."

I nodded. I got out one of my business cards, handed it to him. "If Melissa Alonzo does contact you, I'd appreciate it if you'd let me know."

"You got it. Anything I can do, man."

I WAS ANGRY as I drove off down the track from the weathered old house. If Sam had made a single telephone call back when Melissa had failed to appear at the commune, then perhaps someone in the Underground Railroad would've set in motion a search for her.

Maybe they didn't have the resources to check up on missing women. But maybe, when I spoke with Elizabeth Drewer earlier in the week, she might've told me the truth, and today I would be that much closer to Melissa.

I was still angry when I reached the main road. I drove back to the small general store and used the pay phone to call Norman Montoya. Once again, he answered the telephone himself.

"Ah, Mr. Croft. It is good that you call." His voice was light, relaxed.

"How's that?" I said.

"The telephone line is clear?"

An isolated pay phone in an isolated northern New Mexico town? Probably, but I didn't know, and I told him so.

"Ah," he said. "Well. The package you were asking about. It has arrived."

TWENTY-FOUR

"SHE IS IN THE GUEST HOUSE," Norman Montoya told me. "She arrived less than two hours ago."

"Is she all right?"

He nodded. "Yes, but she is quite tired. She has been under considerable strain."

He and I were in his living room, me sitting on one end of a long white sectional couch, he sitting upright, spine straight, in a white padded armchair. To my right, the wall of glass looked out over a spectacular vista of steep river valley and snow-wrapped pines, all of it drifting down into shadow now as the last of the sunlight drained from the sky.

Montoya was wearing brogues again—maybe he always wore brogues—and also a pair of neatly pressed black wool slacks and a white dress shirt. The shirt was opened at the neck but the sleeves were buttoned. He was not an informal man.

I said, "She's awake, though."

"Oh yes. She is anxious to speak with you."

"Have you talked to her yourself?"

"Only in the most general way. To ascertain that she was all right, and to assure her that she is quite safe here."

He wasn't exaggerating about her safety. Coming up the forest road above Las Mujeras, I had seen two cars backed into side trails in the woods. In both, the drivers had watched me pass while they spoke into telephones. No one had tried to stop me. I had told Montoya, when I spoke to him from Palo Verde, what time I would be arriving and what kind of vehicle I would be driving.

Montoya said, "From what she tells me, she does not know where Melissa and Winona are."

I nodded. "We'll see."

ANOTHER GUARD, a short stocky man wearing black boots, black slacks, a black leather coat, and a black cowboy hat, stood outside the guest house door. As I approached, he said something into a small walkie-talkie, then slipped the device into his coat pocket and nodded to me, unsmiling.

I knocked at the guest house door. After a moment, Juanita Carrera opened it. She took a quick drag from her cigarette and, blowing smoke, she said, "You are Croft?"

"Yes."

"Come in."

Inside, the guest house was one large, spacious room. Behind a counter at one corner, to my left, was a small kitchenette. The living area, on this side of the counter, held a white leather chair, a small white leather sofa, a glass coffee table that supported some glossy magazines and a portable television. To my right was a king-size bed in an oak frame; beside that, an oak dresser. Farther to the right, a door led off into a bathroom. The curtains were drawn at the windows and the light in the room came from behind a white cornice that ran along the top of the white walls.

For a moment, the two of us stood there staring at each other.

Up until then, ever since I drove up the mountain road from Las Mujeras, I had been feeling a dull, almost dreamlike sense of unreality, similar to what I'd felt at Deirdre Polk's house. I had been feeling somewhat unreal, in fact, since all this began; and everything I had learned as I stumbled along, everything I had confronted, had seemed only to intensify the feeling. Roy Alonzo's glib sincerity in my office, the glitter and humbug of Los Angeles, the petty but brutal bigotry of Bill Arnstead and Rebecca Carlson. The endless veils of secrecy behind which Melissa Alonzo appeared to live and move and hide. Salvadoran assassins, two innocent women brutally murdered, inconclusive shoot-outs in the wide white wilderness. Aging hippies so laid back they couldn't make a simple phone call. Burly guards murmuring into car phones and walkie-talkies. And, at last, a melodramatic meeting with a frightened woman who might be able to lead me to Melissa Alonzo.

Juanita Carrera *was* frightened, desperately frightened, and the sense of unreality dropped away like cobwebs falling from my shoulders.

She wore black pumps, a black skirt, a wrinkled white rayon blouse, and she was hugging herself as she looked at me, shoulders hunched, one arm beneath her breasts, the other upraised to hold her cigarette. The cigarette was trembling slightly, as if she were chilled. Her entire body was rigid, poised for flight.

She was also, despite the stiffness of her body and the tension showing at the corners of her mouth, despite the smudges of exhaustion below her eyes and the gauntness of her cheeks, a remarkably beautiful woman. Her hair was thick and long and black, her face perfectly proportioned, her features perfectly shaped: the rich red mouth, the thin and aristocratic nose, the large dark eyes hooded by delicate and slightly slanted, almost Oriental lids.

I said, "May I sit down?"

"Yes, yes, of course." She sucked on the cigarette. "Please," she said, and waved her cigarette at the sofa. The *please* was an afterthought, a politeness remembered because it had been automatic in better times.

I sat. Moving swiftly, jerkily, she sat to my left in the chair, and then she leaned forward, feet together, knees together. I noticed that there was a long run in her sheer nylon stockings.

She reached to the coffee table, picked up a pack of Kools, held them out to me. "You smoke?"

"No. Thanks."

She tossed the pack to the table. "Five years," she said. "No cigarettes for five years. And now, again, I smoke three packs a day." She looked at the cigarette in her hand, leaned forward, and stabbed it out in a circular glass ashtray already nearly filled with half-smoked butts.

It was as though by putting out the cigarette, she had also extinguished, at least temporarily, the smoldering nerve ends on which she had been surviving. With a small tired sigh, she laid her arms along her thighs, wrist atop wrist, hands limp, and lowered her head, her thick black hair sweeping forward, off her twin shoulders.

I said nothing.

At last, slowly, she raised her head and looked at me over her crossed wrists. Her beautiful face was utterly blank. "Perhaps," she said, "as this Mr. Montoya insists, it is safe to speak with you. Perhaps it is not. I do not know. But I think I no longer care." She sat back against the chair.

"You're safe here," I told her. "No one can get to you here."

She shrugged. It wasn't a shrug of resignation. Whatever she felt, it was something that existed out in the cold bleak empty reaches far beyond resignation, and light-years beyond hope. "For now, perhaps," she said.

"Mr. Montoya will see to it that you're protected. He can do that. He's a powerful man."

"He is a gangster," she said, her voice flat, affectless. "The people I was staying with were much impressed that he wished to help me. They are Salvadorans, and of course they have much respect for power."

"He told you that I'm trying to find Melissa and her daughter?"

She nodded.

"Something happened down in El Salvador?" I said. "While Melissa was there. What was it?"

She reached forward, picked up the pack of Kools, tapped a cigarette out, put it between her lips, lit it with a Bic lighter. She sat back, once again folding her left arm beneath her breasts, her left hand clutching at the upper part of her right arm. She plucked the cigarette from her mouth and pursing her lips, exhaled downward. "My sister and the priest she worked with were killed. Melissa was there. She saw them being taken away, my sister and the priest. She saw who was responsible."

Although Rita had proposed the idea several days ago, and although I had grown more and more inclined to believe it myself, I was still surprised to hear it turned, and turned so flatly, so clinically, into fact. I said, "Your sister was Maria . . ." I couldn't remember the woman's last name, and I felt a small sad stab of guilt.

Juanita Carrera didn't seem to care. "Vasquez. My maiden name. She was staying with the priest, Father Cisneros, helping him."

"Why was Melissa there? At the home of Father Cisneros?"

"She had an airplane ticket for Maria. And papers. False papers, you understand? A United States passport with a departure stamp from this country. She had obtained it from people she knew in Los Angeles, people who help women and their children."

"People involved with the Underground Railroad."

"This, yes. Someone in customs, a friend of Maria's, had stamped it with a Salvadoran entry visa while Melissa was in the capital. Also, he had put Maria's fake name on the list of visitors to the country. When she left, no questions would be asked."

"Melissa told you what happened?"

"Yes." She sucked on the cigarette, exhaled.

"Can you talk about it?"

She made again that empty shrug. "It is only one more piece of violence, one more small horror. After a time, the heart grows numb." Another drag from the cigarette. "But if you wish to hear of it."

"Please."

She told me.

Melissa had arrived at the village of Cureiro on the evening of August 16, after dark. As she had been instructed, she had come alone; and, as instructed, she had hidden her rental car behind a grove of palm trees outside the tiny hamlet. Careful not to be seen, she had walked to the priest's house, where Father Cisneros and Maria were waiting.

I asked Juanita, "Had she met Maria before?"

"Yes. A year before, on an earlier visit. They had planned this, the two of them, since that time. They communicated through letters. Melissa would send letters to a woman she knew in Santa Isabel, letters written in a code, and the woman would get them to Maria. Santa Isabel is not far from Cureiro."

I nodded.

Juanita told me that when Melissa arrived at Father Cisnero's, Maria embraced her, laughing. The two women sat down for a parting glass of wine with the priest. They were still celebrating when they heard the truck drive up.

"It was a death squad," Juanita said. "The Esquadron de la Muerte. You know of these people?" She leaned forward, watching me, and stubbed out her cigarette.

"I've read about them."

Sitting back, she nodded slightly. "Yes, of course. Read about them." There was no sarcasm in the words, no bitterness. Only a stony recognition of the huge gulf that separated her experience and mine.

"Why did they come that night?" I asked her.

"Someone had talked. Intentionally or not, someone had revealed that Maria was to leave the country." She shrugged. "Perhaps Maria spoke of it to the wrong person."

"Was Maria involved in politics?"

For the first time, Juanita smiled. It was the scant, grim smile of pity. "To live in El Salvador," she said, "is to be involved in politics. It is to suffer, every day, endlessly, from the terror and the cruelty. My father was a doctor, a liberal. He protested the treatment of the farmers. He and my mother disappeared in 1984. They were killed, of course. My brother was killed in 1985, murdered in his bed and mutilated because he had dared, in public, to call a National Guard officer a swine. I escaped in 1989, leaving my husband behind. He died in November of that year, when the FMLN attempted to capture San Salvador. Only Maria remained."

She reached for another cigarette, lit it, sat back exhaling. "Was she political? Oh yes, she was that very dangerous thing, a liberal. Not an activist, not a Communist, not a rebel. Only a *liberal*. She had trained as a nurse. She cared for people. She attempted to ease their pain. A very dangerous person."

She sucked again on the Kool, blew smoke downward. "A liberal. Such a dirty word here in the United States. A dirty word, also, in El Salvador."

"Why would they want to kill her?"

"Because she was leaving. To leave is to suggest that El Salvador is not the paradise which the government claims it is. Therefore, no one is permitted to leave. If someone attempts to do so, and she is caught, an example is made."

I nodded. "Go on," I said. "The truck arrived at Father Cisnero's house."

Juanita told me that as soon as the truck pulled into the dirt driveway, Maria knew, or suspected, what it signified. Quickly she swept the third glass from the table and dragged Melissa into the bedroom. The bedroom light was on; probably Maria didn't dare now to turn it off. She pushed Melissa into a closet and forced her to the floor, ripped some of the priest's clothing from hangers and hurled them over the woman. Told her, in a hurried hiss, not to speak, not to reveal herself, no matter what she heard, no matter what happened. Melissa's life, Maria told her, depended on it. Maria pushed the door shut, but it swung slightly open, and in her haste she failed to notice this.

Poking her head above the priest's worn robes and surplices, Melissa was able to see a thin wedge of the bedroom: a corner of the bed, a narrow rectangular section of the white plaster wall. She was too frightened, Juanita said, to pull the door shut again. She could shut only her eyes.

She heard them come to the front door, heard Father Cisneros protest, heard the thud of the rifle butts against his body as they clubbed him. She heard a struggle, a shouted curse from Maria, the sharp crack of an open-handed slap, and then laughter and a confused thumping, a scrambling and clatter of shoes.

And then the soldiers, some of them, were in the bedroom with Maria. Melissa had kept her eyes shut—in the atavistic belief, perhaps, that if she couldn't see them, they couldn't see her. But now her eyes snapped open of themselves. She saw flashes of Maria's long dark skirt swirling amid a flurry of khaki legs and black leather paratrooper boots. Heard Maria cursing and spitting, heard the rough bark of male laughter. Heard the sudden creak of the bed, a female gasp, male grunts, fists smacking against flesh. Saw, from only five feet away, a pair of khaki trousers drop to reveal pale hairy legs. More khaki trousers crowding around. More curses from Maria, harsh, defiant. More laughter from the men. Then the bedsprings squealing rhythmically, wheezing like an asthmatic old man. Loud shouts of encouragement, still more laughter. And then they did something to Maria, something painful, and her curses suddenly stopped and she began a long shrill wavering shriek.

"It went on for many minutes," said Juanita. "Perhaps for half an hour. Melissa said that she wet herself. She bit through her lip to keep from screaming. There is still a small scar."

I nodded, but I was looking past her bald, unemotional recital to Melissa in that closet. It would be hot in there—August in El Salvador, yes, it would be stifling. There would be the smell of camphor, to keep away the heavy-bodied moths, and perhaps the smell of the priest's talcum and of the incense he burned at mass. And the smell of her own body, the smell of panic, and the sounds of her body as well, the roaring of her heart, the tight clenching and unclenching of her lungs. And, throughout it all, there would be the unbearable, mind-scorching terror of discovery.

"After a time," Juanita said, "an officer came into the room, and the men stopped. The officer stood against the far wall, and she could see him clearly. She recognized him. He was a colonel with the Atlactl Battalion. You know of this group?"

"No." My voice was raspy. I cleared it.

"An elite unit. It was a soldier from this battalion who shot Archbishop Romero. They are trained by advisers from the United States, of course."

I nodded. Of course. And these advisers would be brave men, even honorable, men, but men—or so I wanted to believe—who had no real understanding of the people to whom they taught their cool, efficient skills.

"He ordered the men out," said Juanita. "They carried Maria from the room—she was unconscious by this time. Melissa waited in the closet."

She waited there for hours, perhaps, after the soldiers left and silence slowly filled the house. She was unable to move. But finally she made herself get up. Moving slowly, as though underwater, she left the house and walked back to the car. It was nearly two in the morning when she started for Santa Isabel. Halfway there, she was stopped by a roadblock, two young National

Guardsmen. She was able to talk her way through, but the Guardsmen took her name.

She knew that someone would be coming for her. The authorities had her name, and the authorities sanctioned the death squads. They knew about her Sanctuary involvement, and knew that she might represent a threat. They would want to question her about the attack on Maria and Father Cisneros. She knew she would never be able to withstand interrogation—sooner or later she would confess that she had seen a high-ranking Atlactl officer. There would be a "regrettable accident."

Back at her hotel, she gathered her clothes and packed, left a message for the other Sanctuary volunteers, and then drove to San Salvador and caught the first plane back to the States, a flight to Houston. From there, she had flown to Los Angeles. Her car was still at the airport, but she had left it there, taken a cab to her house for a change of clothes, and taken another cab to her sister's, to pick up her daughter. And then she had vanished into the Underground Railroad.

"Why didn't she go to someone?" I asked. "Explain what she'd seen. The police. Someone in the federal government."

Again Juanita smiled her small smile of pity. "The federal government? Your federal government is committed to the lie that the government in El Salvador is peaceful and democratic. Over the past ten years your federal government has provided four billion dollars of military aid to the regime. Your FBI routinely cooperates with agents of the Salvadoran security forces. Melissa had no reason to trust your federal government."

"The police, then."

"The police would have simply turned her over to the federal government." She sucked on her cigarette, exhaled. "And you must remember that Melissa had already been called a liar in the courts. To many people she was merely a hysterical woman, a woman who had unjustly accused her former husband of a terrible crime. She felt that no one would believe her. But perhaps most of all, she was concerned about her daughter. If the Salvadoran government sent someone to this country to silence her, Winona would be silenced also."

"But if no one would believe her, then the Salvadoran government had no reason to silence her."

"It was Melissa who felt that no one would believe her. The government in Salvador felt otherwise. Because they did send someone. He killed her sister."

TWENTY-FIVE

I SAID, "HOW DID YOU learn about Cathryn Bigelow's death?"

She took another deep drag from her cigarette, exhaled. The room was foggy now with smoke and my eyes were beginning to sting.

"A friend in Los Angeles," she said. "A Salvadoran. She knew of my connection to Melissa. The television and the newspapers in Los Angeles, they made of it a very big thing, the death of Cathryn. She was Melissa's sister, and Melissa was still missing."

I'd glanced through the newspaper clippings about Cathryn's death, in the material I'd received from Ed Norman. The papers had covered the death heavily because Calvin Bigelow was such a honcho in Los Angeles money circles, and because he and his wife had already been forced to deal with the mysterious disappearance, only months before, of their other daughter. Like the L.A. police, the newspapers had downplayed, or ignored, the possibility of any connection between the two events.

Juanita Carrera said, "My friend telephoned to me because she was afraid I might be in danger."

"When was this?" I asked her.

"Last Wednesday. In the evening." She took a drag, leaned forward, ground out the cigarette, and leaned back, exhaling.

"And you left that night."

"Yes. I knew some people who were safe. Here in Santa Fe. I went to them."

"You were certain that Cathryn had been killed on orders from El Salvador."

She moved her shoulders lightly. "Of course."

"But why would they kill her at the beginning of October? Melissa disappeared in August."

"Melissa told me, when I saw her, that she had written to her sister, to tell her that she was safe. Cathryn must have spoken of this to someone. And that someone told someone else. And someone in El Salvador sent a killer to learn from Cathryn where Melissa was."

"Who would Cathryn have spoken to?"

She shook her head. "I do not know. I never met Cathryn. But it must have happened in this way."

"You met with Melissa on the twenty-third of September?"

"Yes. A Monday."

Melissa's card had been postmarked in Santa Fe on the same day. Cathryn was killed on the second of October. Santa Fe mail could sometimes take a week to reach L.A. The timing was right.

I asked her, "Does the phrase *'The flower in the desert lives'* mean anything to you?"

She frowned as though surprised. "Where did you hear of this?"

"It was what Melissa wrote to her sister, on the postcard."

"Ah." She took a deep breath, and frowned again, sadly now. "Melissa was making, in a way, a joke."

"How?"

She leaned forward, slipped another Kool from the pack, lit it, sat back. "The death squad, sometimes they warn you before they come for you. Sometimes they do not. And sometimes they send only the warning, and they never come. For many people, to receive the warning is enough. The warning is a letter that says, *'The flower in the desert dies.'* It is signed E.M."

"For Esquadron de la Muerte."

"Yes." She inhaled, then exhaled, cigarette smoke.

"And Melissa knew this?"

"Yes. I had told her of it. I had received such a letter myself, before I left Salvador. It was the reason I left."

"Who else would know what the phrase meant?"

A small shrug. "Any Salvadoran. It was common knowledge. There are Salvadorans who have received such letters even while they lived in Los Angeles."

"Tell me this. Why would a death squad come after you?"

"My husband was a fighter with the FMNL. The national liberation front. But, really, you see, they need no reason." She paused, frowned. Finally, she shook her head. "You would not understand."

"Try me," I said.

She inhaled again on the Kool, exhaled, leaned forward, tapped the ash into the ashtray, sat back. She nodded. "I shall tell you a story. Three years ago, before I left Salvador, I went to visit a friend in the countryside. Constancia is her name. I knew her from school in the capital. Her parents had disappeared while she was in school and she had gone back to their village, to live with her aunt. I had seen her only two times since the time of school, when she had come with her uncle to San Salvador."

Another drag on the cigarette. "On this day, I met her family. Her aunt, Tomasina, and her two cousins—these were young girls, not yet sixteen. Constancia had a young son, Gilberto. A baby, eighteen months old. I had met her uncle, of course, before this. Juan. A good man. The husband of Constancia, Carlos, he was gone, off in the hills with the National Front. The others, the seven of them, they lived in a house not much bigger than this room."

Another drag. She leaned forward, tapped off her ash, sat back. "There was work to do, but Tomasina and Juan sent us off, so that we might talk. And we did. We talked for a long time, perhaps for several hours. There was a small river not too far from the village, and we sat there on the rocks, in the shade of the trees, and we talked. Not very much about the war. We talked about small things, unimportant things. The girls we had known in school. What clothes the women wore now in the capital. Constancia always had been fond of fine clothes. She had not owned any herself since she left the capital."

Another drag. "When we returned, the village was silent. There were still some animals in the streets, some chickens and an old dog, but the people were gone. The children, the old people. We went to the house of Juan and Tomasina. I could smell the blood even before we went inside, and I could hear the flies.

"Constancia's family were sitting at a small table in the center of the room. Their heads had been cut off, and each head had been placed in front of the body, and the hands had been placed on top of the head. To make it appear, you see, that they were caressing it. But this had not worked with the hands of the baby, Gilberto. His hands and his arms were too small. And so they had used nails to attach the hands. The hammer was lying on the table. It was beside a plastic bowl, a large plastic bowl, and the bowl was filled with blood."

I took a deep breath. My chest was tight. "Why?" I asked her. Even as I asked it, I knew that this was, finally, the same question that Melissa Alonzo's mother had asked me in California, and I knew that once again it was, finally, unanswerable.

She shrugged her bleak, empty shrug. "To terrify. To exercise their power. All the power in my country is held by the landowners, and a small portion of this they hand over to the government. Which in turn hands over a small portion to the security forces. The National Guard, the Treasury Police. Do you know how the security forces recruit new members?"

I shook my head.

She leaned forward, slipped another cigarette from the pack, lit it with the one she was already smoking, stubbed out the old one in the ashtray. She sat back. "No one, none of the sons of the farmers or the workmen, will join them voluntarily. So they kidnap young boys, boys fifteen and sixteen, and they rape them. Some of these brave soldiers enjoy this, of course. It is their sexual preference. Others do it coldly, deliberately, as a part of their job. Sometimes they use wooden instruments. It sounds grotesque, I know. It sounds impossible. But Salvador is a country of the grotesque and the impossible."

She sucked on the cigarette. "By doing this, they steal from these boys, their sense of themselves, of their humanity, and they give them a sense of shame. The only way the boys can wipe this away is by doing to someone else that which was done to them. And they are indoctrinated to believe that doing this, inflicting this brutality, is patriotic and noble. The boys are first shown how powerless they are, then given a small measure of power, and then encouraged to take their revenge. Not upon the people who shamed them, but upon their own people."

Another drag from the cigarette. "This small power of theirs conceals their shame from themselves. But it is an insidious thing, this power. It must be exercised in order to be felt, and the more it is exercised by brutalizing others, the more they brutalize themselves. At last they are empty entirely. They become monsters." She shook her head. "It is sick. It is insane."

I agreed with her. It was insane. But as with most of the insanity in the world, there was little I could do about it at the moment. At the moment, my concern had to be somewhere else.

"About Melissa," I said. "When you saw her on the twenty-third, did she tell you where she was staying?"

"With a young couple, she said. Here in Santa Fe. I did not ask her their names and she did not give them to me."

"She came back to Santa Fe to see you."

"Yes. She wished to speak with me about Maria. To tell me what had happened."

"Did she talk with you after the twenty-third?"

"She telephoned me one time. To tell me that she had left the couple and that she would soon be moving to another safe place, nearby. She did not say where this was."

"When did she call you?"

"On the twenty-seventh. A Friday."

"Did she say where she was calling from?"

"No. We were always careful on the telephone."

"If Melissa had seen you and said what she had to say, why didn't she leave the area?"

Juanita Carrera frowned. "I believe, now, that she should have. It is my fault, perhaps, that she did not."

"How?"

"I know of a reporter. A good man, I think. He works in Los Angeles, and we had talked some time ago, when I first arrived from Salvador. He was writing then a story about refugees from my country. Melissa knew of my friendship with this man, and wanted me to contact him. She wanted to leave a written account of what she had seen in Cureiro. She thought that he could publish this, and the truth would be known. I agreed. I thought then that this was a good idea. But the man was in Central America, Honduras, and he would not be back in California until the first week of October."

"Did Melissa give you the account?"

"No. She was to call me at the end of September, on the thirtieth. She did not. I was worried, of course. And then, on the second of October, I learned of her sister's death." She shrugged. "I think now that Melissa, too, is dead." She said it as flatly as she had said everything else, and then she inhaled on the cigarette.

"I don't think so," I said. "The man who killed Cathryn is still looking for her."

"If she were still alive," she said, exhaling smoke, "she would have contacted me."

"She has no way to contact you. You've been hiding since last week. Is there anyone else she might contact?"

Another drag. "She spoke once of a woman friend. An artist. I cannot recall the name."

"Deirdre Polk. She's dead. Killed the same way Cathryn was."

She closed her eyes. For a moment she didn't move.

I said, "Yesterday. Last night." It didn't seem possible that the woman had died less than twenty-four hours ago.

Juanita Carrera opened her eyes. "These people never stop," she said.

We talked for a while longer, but she possessed no information that might help me locate Melissa. As I was about to leave, I asked her, "Your friend, Constancia. What happened to her?"

She inhaled on her cigarette. "It was she who called me from Los Angeles."

"She came with you when you escaped from Salvador?"

"Yes."

"Good," I said.

She shrugged. Emptily. Blankly. "There were many others," she said, "who could not escape."

I SPOKE WITH Norman Montoya, told him what I'd learned, and told him I was on my way to Taos to see if I could pick up Melissa's trail. I asked him if Juanita could stay in the guest house for a while longer. He said that she was welcome to stay for as long as she liked. Afterward, I called Rita and told her that she'd been right about Melissa Alonzo and El Salvador. She was kind enough not to point out that she was usually right. She said that Roy Alonzo had called, several times, asking for me to call him back.

I left Las Mujeras at a little after eight, and arrived in Taos a little before nine. Taos is smaller than Santa Fe and has fewer motels. I stopped and asked questions at only three of them before I found a night clerk who thought he recognized Melissa from the picture I showed him.

He'd seen a woman who looked like her, except that her hair was shorter and darker. She had been with a small girl, and she had stayed at the motel at approximately the right time. It cost me twenty dollars to learn that the woman had checked in on the twenty-seventh of September and checked out on the thirtieth. She had paid cash and she had used the name Linda Lattimore. She had described her car as a Honda Civic.

Melissa.

It cost me another twenty to learn that she'd made no phone calls from her room. If it was from Taos that she'd called Juanita Carrera, she hadn't called from the motel.

The clerk told me that it had probably been the day clerk who checked the woman in and out. The day clerk was unavailable until morning, and the clerk wouldn't give out her home telephone number or her address, no matter what I offered him. He seemed afraid of her. I bought a room for the night, drove the borrowed Jeep over to it, took possession. When I finished my shower, the time was nearly ten thirty. I called Rita, told her where I was, what I was planning to do. Then I called Roy Alonzo.

"Croft," he said, and I could hear, over the line, the long sibilant intake of his breath. "Can you tell me what's going on?" He sounded like someone who was trying hard to keep his emotions in check, or like someone who was trying hard to sound like that. I couldn't tell which it was, and just then I didn't much care.

"I haven't found her yet," I said.

"Jesus Christ, man. First Cathryn and now this Polk woman up in Hartley. What's happening here?"

"I'm not sure. It looks like someone else is looking for Melissa."

"Why?"

"Apparently she may've seen something when she was in El Salvador."

"What, for God's sake?"

"A murder."

"Jesus *Christ!* What the hell *is* this?"

"Where were you last night between seven thirty and ten thirty?"

"*What?*"

"Sounded like a fairly simple question to me."

"It's the same goddamn question the state police asked me. And it's none of your goddamn business."

"Fine. Goodbye."

"Hold on, hold on. You don't really think I *killed* that woman?"

"I'm tired," I said. "Right now I'm not capable of thinking anything. If you don't want to answer the question, don't answer it. But do me a favor and get off the phone so I can go to sleep."

"I was at the Palace last night, for dinner. With Shana. Shana Eberle. I told you about her."

"Shana's in town, is she?"

"I resent your tone, Croft."

"A lot of people do. I stay up nights, sometimes, trying to change it. When were you at the Palace?"

"From about seven till about ten. Look, Croft, why are you being so hard-headed about this? I'm just trying to find out what's happened to Melissa and Winona. I'm worried, goddamn it. Does that make me such a total putz?"

"No," I admitted. "It doesn't. If I learn anything, I'll get it to your uncle. In the meantime—"

"But who's killing these people?"

"A Salvadoran, I think. I don't know anything for certain now. I—"

"Is anyone doing anything about this? Have the police been notified?"

"Yeah."

"Is there anything I can do?"

"Nothing. I'm sorry." I felt uncomfortable apologizing to Alonzo: as though the apology signaled a forgiveness for the things I had come to believe he had done. But if he were faking his concern now, he was a better actor than he'd ever been on "Valdez!"

"Maybe if I talked to someone," he said. "I know people in this town. Important people."

"I remember. But I don't think that in this case they're the right people. Like I said, as soon as I know anything, I'll get it to your uncle. You're just going to have to hang in there."

I heard him take another long breath. "All right. All right. But if I *can* do anything, you let me know."

"I'll do that. Good night."

DESPITE MY EXHAUSTION, I had thought that I wouldn't be able to sleep. But as soon as I turned out the light, the long day caught up with me, and I was out.

I dreamed of people walking down the narrow dirt road of a village in a clearing in the jungle. Tiny whitewashed shacks, roofed with thatch, leaned one against the other. The people, men and women of all ages, children of all sizes, wore the tattered clothes of impoverished farmers—cheap huaraches, frayed serapes. They went, all of them, about their business—tending chickens, leading goats to the stable, grinding corn—as though nothing were wrong, as though there were nothing unusual going on. But the eyes of all of them were narrowed, and all their mouths were stretched wide open in an agonized but absolutely silent scream.

The dream woke me up, and for a long time I couldn't get back to sleep.

TWENTY-SIX

"WHY ARE YOU looking for her?" the woman asked, glaring at me over the counter.

"Because she's in trouble and I want to find her before the trouble gets worse."

"That's none of my business."

"I understand that. All I'm asking for is information."

Only a few women in the world can be accurately described as barrel-chested, but Margery Helms, the day clerk at the motel, was one of them. She wore a gray wool blazer over a black rayon top that was tight against her heavy breasts and her heavy tubular belly. A strand of imitation pearls lay along the taut fabric, a string of golf balls on a black trampoline, and they moved slowly up and down as she breathed. The blazer had shoulder pads, but she didn't need them. Beneath her blue-rinsed hair, her round face was lacquered with cosmetics that glistened like bacon fat. She was in her fifties and she could have been J. Edgar Hoover's sister, except that probably she would have killed J. Edgar when he was a little boy. With her bare hands. I could understand why she might've frightened the night clerk. She frightened me.

Her hard gray eyes glared at me as she said, "I'm not going to give you any."

"Did you read about the woman in Hartley?" I asked her. "The one who was killed two days ago? She was a friend of the woman I'm looking for."

I was standing on the customer side of the front desk. Glancing to my left, I saw that the Hispanic maid who'd been tidying the rack of postcards was watching me. I lowered my voice. "Look, Mrs. Helms, this woman's in trouble. All I want to do is find her. And help her."

"I'm sorry," she said. "But I'm not going to reveal any information about any of our guests. It's against company policy. Now, will you be checking out this morning?"

I didn't think she was sorry. I thought she was rather pleased. I thought, as Juanita Carrera might put it, that she was exercising her small measure of power.

"Soon," I said. "May I talk to the manager?"

She smiled, and there was triumph in the smile. "Mr. O'Hara is in Albuquerque, at a meeting."

"When will he be back?"

Another smile. "I really couldn't say."

I nodded. "Were you ever in the Wehrmacht?" I asked her.

She frowned, puzzled. "And where might that be?"

"Outside Cleveland."

She said dismissively, "I've never been to Cleveland."

You should go, I almost said. *Now.*

But I didn't. She was, after all, only doing her job. Instead, I thanked her—sourly—then walked back across the parking lot to the rented room, carrying the disposable razor, the toothpaste, and the toothbrush I'd bought in the tiny gift shop. I'd left my emergency toiletries bag in the Subaru when I picked up the Jeep. I had thought I'd be back for the car yesterday afternoon.

I had just finished shaving when a knock came at the door. I toweled my face dry, saw that I'd nicked myself along the jaw, and walked to the door, dabbing the towel at the wound.

It was the maid from the lobby. "Do you speak Spanish?" she asked me.

"Poquito," I said.

She glanced quickly around her, then asked me, in Spanish, "May I come in?"

"Of course."

Forty or so years old. A dark, broad face that had seen some bad weather and some bad times. Black hair that looked dyed but probably wasn't, pulled back behind her small ears below a starched white maid's cap. A stocky, muscular body inside the green and white uniform.

She looked about her uneasily as she stepped into the room. Probably she wasn't comfortable entering the room of a male guest. I closed the door and asked her, "Would you like to sit?"

She had moved to the center of the room. She turned to me. "No. I will stand. Thank you." She put her hands in the pockets of her uniform. "Senora Linda. She is in trouble?"

"Yes," I said. I swung the towel over my shoulder, leaned back against the door, crossed my arms. "Yes, I believe she is. Did you hear me talking, at the desk?"

"I did not mean to listen," she said. "But yes, I heard. My English for speaking is not good, but I can understand it well."

"My name is Croft," I told her. "Joshua Croft. And what is your name?"

"Rodriques." She held her head a little bit higher. "Senora Rodriques."

"Senora Rodriques, I thank you for coming to see me. Did you meet Senora Linda?"

"Yes. Her and the little one. Mary."

So now I knew that Winona had a new name, and I knew what it was. I wondered if Melissa had intentionally given her the English version of Juanita's sister's name. "Did you speak with her often, while she was here?"

"Not often, no. But several times. I liked her, but I felt badly for her. She was a troubled woman, I think."

"Why did you think so, senora?"

"She never went out. She and the little one stayed always in their room, except to go for small walks through the town. Often, they ate here. They watched the television all day and all night."

"But you said you talked to her."

"When I came to do the cleaning of the room. Only for a few moments at a time. She and the little one would leave, and she would take her book with her, but soon they would return, sometimes before I was finished."

"Her book?"

"She said she was a writer. She spoke excellent Spanish. Mexican Spanish, not the kind from Spain. She said that her book was the reason she spent so much of her time in her room. But to stay in a small room like this all day, that is not good for a small child."

"How did the child seem to you?"

"Quiet. Very quiet. It was not good for her, being here like that."

"What kind of book did the senora have?"

"A small book, but thick. Red. Like a diary."

"Did you ever see her writing in it?"

"No. But sometimes, when I came to clean, it was lying beside her on the bed, closed, with a pen on top of it. It seemed to me that she had been writing before I arrived."

"Always she took this book with her when she left the room?"

"Yes."

"Did the senora tell you where she would be going after she left Taos?"

"No."

"Did you see her leave, when she left for the last time?"

"Yes. I was crossing the courtyard when I saw her car. She waved to me. So did the little one."

"Which way did the car go? North or south?" South was the direction Melissa would've taken to reach the commune in Palo Verde.

"North," she said. "But often they went for breakfast at the McDonald's. That is north of here. And they had not eaten yet, that day. Perhaps they went there."

I nodded. "Is there anything else you can tell me, Senora Rodriques?" So far as I knew, Mrs. Rodriques was the last person to have seen Melissa and Winona before they disappeared.

She shook her head. "No. Will they be all right? She and the little one?"

"I hope so. I thank you very much." I reached back and tugged out my wallet. "May I offer you something for your assistance?"

She took her hands from her pockets and waved them. "No, no. I want no money."

"Senora, please. You have been of great help to me."

"No, no. I wanted to help the senora only. And the child. Thank you very much, but no."

I nodded. "As you wish. Do you intend to clean this room now?"

"You are leaving very soon?"

"Yes."

"I will return. There is another I must clean first."

"Very well. Thank you again, senora."

"For nothing, I, too, hope that the senora and Mary are well."

After she left, I put two twenties on the top of the dresser.

"The book," Rita said. "The diary. Melissa was using it to write her account of what happened in Cureiro."

I shrugged. "She told Juanita she'd be writing an account. So, yeah, probably."

"And you checked the McDonald's?"

"Yeah. One of the girls there remembered her from the picture, said she'd come in a couple of times for breakfast. But the girl couldn't remember what days she'd been there. And naturally, she didn't pay any attention to which direction Melissa took when she drove away. She was too busy."

"Which is no doubt why Melissa ate there in the first place."

I nodded.

We were sitting on the sofa again. Rita wore a white blouse this morning, and a blue skirt that, like the others, reached to her ankles. We were both drinking tea.

I said, "The woman from Albuquerque. The S and M queen. She couldn't tell you anything useful?"

Rita shook her head. "She hasn't seen Melissa for three years, and Melissa and Roy went to only a couple of meetings back then, before their divorce."

"Meetings?"

She smiled. "Not orgies. The group down there is more of a discussion group. They sound a fairly sedate bunch. They have pot luck dinners once a month."

"What do they bring? Chicken in Chains? Roast Beef Torquemada?"

"Joshua. You're not very tolerant today."

"I'm pissed off. I've run out of places to look and people to talk to. This is a mess, Rita. Stamworth, the Salvadoran, death squads. And now Melissa and Winona have vanished into thin air." I drank some tea.

"Let's put Melissa and Winona aside for the moment," she said, "and deal with the others, one at a time. Starting with Stamworth. What do we know about him? When did he first show up?"

"Sometime toward the end of September. In L.A."

"Before Cathryn was killed."

"Right."

"We don't think he killed Cathryn."

"I don't, no. I think that was the Salvadoran."

"And we don't think that Stamworth's really with the FBI."

"No."

"But we don't know with whom he might actually be working."

"No."

"He showed up next here in Santa Fe, last week, just after Cathryn was killed. He talked to Deirdre Polk, Rebecca Carlson, and your friend Arnstead, at Juanita Carrera's apartment."

"Right."

"We're assuming that he knew about Polk and Carrera from Melissa's phone bill."

"Right."

She sipped at her tea. "Next time we hear about him, he's in Los Angeles, talking to you."

"Right. On Tuesday night."

"We don't know how he knew about you."

I shrugged. "Someone must've told him."

"Perhaps. Or perhaps one of the people you spoke to was being watched."

"A stakeout?" Maybe. "And Stamworth, or someone working with him, gets the license number off the rental I was driving. And then gets my name from the rental company."

She nodded. "Someone working with him, I should think. Stamworth was probably still here, in Santa Fe, while you were asking questions on Tuesday."

"Why?"

"Because it was from here that Melissa sent her postcard to Cathryn. He would've known about the postcard from the Los Angeles police. Why return to Los Angeles unless you suddenly appear over there, asking questions?"

I nodded. "L.A. is only a few hours away. He could've flown there Tuesday night. But we still don't know why Stamworth is looking for Melissa."

"For the same reason, perhaps, that the Salvadoran is looking for her."

"To kill her?" I finished off my tea.

"Not necessarily to kill her. To contain her, possibly. Possibly he's learned about what Melissa saw in El Salvador. Possibly someone in the government, our government, felt that Melissa represented a possible embarrassment, and sent Stamworth to track her down."

"But he was looking for her *before* Cathryn was killed. Before anyone knew where Melissa might be."

She sipped her tea. "We're assuming that Cathryn talked to someone about the card from Melissa. We don't know for certain who that was or—"

"I've got an idea about that," I said. "About who she talked to."

She nodded. "Charles Hatfield. The man you talked to in Los Angeles. At Sanctuary."

I looked at her. "Rita. I wish you wouldn't do that."

She smiled. "He knew Cathryn, he admitted that."

"So did Edie Carpenter. And Chuck Arthur."

"Each of them said they only met her once. Hatfield admitted to seeing her several times, around the Sanctuary offices. And if Cathryn were going to talk to anyone about receiving a postcard from Melissa, wouldn't Hatfield be the obvious choice? He was the man Melissa worked for. He was—ostensibly, anyway—as dedicated as Melissa to the cause."

"He was also a liar," I said.

"In what way?"

"That phrase Melissa used in her card to Cathryn— *'The flower in the desert lives.'* He told me he'd never heard it, that it didn't mean anything to him. Juanita Carrera told me last night that it was a standard phrase used by the death squads. They've even used it in letters sent to Salvadorans in Los Angeles. Hatfield had to know about it."

"He probably lied, too, about receiving a message from Melissa. We know she sent at least two postcards toward the end of September, and probably both on the same day, the twenty-third. One to Cathryn, one to her mother."

"And probably one to Edie Carpenter," I said. "I think she was lying about not hearing from Melissa."

"And probably one to Hatfield."

"But if Hatfield already had a postcard from Melissa, if he already knew she was in Santa Fe, or at least in New Mexico, it doesn't matter whether Cathryn called him."

"Of course it does. If all the card said was *'The flower in the desert lives,'* then it didn't tell Hatfield where Melissa might be. It told him only, from the postmark, that she was somewhere near Santa Fe."

I nodded. "And there was a possibility that Cathryn might know more. So as soon as she called him, told him she'd heard from Melissa, she put herself in jeopardy."

She nodded, sipped at her tea. "And let's not forget that Maria Vasquez and Father Cisneros were killed because someone informed on Maria. Someone notified someone in El Salvador that Maria was leaving."

"But if it was Hatfield, why didn't the death squad that went up to Cisneros's house pick up Melissa, too? They never searched the place."

"Perhaps Hatfield never mentioned Melissa's name. Perhaps he simply said that Maria Vasquez was preparing to leave."

I shook my head, dubious. "I don't know, Rita."

"All right. We'll forget about Hatfield informing on Melissa and Maria. For now. But you'll admit that he's most likely the one who informed on Cathryn."

"Yeah," I said. "He looks good for that. But why would he do it?"

"Who knows? Money, possibly. We don't need motive, Joshua. We're not a court of law. Let's suppose it went something like this—Hatfield receives a postcard from Melissa sometime toward the end of September. Then Cathryn calls him and tells him that she's heard from Melissa. Hatfield notifies someone in El Salvador, and they send up the two men you saw yesterday."

She sipped at her tea. "Let's suppose that someone in the American government learns about this. Learns that Melissa has been located somewhere near Santa Fe, and that the Salvadoran government is sending up an assassination team. There are Americans all over El Salvador. Military advisers. Intelligence agents. Maybe someone in the Salvadoran government leaked the plan to one of them."

"But if someone in the American government wanted Melissa removed, why didn't he just let the Salvadorans do it for him?"

"As I say, maybe they wanted only to contain her. Neutralize her somehow. Maybe they decided to find her before the Salvadorans tried to kill her. What if the Salvadorans botched the job? Then the American government would have not only the embarrassment of Melissa, but the further embarrassment of a foreign assassin attempting to kill an American citizen on American soil."

"So they, whoever they are, send Stamworth to L.A. And he gets there before the Salvadorans do, and he starts asking his questions."

"And then Cathryn is killed, and the police find the New Mexico postcard and Stamworth comes out here."

"You're always telling me that I'm too easily inclined toward speculation, Rita. Isn't it pure speculation, all of this?"

"We're trying to construct a scenario that accepts all the facts as we know them. And this scenario, as you like to put it"—she smiled—"it fits."

"Maybe. One thing's been bothering me. Why didn't the Salvadorans take the postcard from Cathryn's house, after they killed her? It was a lead to where Melissa might be."

"From Hatfield's point of view, and probably from the Salvadorans', the postcard wasn't important. If I'm right, Hatfield knew that there were at least two postcards, the one he'd received and the one Cathryn had received. He had no idea how many others Melissa had sent. There could've been twenty or thirty of them."

"Why didn't the Salvadorans go to Melissa's mother? She got a postcard from Melissa."

"But neither Hatfield nor the Salvadorans could know that. And Hatfield couldn't contact her without drawing attention to himself. Neither could the Salvadorans. Melissa's mother lives a relatively public life. And she has servants. Cathryn lived alone."

I sat back. "Okay," I said. "It fits. So what do we do about it?"

Rita had an idea.

TWENTY-SEVEN

"MR. HATFIELD?"

"Yes."

"This is Joshua Croft."

"Sorry?"

"Joshua Croft. From Santa Fe. I've been trying to locate Melissa Alonzo?" I looked down at Leroy's little black box, beside the telephone. The green light was off. The line was tapped. But I'd already known that—I'd arranged for it myself.

"Yes, yes," said Hatfield. "Of course. Croft. Good to hear from you. How are you?"

"Fine. I apologize for bothering you on a weekend."

"Not at all, not at all. No rest for the wicked, eh? Back in New Mexico, are you? Had any luck with your quest?"

"Yeah, as a matter of fact, I have. I've heard from Melissa."

"Good Lord. Have you indeed? Is she all right?"

"She seems to be."

"Thank heavens for that." Hatfield was good. There was nothing in his voice but relief and pleasure.

But maybe that was all he felt. Maybe Rita and I were wrong.

"Where is she?" Hatfield asked me.

"She wouldn't say. She's nearby, here in Santa Fe, but she's being cautious. That's why I'm calling you. She won't meet with me unless I can prove I'm who I say I am. I need something from you, a piece of information, anything. Something I can give to Melissa to show her that I've been in contact with you, and that you're working with me on this. She trusts you. She'll be calling me back at two thirty."

There was a pause. Then: "Well, you know, old man, no offense, but I'm not entirely sure you should do that. After all, I've only your word myself that you *are* who you say you are."

He was good. Or Rita and I were wrong.

"Mr. Hatfield," I said, "I can provide you with the name of a lawyer here in Santa Fe who'll verify what I told you in Los Angeles. I can also provide you the name of a high-ranking Santa Fe law enforcement official.''

"Well, look," he said. "Why don't we just do this. Why don't you tell Melissa to give me a jingle? That way, she and I can chat for a bit, I can get the lay of the land."

"I suggested that. She wants to do it this way. I don't know why."

"Hmmm. Puts me in a bit of a spot, doesn't it." He was silent for a moment. "All right. You're on, Croft. Got to think of Melissa, don't we. Let's see . . . Hmmm . . . Got it. Perfect thing. Tell her about Jorge Mirandez. Tell her that Jorge Mirandez's second wife, Sophia, says hello."

"She'll know what that means?"

He chuckled. "Oh yes. Mexican chap. Brought his wife and kids over, applied for a residence visa. Week later, his other wife shows up, with another set of kids. Turns out he was a bigamist. Both wives knew about each other. Took turns watching the children. Extraordinary. Melissa handled the paperwork. She and I had a laugh or two. She'll know what it means."

"Fine. That's exactly what I need. I'm very grateful, Mr. Hatfield."

"Not at all. Glad to help. Wonderful news. Give Melissa my love, would you? Have her get in touch when she can."

"I'll do that. Thanks again."

"Nothing. Bye now."

"Goodbye."

I hung up and turned to Hector Ramirez. "He bought it."

Sitting across the room at the end of my sofa, Hector nodded. "A high-ranking law enforcement official? Who would that be, exactly?"

"You got promoted. When do the L.A. cops call you?"

He shrugged his heavy shoulders. He was in shirtsleeves again, a pale yellow shirt with thin gray pinstripes that matched his gray silk tie. "Soon as he makes a move," he said.

"I hope the bastard doesn't call from a pay phone."

"He may not call them at all."

"Right. Look on the bright side."

"All we can do is wait, Josh."

"Yeah. I know, Hector."

I glanced at my watch. Ten minutes after one.

It was Sunday. Yesterday afternoon, Rita had persuaded Hector to arrange all this. He'd spent most of the evening trying to persuade Sergeant Bradley, in Los Angeles, to go along. Bradley had been reluctant; there was no real evidence linking Hatfield to Cathryn Bigelow's death. But finally he'd agreed to look for a judge willing to sign a court order authorizing a one-day tap on Hatfield's phone. He'd found one this morning.

Outside, the sun was shining. The air was warm. Most of the snow had melted, but water still dripped from the Russian olive by the window.

"Cards?" Hector suggested.

"Yeah. Sure."

I got up from the leather chair, walked across to the bookcase, lifted the small wooden turntable that held the cards and the chips, carried it over to the coffee table, set it there. Hector slid out a deck, began shuffling the cards as I maneuvered the leather chair to the table.

He said, "The whites are fifties, the blues hundreds, and the reds five hundreds."

"And you're going to make good on your bets."

"Got to," he said. He smiled. "I'm a cop."

The telephone rang.

I crossed the room, lifted the receiver. "Hello?"

"Sergeant Ramirez." A gruff voice I didn't recognize.

I brought the phone over to Hector, handed it to him, sat down in the chair.

"Ramirez," he said into the speaker. He listened for a moment, then said, "Right . . . Right. Let me know."

He hung up the receiver, set the phone on the end table, beside the two radio transceivers. "Hatfield just left his house. Driving. He didn't make any calls."

I frowned. "Terrific."

Hector shrugged. "Someone's on him now. We'll see where he goes."

"If he uses a pay phone, we won't be able to nail him on this."

"We'll nail him," Hector said. He spoke with the same certainty I'd heard in my own voice when I told people that I would find Melissa Alonzo. So far I hadn't found her.

He slapped the deck to the table. "Cut."

We played five-card stud. After ten minutes, Hector was into me for three hundred and fifty dollars.

The phone rang. Hector handed it to me. I lifted the receiver. "Hello."

"Ramirez." The same voice.

I gave the phone to Hector. Once again, he listened. "Okay," he said. "Thanks. Forget this phone number. Anything happens at that end, call it to the other number. They'll patch it through to me. And tell Sergeant Bradford I said thanks. Tell him I'll get back to him."

He hung up the phone, returned it to the end table, looked at me. "He used a phone at a 7 Eleven."

"So we're on," I said.

He nodded. He picked up one of the transceivers, fiddled with some buttons, held it to his mouth. "Diego?" he said. "You out there?"

A rattle of static, and then a thin voice came rasping from the transceiver's speaker: "Yo, Sarge."

"It's a go," Hector said. "You set?"

"Sure," came the gravelly voice. "Hey, Sarge. How come we don't get to be like Alpha One and Charlie Two and like that? That's the way Schwarzenegger would of done it."

"Diego?"

"I know. Cut the shit."

"Yeah."

"You got no sense of humor, Sarge."

"Keep your eyes open."

"You got it."

Hector fiddled with the buttons again. "Monahan?"

More static, then: "Got you, Sarge."

"You heard?"

"Yeah. We're ready."

"Okay."

"Hernandez," Hector said.

"Yeah." The voice of the state police officer sounded bored and flat.

"You people ready?"

"Yeah. This better work."

"I'll let you know when Croft leaves."

"I can hardly wait."

Hector punched some buttons, put the transceiver on the end table.

HALF AN HOUR LATER, Hector was into me for $4300. He was showing a six of clubs and a three of hearts. I was showing a pair of tens and my hole card was the ace of hearts. "Pair of tens bets fifty," I said, tossing a chip into the kitty.

"See that," Hector said, and tossed in a chip.

"Hector," I said. "You're already beat on the board."

"And up fifty," he said, tossing in another chip.

"Maybe you'd be interested in this bridge I've been trying to sell."

"Deal the cards."

I dealt. Ace of spades for Hector, three of spades for me. I tossed in two chips. "A hundred," I said.

Hector picked up a red chip, tossed it into the kitty. "And up four."

I took four blue chips, tossed them onto the pile. "Does your heart do a little leap when you get a letter from Ed McMahon?"

"Deal."

Hector's last card was the ace of hearts. He grinned. My last card was the four of diamonds.

"Pair of aces bets a grand," he said, tossing in two red chips.

"It's yours," I told him.

Hector scooped the chips toward him. "The Lord takes care of his own."

"You and the Lord owe me four grand."

He gathered the cards, began shuffling the deck. "Prepare to taste the agony of defeat."

The transceiver suddenly crackled. "Sarge?"

Holding the deck of cards in his left hand, Hector picked up the transceiver with his right. "Go ahead, Diego."

"What we got here is a Chevy Blazer, a new one, gray. Looks like two males inside, but the windows are tinted. Came up the street past the van, turned around, drove back. They're parked about fifty yards down from the house."

"You run the plates?"

"I just called them in. They're not rentals."

"The men get out of the car, come toward the house, you let me know."

"Right."

"Okay, Diego. Thanks."

He put down the transceiver, set the cards in the center of the coffee table. "Cut," he said.

Three minutes later, the transceiver crackled again. "Sarge. This is Alpha One."

Hector picked up the transceiver. "Stop fucking around, Diego."

"Just got the word on those plates. They don't belong on the Blazer. They belong to an eighty-nine Oldsmobile registered to a Timothy Griegos. You want I should inform these guys someone made a mistake and put the wrong plates on their car?"

"They're still inside the Blazer?"

"Yeah."

"Hang loose. Monahan?"

"Yeah, Sarge."

"Another fifteen, twenty minutes."

"Okay."

Hector put aside the transceiver. He looked down at the cards. "Your bet."

I was showing ace high. My jack of hearts was paired to the jack of clubs in the hole. I tossed in a chip. "Fifty," I said.

Hector threw in two chips. "And up fifty."

"It's a privilege watching you work."

Fifteen minutes later, when Hector was into me for another two thousand dollars, he looked at his watch. He tossed his cards to the table. "Showtime," he said.

"Let me call Rita."

He nodded.

I picked up the phone, dialed her number.

She answered on the first ring. "Hello."

"Hi. My performance is about to begin."

"Don't do anything stupid."

"Do I ever?"

"And call me afterward. I found out something you should know."

"What?"

"Later. Call me. Hello to Hector."

"Bye."

"Be careful, Joshua."

"Yes dear."

She hung up.

I put down the phone, stood up, walked around the coffee table, lifted the sheepskin jacket from the sofa. "Rita says hello," I told Hector.

He nodded, picked up one of the transceivers, held it out to me. I took it, slipped it into the jacket's right-hand pocket.

"No improvising," he said. "Stick to the script."

"Right."

He lifted the other transceiver, spoke into it. "Diego?"

"Yo."

"He's leaving now."

"Gotcha."

"Monahan?"

"With you, Sarge."

"Hernandez?"

"We're ready."

He looked at me. "Okay."

I said, "You owe me six thousand dollars."

"We'll cut for it. Double or nothing." He scooped up the cards, shuffled them, put the deck on the table. He cut, showed me a ten of clubs, put the deck back together. I leaned over, cut the deck. Seven of spades.

Hector smiled. "Not your lucky day."

THE TWO MEN in the Blazer made no effort to hide. But they didn't pay any attention to me, either, as I drove past them. They simply sat there, chatting calmly. I didn't turn to look.

Beside me on the seat, the transceiver crackled. Diego's voice: "And they're off."

Hector's voice: "Monahan?"

Monahan: "I got 'em."

At Acequia Madre I stopped and glanced in the rearview mirror. The Blazer was about seventy yards back, and moving closer.

I signaled a left turn, and then made it.

Monahan: "They're stopping at the sign, signaling a left."

Hector: "Diego, come and get me."

Diego: "On my way."

Monahan: "They're turning left onto Acequia."

In the mirror, I saw the nose of the Blazer edge out onto the road.

I drove.

Monahan: "Proceeding down Acequia. Got 'em in sight."

Hector: "Don't get too close."

Monahan: "Piece of cake, Sarge."

At Paseo de Peralta I turned right.

Monahan: "Approaching Paseo. They're turning right."

I had them in the mirror. I followed Paseo around town, and the Blazer stayed sixty or seventy yards behind.

Monahan: "Proceeding down Paseo."

At Washington, I caught the red light. I signaled a right turn. The Blazer was three cars back, behind a Ford wagon and a Mercedes sedan.

Monahan: "Stopped at the light on Washington. They're two cars ahead."

I made my turn.

Monahan: "Okay. They're still behind Croft. Turning right onto Washington."

I signaled the turn for the Ski Basin Road. A few moments later, Monahan said, "They're heading up toward the basin."

Hector: "I've got you in sight, Monahan."

I drove east, climbing the mountainside. Rita's house was off to the right, invisible from the road among the trees, but I knew that if she were out on the patio, she could've been watching our little parade in comfort.

There was very little traffic coming from the other direction. Tourist season was over and the ski season wouldn't begin until after Thanksgiving.

Hector's voice came from the transceiver. "Okay, Monahan, fall back. We'll take it in the van."

I passed Ten Thousand Waves, a Japanese bathhouse that offered hot tubs and massages, and that was pretty much the last sign of civilization for a while. No homes, no commercial buildings. Just the forest and me and the two men in the the Chevy Blazer. And, behind them, Hector and Diego in the unmarked blue van. And, behind them, Monahan and his partner.

Hector: "Hernandez."

Hernandez: "Yeah."

Hector: "We're about three miles from your position."

"I hear you."

Hector: "Josh, as soon as you stop the car, you jump out and you get down and stay down."

The air was colder up here, and snow still covered the ground between the pine trees. I passed the Evergreen Restaurant, perched up on the hillside among the ponderosas. Only two cars were parked in the lot.

Hector: "Hernandez."

"Yeah."

"Less than a mile."

"We're ready."

The road became more winding, twisting back on itself through the forest. The mountain dropped off to my left, giving me a view of snowy, pine-studded hills rolling off into the distance. I passed a stand of aspens, their leaves faded to a dull brown now, their knobby white trunks skeletal against the snow, bones on a bedsheet. Then I made a turn and the state police cruiser was parked directly across the road, fifty yards away. I pulled up beside it, braked, jumped from the Jeep.

Hernandez and Green were behind the cruiser, both holding guns, and Hernandez was waving at me. *"C'mon, c'mon!"*

I ran around the car and looked back.

The Blazer had just made the turn and the driver was braking. Suddenly, behind him, the blue van appeared. Diego swung it around to block the road and then Hector was out of the door and standing in a crouch, gun upraised. *"Police!"* I heard him shout. *"Out of the car!"* Diego came around the van, gun in hand, just as another unmarked car—Monahan's—pulled up behind it, lurching to a stop. Two men jumped out, both armed.

The driver of the Blazer didn't hesitate. He slammed into reverse, spun around, and aimed the big car directly at Hector.

Hector fired, one burst of two rounds, and then another. The Blazer kept coming. Then all four cops were firing, the sound of their gunshots rattling the still air, and suddenly the Blazer careened off to the right and left the road and sailed for a moment through the air before it crashed back down and then spun over on its side, once, twice, and then smashed broadside into a pair of ponderosa pines. The trees snapped like Popsicle sticks, their green branches collapsing over the Blazer as though enfolding it in an embrace.

TWENTY-EIGHT

"HI, RITA. IT'S ME. It's all over."

"You're all right?"

"I'm fine."

"Where are you?"

"At the Evergreen."

"The Salvadorans?"

"They tried to run. One of them's dead. The other's pretty busted up, but it looks like he'll live. The ambulance is on its way."

"Is Hector all right?"

"He's fine. Everybody's fine. The bad guys are the only ones who got hurt."

I heard her let out her breath. "Good."

"What was it you wanted to tell me?"

"Sam Davenport."

"Who?"

"Sam Davenport. The leader of the commune up in Palo Verde."

"What about him?"

"He has an interesting past. Do you know where he was, about twenty-five years ago?"

"Is this something hot off the computer?"

"Yes."

"All right. Where was he?"

She told me. We discussed it for a bit.

I said, "It's not proof of anything."

"No," she said. "But it's suggestive."

"Yeah, it's suggestive, all right. I think I'm going to go talk to the Coopers."

"Why the Coopers?"

"It could be that I've been showing people the wrong photograph."

"Would you like to explain that?"

I did.

"A PHOTOGRAPH of Winona?" Larry Cooper asked me.

"Yeah," I said. "The only picture I've seen of her was taken when she was a baby. I have no idea what she looks like now, and I'm looking for her just as much as I'm looking for Melissa. I thought that maybe you might have a photograph."

He looked at his wife. The two of them sat opposite me, on their sofa. He looked back at me. "I'm sorry, but I don't take the kind of photographs you're talking about. Candid stuff. Family stuff."

"But I do," Sarah said. "And I think I do have a picture of Winona. I know I do." She stood up. "I'll go get it." She crossed the room, passed through the door that led to the rest of the house.

Larry Cooper asked me, "Are you any closer to finding Melissa?"

"I don't know. Maybe."

"This is such an awful mess. I wish there was something more we could do."

I wished the same for myself.

Sarah returned to the living room, crossed the room. She handed me a color print, and then pointed to one of the two small figures it showed. "That's Julia, our daughter. And that's Winona."

Both girls stood facing the camera, spectacularly grinning in the sunshine. They were standing outside the house, in front of the woodpile. Julia was slightly shorter than Winona and wore her black hair in braids. Winona was blond, like her mother. Clutched under her arm was a large stuffed panda.

I had seen her, and the panda, two days before. With her hair cropped short, and wearing a pair of boy's pants instead of the pink dress she wore in the picture, she had been one of the two children I'd seen standing outside the commune's barn in Palo Verde.

I asked the Coopers if I could use their phone. Sarah told me that if it was a private call, I could use the extension in their bedroom.

"JOSHUA," Rita said, "I don't think you should go up there on your own."

"It's out of Hector's jurisdiction, Rita. He can't do anything."

"What about the state police?"

"What can I bring to the state police? A photograph? And if they were willing to go in there, they'd probably have to notify the sheriff's department. According to Sam, he and the sheriff ge along real well. Someone might warn him. If Melissa's there with Winona, they could both take off before I get to them.''

"If Melissa's there, why hasn't she contacted you? Why has she abandoned the Underground Railroad?"

"Maybe she's frightened. Maybe she spotted the Salvadorans and decided to stay hidden. I don't know. Listen. It's four o'clock now. By the time I get up there, it'll be dark. I'll take a look around. I'll be careful. But maybe I can find out what's going on."

"I don't like it," she said.

"I'll call you when I reach Palo Verde."

"Call me *before* you go in."

"Right."

"Do you have your gun?"

''Yeah. It's in the car.'

"Good."

BY QUARTER TO SIX I was back in Palo Verde. I called Rita from the pay phone at the deserted general store, told her I was going in. She told me to call back in an hour.

I kept the headlights on until the track swooped down out of the hills into the broad moonlit valley. After I turned them off, there was enough light reflecting off the snow for me to make out the ruts of the cars that had passed here before mine.

About seventy-five yards from the cluster of buildings, a dark stand of pines stood to the right of the road. I drove off the track, turned the car around, backed into the trees. Thinking that later I might want—or need—to leave in a hurry, I turned off the engine but left the key in the ignition. I opened the glove compartment, took out the revolver, slipped it into my jacket pocket. I opened the door as quietly as I could and stepped out into the snow.

There were lights burning in three of the buildings—in the main house and in two of the dormitories, including the dorm where, according to Sam, the children slept.

A direct approach would take me across an open field. I might be seen by anyone glancing out a window or stepping outside for a breath of fresh air. Crouching low, I scurried off to the right, toward the base of the hill and the black shadows of the tall pines. I felt extremely exposed as I scooted across the snow, but no one called out, no one took a shot at me.

I was wearing a pair of Justin muleskins—nice boots, but they weren't insulated and they weren't designed for scuttling through the drifts. A cold dampness began to reach my feet.

When I hit the trees, I slid between them, the boots slipping in the snow as I clambered up the slope. When I was ten yards into cover, I began to move along the flank of the hillside, toward the rear of the barn and the house. The inclined ground was rocky beneath the snow, and pitted with hidden holes. Twice my foot went plunging into drifts that climbed up to my thighs.

Behind the house, still among the trees, I could see through the back door into the illuminated kitchen. Four people sat at the table. I recognized three of them as workmen I'd seen coming from the meditation hall on Friday. No Sam. No Bilbo. No Freddy.

When I was behind the children's dormitory, I left the trees. Snow crunching loudly beneath me, I approached the building. A light was on beyond a long narrow window at eye level. Cautiously, I peered in.

Children sat on cushions on the floor, listening, as Freddy, who sat in an antique wooden rocker, read to them from a thin cardboard-bound book opened on her lap. Metal bunk beds, three of them, ran along the far wall. All the children were girls, ranging in age from three or four to ten or eleven, and all of them wore cotton pyjamas. One of them was Winona. She sat somewhat apart from the others, the stuffed panda resting on her crossed legs.

I could see why, two days earlier, I hadn't realized that there was a girl beneath her boy's clothes. Without being at all unfeminine, her face owed something to her father's—her features were stronger than Melissa's, her jaw proportionally wider, her chin firmer. She would be a striking woman one day.

I backed away from the window and spent a few moments deciding how to handle this. I could keep skulking around, see if I could locate Melissa. I could wait until Freddy left, then wait some more to see if somehow I could isolate Winona.

But maybe Freddy wouldn't leave. Maybe she slept out here with the children.

And my feet were cold.

Might as well get this over with.

I circled the dorm. The building had two entrances, one at the far side that presumably led into the boys' section, and the one beside which I stood now. I slipped my hand into my pocket, wrapped my gloved fingers around the reassuring shape of the Smith & Wesson. I figured that with the revolver I was an even match for a single mother and six preadolescent girls. Keeping the gun in my pocket, I reached out my left hand and turned the doorknob. I pushed open the door and stepped into the room.

For a moment there was absolute silence.

Then a girl screamed.

It wasn't a terrified scream—it was more the sort of wild theatrical scream young girls make when young boys invade the pyjama party.

But it set some of the others to squealing and giggling.

"Quiet," Freddy snapped. Calmly, she closed the book on her lap and then said to me, "What on earth are you doing here?"

I said, "You weren't entirely truthful with me, Freddy. I'm disappointed."

A girl tittered. Another girl slapped her lightly.

"You're trespassing on private property," Freddy said. She ran her hand back through her untamed gray hair. She was wearing the same kind of bulky clothing she had worn two days before: a long dress, a man's shapeless brown sweater.

"Winona," I said. "Where's your mother?"

The young girl had clutched the panda to her chest, her hands pressed tight against its black and white fur. She looked from me to Freddy, then back to me.

Freddy said to the girl, "Mary, you don't—"

Winona said to me, "She got sick."

I don't remember any more. It's possible that Bilbo said something before he clubbed me, possible that he warned me, or threatened me, but I doubt it.

I WAS LYING ON MY SIDE and I couldn't figure out what was wrong with my hands. My wrists hurt, but I couldn't bring them around in front of me to see what the problem was. The air held the strong ammoniac smell of goats, and it was cold.

I opened my eyes. In the wavering yellow lantern light, I could see across the dirt floor of the barn, strewn with straw and spotted with goat droppings, to where Bilbo and Sam sat on some bales of hay.

My head felt as though someone had kicked it down a stairway. I took a breath and, abruptly, I was nauseated. I vomited, and then, coughing, hacking, I rolled away from the mess I'd made. I tried to sit up, and my wrists screeched at me. They were tied together. I felt around with my fingers. Tied not with rope but with wire.

Sam looked at me over his shoulder, his gray ponytail swaying along his red mackinaw. He stood up from the bale of hay and crossed the dirt flooring and looked down at me. He shook his head sadly. "Jesus, man, what'd you have to come back here for?"

Bilbo still sat on the hay, eyeing me silently.

"Could you help me sit up," I said to Sam.

He squatted down, eased my shoulder up, gently eased me back against another bale of hay. Leaning on it seemed to tighten the wire at my wrists, but it was better than lying in the dirt.

Sam stood up, put his hands in his pockets.

"This isn't good, Sam," I told him. "People know where I am."

"What the fuck you have to come back here for?" The barn door was wide open, letting in the cold black night, and Sam's breath made a cloud of white vapor before his face.

"For Winona," I said. "And Melissa. Where's Melissa, Sam?"

He said nothing.

"Is she dead, Sam?"

He said nothing.

"We should off him," Bilbo said.

"Shut up," Sam told him. "We'll wait."

Bilbo shrugged. "You know what the man's gonna say."

I said, "Bilbo the one who hit me?"

Sam nodded.

"What did he use?"

"Gun." He smiled, and the smile seemed almost embarrassed. "He doesn't like you very much, I guess."

"That's a shame. I've gotten real fond of him."

Bilbo seemed indifferent to this.

I asked Sam, "How long was I out?"

Sam took a brass railroad watch from his front coverall pocket. "Almost three hours."

"Three hours? From a hit on the head?"

"Freddy gave you a shot."

"A shot of what?"

He shrugged. "Some downer. She said it was safe."

"She's a real Mother Teresa, that Freddy."

He shrugged again. "She knows about drugs."

I nodded. "You know, Sam, you're too smart a guy to be in this position. My partner knows I was coming out here. I was supposed to call her a couple of hours ago. By now she's notified the police."

Sam looked around. "Don't see any police."

But I could hear a car coming and so, now, could Sam: the thin whine of an engine came drifting through the barn door. He turned to Bilbo. "It's probably him. Go check."

Bilbo got up from his bale of hay, slipped his hands into his pockets, and sauntered to the doorway. Without a glance back, he disappeared out into the night.

"Sam," I said. "It's over. In a little while this place'll be crawling with cops."

He shook his head. "Anything like that about to go down, I'd get a call from the sheriff. Got a CB in the house."

I heard a car door slam outside.

I said, "Did he kill her, Sam? Is that what this is all about?"

Sam said, "You never should've come back here, man." He shook his head again. "That was a bad mistake."

Bilbo walked through the barn door, followed by Roy Alonzo.

Alonzo wore a full-length black topcoat, a white scarf draped outside the upraised collar. Gestapo night at the opera. Hands in his pockets, he walked up to me and said, "You are one world-class putz, Croft."

I said nothing.

Without looking away from me, Alonzo said to Sam, "He have a gun?"

"Bilbo's got it."

Not taking his glance off me, he held his hand out from his side and said, "Bilbo?" Bilbo came up behind him and put my revolver in his hand. It was a nice piece of stage business. I think I saw it once on an episode of "The Man from UNCLE."

He grinned down at the pistol. "A Smith and Wesson. Good gun."

I said, "I'll tell you the same thing I told Sam. My partner knows I'm here. By now she's called the police."

He grinned at me, the same dauntless, devil-may-care grin that Rick Valdez had always grinned in the face of adversity. Flawless teeth, dimples in his cheeks. "This'll all be over in a few minutes."

He unbuttoned his coat, squatted down on his haunches so that we were at eye level. He grinned again, tapped the barrel of the pistol lightly against the ankle of his black leather boot. "You know, usually I'm the one in your position. Trussed up, surrounded by enemies. All hope gone, and only a minute or two left until the pizza commercial. I have to admit, in real life I prefer being on this side of the gun."

"You won't be able to enjoy it for long."

Another grin. "Longer than you." He tapped the pistol against his boot. "Why'd you come back here?"

"I found out that you and Sam were old buddies. Went to college together out in Oregon. Even acted together. A mime troupe."

He smiled. "One of my first gigs." He looked up at Sam. "Good times, eh, Sam?"

"Of all the places that Melissa could've come to," I said, "this was probably the worst. Sam knew you. All he had to do was let you know that Melissa and Winona had shown up here." I turned to Sam. "What was it, Sam? Money? You needed cash for your nifty new meditation hall?"

Sam said nothing. I turned back to Alonzo. He was still grinning, still enjoying the denouement of the piece. "And so you came out here," I told him. "And you killed her."

His smile vanished. "It was an accident. She got hysterical. I was just trying to calm her down."

I let out my breath. I hadn't realized that I'd been holding it.

The long-haired woman squinting into the New Mexico sun. The friend to Deirdre Polk and Juanita Carrera. Mother to Winona. Dead.

I said, "And I'll be another accident."

"No." He grinned. "You'll be a pleasure. Wiseass prick."

"The cops'll figure it out."

"I'll be gone. Winona and I. I've got money hidden, we'll go to Europe. Brazil. Someplace where we can start living our lives again. I'll take care of her."

"Right. Take care of her. You're destroying her."

His face hardened. "You scumbag. You don't know what you're talking about. I love her, and she loves me. What Winona and I have is something special, something that a sleazeball like you could never understand."

"You're right about that."

He stood up, held out the gun, grinned at me. "Say good night, Gracie."

Sam said, "Roy, wait a minute, man. What about the cops?"

Without looking at him, Alonzo said, "He's full of shit. There aren't any cops. He never called anyone."

From the doorway, Rita said, "Drop the gun."

Alonzo didn't, and she shot him.

TWENTY-NINE

ON THE NEXT DAY, Monday, two visitors came to the office. The first of them arrived in the morning, at eleven thirty. I was on the phone with Hector when the man opened the door and walked in.

"I'll call you back, Hector." I hung up the phone.

Beneath a neatly pressed tan trench coat, Jim Stamworth was wearing another beautifully tailored suit, this one made of cashmere. He showed me his polite smile. "May I sit down?"

"It's a free country."

He smiled again and sat in one of the clients' chairs, lightly tugging up the creases of his slacks. He folded his hands together on his lap. His fingers were still nicely manicured. "So you found Melissa Alonzo."

"I found her body."

They had buried her there, at the commune. The state police, sent there by Hector, had arrived shortly after Rita did, and it didn't take them long to persuade Sam to tell them everything he knew.

Stamworth said, "You've been a busy man, Mr. Croft."

"Yeah."

"You were also instrumental in the capture of two Salvadoran assassins, I hear."

"The capture of one. The death of the other."

"The Los Angeles police have arrested Charles Hatfield. You apparently had something to do with that as well."

"Idle hands are the devil's workshop."

The second Salvadoran had implicated Hatfield, whose motive, as Rita suggested, had been money. Questioned by the L.A. cops, Hatfield had folded almost immediately.

He said, "I understand that Mrs. Mondragón shot Roy Alonzo."

I nodded. "Mrs. Mondragón is pretty good with a handgun. Alonzo won't be using that arm for a while."

"He's claiming, I understand, that he killed his ex-wife by accident."

"That won't sell. He'll spend a long time in the prison system. And he should be very popular there. The residents have a real fondness for child molesters."

Stamworth shook his head. "It's been a terrible thing, hasn't it?" he said. "A tragedy."

"But fairly convenient for you, I'd say."

He raised an eyebrow. His left. "How so?"

"Now Melissa Alonzo won't be able to tell anyone about what she saw in El Salvador."

"And what was that?"

"She saw a squad of soldiers from the Atlactl Battalion rape a woman. She saw them drive the woman and a priest off to be executed. The government of the United States is still claiming that El Salvador's a constitutional democracy. It was members of the Atlactl Battalion, American trained, who killed those five priests down there a few years ago. Another couple of killings by the same troop of Boy Scouts might be an embarrassment right now."

He shrugged. "What makes you think that I have any interest in El Salvador?"

"Let me tell you what I think. I think some spook down in Salvador found out that the Salvadorans were sending a couple of goons up here to kill Melissa Alonzo. I think some other spook sent you out to find her before they did. I'm not sure why. But whatever the reasons were, I don't think you had Melissa's best interests at heart. You were working undercover. You lied to the L.A. cops. You lied to me. I think you wanted to find her and tuck her away somewhere. Neutralize her before she told her story."

He smiled. "Even if what you say were true, I might simply have been trying to locate her in order to protect her. I might've been able to guarantee her safety, and the safety of the child."

"Maybe. If she kept her mouth shut about what happened down there."

He shrugged again. "As you say, it's all academic now."

"I didn't say that." I opened the drawer, took out the sheets of copy paper. I tossed them across the desk.

He leaned forward, picked them up, sat back, started to read. He glanced over at me once, expressionless, then continued his reading. I waited. He read them through, all eight of them. When he was finished, he tapped them against his thigh, to straighten them, then leaned forward and set them carefully on the desk. He sat back. "Where are the originals?" he asked.

"I have them."

"How did you find them?"

"Melissa wrote them in a diary, a small red book about four inches by six. Maybe an inch thick. Before she went to the commune in Palo Verde, she hid it inside her daughter's stuffed toy panda. Winona gave it to me last night, after we came to Santa Fe."

"Who's seen them?"

"I have."

He smiled politely. "You're out of your element here, Croft. You might possibly find yourself in serious trouble."

"Possibly."

He nodded. "What do you want?"

"Juanita Carrera."

"What about her?"

"I'm assuming that she's your reason for coming here now. She's a loose end. We can't have that, now can we?"

"Spare me the sarcasm. What do you want?"

"I want her protected. She calls me once a month to tell me she's all right, and I keep those buried. Something happens to her, *any-thing* happens to her, I give them to a reporter I know and then the whole world finds out what Melissa saw down in El Salvador, all of it nicely drafted in her own handwriting. Something happens to me, the reporter gets them anyway."

He gave me another polite smile. "And what if something happens to Carrera accidentally? Or happens to you?"

I gave him my own smile. I suppose it wasn't particularly polite. "I'll try real hard to be careful. I'll recommend to Juanita that she do the same."

He nodded. "There's a possibility that something might be arranged."

"Let me know."

He nodded again, then stood. He brushed nonexistent wrinkles from his trousers. He smiled politely one more time and said, "Perhaps we'll meet again."

"Perhaps."

I DIDN'T GO OUT for lunch. I wasn't hungry. I put the copy of Melissa's account back in the drawer and I sat back in the office chair, my feet on the windowsill, and I stared up at the white mountains and I thought about Melissa Alonzo and her daughter.

I was still sitting there at one thirty, when Melissa's father, Calvin Bigelow, arrived at the office. I'd been expecting him, now that Melissa was no longer around to protect Winona, but I hadn't expected him so soon.

He wore a black doublebreasted suit, a long black wool topcoat. He was either in mourning or he was about to negotiate a merger. The black made his hair seem whiter and his face seem more red than I remembered.

"I just spoke to the people who have my granddaughter," he announced. "The Cooper people. They insisted I talk to you."

"Have a seat," I told him.

He sat down stiffly, his back upright, his arms along the arm of the chair. "This is outrageous," he said. "Winona's my flesh and blood. Those people have no right to keep her from me. After everything she's been through, she needs the protection of her family. I don't know what you think you're up to, Croft, but I can tell you I've already notified my lawyer."

I opened the drawer that held the copies taken from Melissa's book. Below the sheaf of papers I'd showed Stamworth were four more sheets. I slipped them out, leaned forward, laid them on the desk in front of Bigelow. "Read that," I said.

He looked at the papers, looked at me, reached out and took them from the desk.

He read a few paragraphs. He frowned. Suddenly he looked up at me. "This is libelous! This is *vile!* How dare you!" His mouth moved some more, but no sounds came out.

"Mr. Bigelow," I said.

He stood, his face a brighter shade of red now, the papers trembling in his hand. "You cheap, penny-ante...you no-account, low-life swine...!" He was sputtering, spraying bits of spittle.

"Mr. Bigelow," I said. "Sit down."

He gasped, and then, his mouth still opening and closing, he sat back in the chair and put his left hand to his chest. The hand was twitching. Maybe he was about to keel over dead in my office.

Good. It would save me from having to make another deal with another devil.

"Mr. Bigelow," I said, "what you've got there is an account, written in your daughter Melissa's handwriting, of how you systematically abused her sexually from the time she was nine years old until the time she was thirteen. If you read through it, you'll see that it's a very graphic account. She gives details. She also talks about your abusing her sister, Cathryn. Those are copies. I have the originals. Now here's what you're going to do. You're going to book yourself a flight out of New Mexico, and you're going to go back to Los Angeles. Today. In a few weeks, when the adoption papers come through from the Coopers, you're going to sign them. If you don't do any of these things, I'm going to send copies of those to every newspaper in Los Angeles, starting with the *Times*."

He had shut his mouth. Now he opened it: "She was...Melissa was hysterical when she wrote this ... It's all a ... figment of her imagination."

"That's not true. And that's not what people are going to think. That's not what they'll say."

"My lawyer . . ." His voice tapered away. He stared off, perhaps into the future. Perhaps he was hearing what people were going to say.

"Mr. Bigelow," I said, "do you know who Norman Montoya is? He's Roy Alonzo's uncle, Winona's great-uncle. He's concerned about Winona. He's the one, after Cathryn died, who persuaded Roy Alonzo to hire me. Roy went along with the idea to humor him—Roy already knew where Melissa was. Now you're a pretty powerful man out in California. But Norman Montoya has a different kind of power, and he's perfectly willing to use it. If you don't do what I'm telling you to do, he's prepared to take action on his own. He doesn't like you. He's got this idea that if you hadn't violated Melissa, none of this would've happened. I don't know that he's right. Maybe not. Maybe Melissa would've still gone off to El Salvador. But I think that if you'd never touched her, she'd never have married someone like Roy Alonzo. So you give that some thought on your way back to Los Angeles."

He looked at me. "I . . ."

"Goodbye, Mr. Bieglow." I wanted him out of the office. I didn't want to feel sorry for the man, and I was beginning to.

He stood up. The papers slipped, unnoticed, to the floor. He turned and walked away, his broad shoulders stooped.

"Do you think Stamworth will do a deal?" Rita asked.

"Yeah," I said. "Probably. It's in the interest of 'national security.'"

She was sitting back against the arm of a small couch, staring out the window, her arms crossed. It was night and the room was dark. Moonlight spilled through the window and splashed against her black hair, her black gown.

"And Bigelow?" she said.

"Him for certain. He doesn't want anyone to know who he is. What he is."

"Poor Melissa," she said, still staring out the window. She breathed in deeply and the pale white light slid along the black silk of the gown. "I keep thinking about those postcards she wrote. *'The flower in the desert still lives.'*"

"She tended to dramatize herself a bit." And that was pretty much all I really knew about Melissa Alonzo. Despite the time I'd spent, the people I'd talked to. I still didn't understand the woman, still didn't know her. Maybe no one did. Maybe no one ever had.

"Yes. But with a childhood like hers, she must've felt all her life like a flower in the desert."

And the flower in the desert dies, I thought. "At least Winona's safe. The Coopers will take good care of her."

She turned to me and smiled. "You looked good with her last night. In the car, coming back."

"You looked pretty good yourself last night, Rita."

And so she had, standing in the doorway, supporting herself on an aluminum cane. One shot had taken care of Roy Alonzo, who lay on the ground amid the goat droppings, clutching his arm and hissing through his expensive teeth. When Rita turned the gun on Sam and Bilbo and told them to raise their hands, both of them were inclined to listen to her.

Later, when everything was over and we had finally returned to her house, she told me that she had actually arrived before Alonzo. She had parked her Volkswagen in the stand of pines beside my borrowed Jeep, and she had just started for the buildings of the commune when she heard Alonzo's car. She had waited in the trees until he reached the barn, then set out after him. Hobbling with the cane across seventy-five yards of snow and ice.

"You could've called Hector," I had told her.

"I did," she said. "And he'd told me he'd try to get the state police there, but I wasn't certain that they'd arrive in time. They needed a warrant."

I had smiled. "It's a good thing someone arrived in time."

Now, in the moonlight, she said to me, smiling. "Maybe you should think about having children of your own."

"It's a lot of work, I hear."

She smiled. "It requires practice."

"Well," I said, "why don't you come back to bed, and we'll practice some more."

She smiled and opened her robe and let it fall and then stood up and walked to me through the moonlight.